The
Shadow
Of The Staff

A Wizard's Revenge

M.A. HADDAD

THE SHADOW OF THE STAFF

OF THE

A WIZARD'S REVENGE

ReadersMagnet, LLC

The Shadow of the Staff: A Wizard's Revenge
Copyright © 2020 by M.A. Haddad

Published in the United States of America
ISBN Paperback: 978-1-952896-85-9
ISBN Hardback: 978-1-952896-86-6
ISBN eBook: 978-1-952896-87-3

ReadersMagnet, LLC
10620 Treena Street, Suite 230 | San Diego, California, 92131 USA
1.619.354.2643 | www.readersmagnet.com

Book design copyright © 2020 by ReadersMagnet, LLC. All rights reserved.
Cover design by Ericka Obando
Interior design by Shemaryl Tampus

DEDICATION

To my mother Audrey, who always believed in me. Thank you!

CONTENTS

PROLOGUE

AS TIME GOES BY

From the beginning of time it has been said that man does not learn from his mistakes and therefore is destined to repeat them. Ever since the days of the awakening, he has been the bane of his own existence. From the moment man first opened his eyes and he looked upon the stars, his heart has been filled with wonder and his fate tied to his ability to reason and to grow. Often it has been stated that man, while both strong and wise, is easily corrupted, and therefore he would make an easily controlled puppet to be used as a tool for conquest and domination. This is how it was in the early days of Hatu.

Hatu is a large continent at the eastern edge of the Great Western Sea. It is surrounded by the Great Western Sea, the Great Northern Ice Sea, and the Great Eastern Sea and is located beyond the farthest mountains. To the south much of the country is still unknown, with few having made the effort to travel or live there. In the Beginning Days the strongest, purest races came from distant lands that are just beyond the next horizon and only remembered by those with a love of days of yore. Many people, Elves and Dwarves, sailed from the west and arrived at the eastern edge of Hatu thousands of years before this story began. Once they landed in Hatu, these many races made their way inland, making wondrous and powerful realms for their different peoples. Some of the Elves made their homes along the coast and became known as the Sea Elves. Sea Elves had love for the water, and their many ports and cities lined the shore from the southern end of the Mystic Mountains to as far south as the realm of Ancintron, beyond the southern mountain range of the Rindors. The city of Malquint is the most notable of their many ports and inlets. These Elves were as tall as 6 feet and had long, flowing brown hair, with piercing green eyes that reflected a bluish hue when upon any body of water.

The High Elves made their way inland as far as the first set of great mountains, the Winderly Mountains, and lived in their main home, a great fortress hidden from the views of man and dwarf and is called Fallquint. High Elves were slightly taller than Sea Elves and usually had light brown or blonde hair. Their eyes were bright blue, as blue as the sky on a clear winters day. High Elves also appeared to have a glow, or aura about them that grew in intensity when in battle, or angered, or using magic. The brighter the glow, the more powerful the Elf was. A few had golden hair and even brighter blue eyes. These were the most noble of all the Elves and they had the greatest magical ability.

The Dark Elves settled in the many forested areas beyond the Winderly Mountains and became an almost forgotten race. They lived in smaller groups and had no city or place that they truly called home; they were a nomadic race that became skilled in the art of war and the making of powerful, magical weapons. These Elves had dark eyes and dark hair. They were built for war and were much stockier then either Sea Elves or High Elves.

The Dwarves that made their way to Hatu had many kings and passed freely throughout the land with two primary homes. Those homes were in the Rolling Hills, which were located far to the east, past both the Winderly Mountains and the forests of the Dark Elves and in The Mystic Mountains, the mountain range directly north and east of the Sea Elves most northern port city of Malquint. The most famous leader of the Dwarves was King Tyrindus, who made his home in Doubblegate, capital of the Mystic Mountains. The Dwarves became accomplished miners, who valued gems and wealth almost as much as life itself. Their most precious mineral is the diamond, which they are able to incorporate into various items such as armor and helm, through a secret process unknown to man or elf. Dwarves were very stocky, stout beings who only stood about 5 foot tall. They had long beards of any color from red to black. Their faces were worn and fierce and they were a testament to the passage of time.

There were many different tribes of Men, and they passed beyond the realms of Elves and Dwarves, settling in kingdoms throughout Hatu. Many of the tribes had no names and made dominions both far and wide. They were simply called Tree People or Hill People or Lake People, depending on the areas that they settled and called their home. Many of these groups of settlers actually lived in the great realms of Forlosha and Ancintron, but because the realms were so vast in size, no formal name was given to the city, or village, in which these people lived. Still, they were organized and had some form of government or leadership. Normally they were led by a mayor or cleric.

In the Beginning Days, a tribe of men, known as Rangers, had a great settlement called Cye, which was a very rare realm, as they cohabitated with the Dwarves of the Mystic Mountains. However, during the reign of terror in the days of Porttia, a renegade wizard, the mighty cities were overthrown and the Rangers were all but destroyed. They settled in small groups and established colonies and villages far from the site of most other beings of Hatu. They were most skilled in hunting and tracking.

Just to the south, and slightly to the east, lay the quiet land of Myopia. Myopians were a race of men who were not as big in stature as most men. They had no armies, nor did they have issues with any who lived outside of their borders. They lived a peaceful existence and with few exceptions, were never seen outside of their lands.

To the Far East, beyond any other tribe of men, lived the Titonians. Very little is known about this tribe except that they made the longest journey of all when man first settled upon Hatu. Their lands stretched from the eastern deserts of the Dwarves to the Great Eastern Sea.

Also journeying to Hatu from the west were the four great wizards. None of the wizards actually took Hatu for his own home, but they spent time with the races of their choice, that is all but Porttia. Quickfoot choose to live with the Elves and Men. Erideous lived with the northern tribes of men in the forest beyond the mountains. Maloneous made the trek across Hatu and resided with the eastern tribes of men, beyond Elf and Dwarf. And the fourth wizard, Porttia, made his own home in a land called Mertain. It is here that he created evil, hideous creatures and formed them into an army that at one time threatened to enslave all of Hatu. However, he was defeated when his Staff of Power, the device through which he channeled his skills and energy, was unmade and his army beaten. While this was a great victory for all who lived in Hatu, the result of the Great War was costly, and it was the Elves and Dwarves who lost much of their power. Many left Hatu for the lands from where they had originally come and vowed never to return, while others who were directly involved with the downfall of Porttia, such as the wizard Quickfoot, left Hatu because the Great War had left them wary, and they knew that their time in this realm had ended.

So, with the passing of Porttia, the Dark King, the Age of Plenty began. Man soon ruled many lands and became the master of all Hatu. King Sinford and King Xandet were great and powerful leaders, and they stood as the pillars of old, like the kings of days long forgotten. Their lands grew rich and their kingdoms prospered, while the other Free Peoples of Hatu grew in wealth and trust. Hope was clear and life was good in ways the world had never seen. From Manfer in the far north to South Isle in the south, to the desert lands in the east, to the great seas to the west, there was peace and the power of mankind grew. In the beginning of the new age, calm embraced all the land and they were one with nature, the beasts of the forest and each other. Be they Elf, Dwarf, or Man, and regardless of where they dwelt, they were all equal and Hatu was a total harmony.

Forlosha, the home of the Horse People, became a land of great strength and commanded much respect from those who were near their borders. They were a proud and just people with a love of horse and rider unparalleled throughout the land. Soon after the defeat of the evil that had plagued the land there came a time of great celebration as Dwarves from the Rolling Hills rebuilt the great fortress of Moewirth Lake. Moewirth Lake had suffered tremendous damage during a great battle against the forces of Porttia in early March of the Forlosha calendar year 4507. While this was a great victory for the Horse People and was worthy of song, it is also marked the beginning of the end of the alliance between all of the free peoples of Hatu.

During the reign of King Xandet, a time of strong and deep-seated respect and admiration of the Dwarves began. They were looked upon with tremendous respect due to their ability to work with earth and stone. Never had the people of Forlosha seen such craftsmanship. They were in awe of the skills of the Dwarves and allowed them to mine within the mountains surrounding Moewirth Lake fortress. Great deposits of diamonds and gold were found deep within the mountains. For several years after the passing of King Xandet, the mighty folk from the Rolling Hills dug and mined the precious minerals and took them for their own. However, as generations passed, and Man did not always remember the past and, in time, tended to repeat his mistakes.

Many kings passed, and as the dominion of Man grew, the numbers of Dwarves diminished. Soon there were but a few hundred left to mine the never-ending supplies of diamonds and gold and return them to their homeland, where they would be forged into armor and other mighty weapons. King Therin of Forlosha, many times removed from the great King Xandet, sent forth an edict that would no longer allow the Dwarves to remove diamonds and gold, but only lesser gemstones of very little worth. This angered Dwarves throughout Hatu, as Dwarves from both the Rolling Hills and Mystic Mountains had relied upon this as their sole source of trade materials. And as we all know, dwarves are extremely greedy and must be dealt with cautiously when it comes to wealth and precious metals. Soon negotiations broke down and Therin demanded the Dwarves leave Forlosha never to return. The Dwarves did this, and soon they were lost to mind and became but a memory, a shadow that lives beneath the mountains, never seen or heard, simply folklore and rumor. And so they settled in their mighty realms in the Rolling Hills and the Mystic Mountains. The great Dwarf city of Doubblegate was created in the Mystic Mountains and stood as the cornerstone of the Dwarf nation. It is here that the direct descendants of Tyrindus and his people were rumored to live.

In Ancintron, time had left its heavy-hearted print on a war-weary land that had never quite recovered from the long and hard fight against the Dark King. During the reign of King Sinford, the people of Ancintron rejoiced in freedom and prosperity, and the great King provided hope to all of his people. Until his death in the common calendar Year of 4504, King Sinford ruled with strength and wisdom. He sent ambassadors too many lands and maintained council with all the peoples of Hatu.

To the Dwarves, he sent emissaries skilled in the ways of construction and gifted in the arts of day long forgotten. They traded in armor and weapons made by the old ways; powerful and magical were these great weapons. However, much of the ability to create mighty weapons such as Steelsmith, the great sword of the Ancintron King, or Glowmaster, the Dark Elven sword wielded in battle by the wizard Quickfoot, was lost. Yet, skilled in craft and the making of things they were. Until the Great Parting, as it was called by the Dwarves, there was a strong friendship between Ancintron and the realms of the great Dwarf kings. After the Great Parting, the resentment of Man grew in the hearts of all Dwarves, and they had very little use for Ancintron or the Realm of Dismay, Forlosha. A great divide grew and all contact with the Dwarves was lost.

To the Elves that remained in Hatu, and did not seek the tranquility of faraway lands, King Sinford sent scholars and musicians who documented the history of all peoples of Hatu; so that there would be a record in both book and song for ages to come of the bonds forged throughout the ages. The Elves were led by the Great Lord Mindeloria, who continued in the ways of his mentor, Lord Nuldoria of Fallquint. With the gracious consent of King Sinford, it was commanded that the once proud city of North Spire be rebuilt and restoration of the timeless library that once had been there be accomplished. This was despite the fact this had once been the stronghold of Porttia in the early years of his rise to power, and was the great city of his most trusted general. North Spire was razed by the Elven army of Fallquint, led by Nuldoria, their mighty lord, in the time of great strife. The remaining Elves maintained a great distance from the other peoples of Hatu, and they became more of a myth then a reality. With few exception, such as Mindeloria, they were neither seen nor heard and walked the land as softly and quietly as they had since the beginning of time. Once the city of North Spire was rebuilt, a great host from Ancintron came from the south, and it became the northern capital of their realm and was re-named after the king becoming the city of Sinford. A great celebration was by the peoples of King Sinford and Lord Mindeloria. However, soon after that, the elves simply disappeared, leaving a golden flag on a golden pole flying high above the city bathed in a soft, never-dimming light.

To the lands of the north, Sinford sent many ambassadors and developed trade and commerce with the men of the northern cities. These men had no allegiance to any king and lived in small communities that were self-governing. Here lived the great wizard Erideous. Erideous was a friend to all of the freemen of the north and had a oneness with any who dwelt in the forests, on the lakes, and on the plains of the realm. After his past battles against Porttia, he retired to the solitude of the forest and lived with the northern men in harmony and friendship. It is said he had suffered greatly in his fight against the Dark King as he was manipulated by Porttia and his powers turned against the forces of the free peoples of the land. Seldom was he seen, and many thought he had left Hatu and returned to distant lands with the sailing of the last ship. Soon his type, the wizards, were forgotten as great seers of truth and justice and were thought to be but simple conjurers and performers of magical tricks. Many compared their great feats with that of illusionists, stating that magic had no place in their lifetime and should be left to the pulling of rabbits from a hat or setting fire to a stick that gave off sparks in the night. The many great deeds of Erideous and Quickfoot, the great wizard and chief architect of the defeat of Porttia, were twisted and misshapen until very few remaining remembered their greatness and power.

The land of hills was declared to be a land free from man and all other races in an effort to give the Hill People the peace they desired and allow them to enjoy their time together, coming and going as they please. They, too, were soon forgotten and had long since faded into the vast expanse of time and history. They became a mere mention in a few books and dry ink on a smattering of pages.

The Tree People disappeared back to the forests from which they had come. Word was soon heard that the tribes had united from various forests throughout Hatu and a great gathering was held. There they remained together as one people. However, the Great War had left the Tree People weary and tired in the ways of the world, and they took leave of man and journeyed deep into the forest, leaving mankind to live as he saw fit, with nary a word to be heard. Soon they became a myth, with just an occasional noise from the distant woods that had with neither shape nor substance.

The kingdoms of Forlosha and Ancintron remained allies through the age of King Sinford and King Xandet and through the passing of many kings after that. Their realms grew to such size and vastness that free, untended land, between them became scarce, and soon there was little room for the growing of food and other necessities. This caused great worry in the kingdom of Forlosha, which needed the land for horse and plow. This conflict undermined the strong relationship between the two powerful domains, and a kind of competition formed between them. Commerce and profit became the weapons of choice, as Ancintron established trade with the lands to the east and north, and Forlosha began to keep its commodities to themselves and cut ties with the outside world. They blamed Ancintron, and the ongoing dispute with the Dwarves, for all their woes. Beneath this silent battle for power a current of jealousy and deceit led to much decay, and the people began to suffer. Ancintron fell victim to a devastating plague during the time of King Anatherian and tens of thousands perished as disease and pestilence ran through the cities of South Spire, Acton, and Wintriton, all once places of great power. People soon began to relocate, and a great void developed where there was once great friendship and trust. Distrust and malice were growing once again. While the two great kingdoms were never enemies or foes, a distance grew between them such as had existed in the time prior to the uprising of Porttia and his reign of terror. The great port city of South Isle was all but in ruins as man turned his back on his love of the sea and the riches once giving hope and aspiration to the men of Ancintron.

And of some men, such as the Myopians, very little is known. They were placed under the watchful eye of the Rangers, and being a quiet, stay-at-home people, were seldom seen outside of their realm. In the time of the King, travelers were guided past the lovely hills and valleys of the Myopia so that they would not disturb the tranquility of these simple, peaceable people.

Yet, it is said a great Myopian from the bloodline of the Great King, Master Milton Brew, had grown into a powerful and strong-willed leader; and that he was skilled in the ways of Elf, Ranger, and Wizard. It is believed that he had taken interest in the realms beyond the borders of this sleepy land and ever attentive and watchful of the world around him has the wandering call of both Brew and Peck in him. However, other folk say he would really rather smoke his pipe and enjoy the simpler things that life has to offer, such as kite flying and other less meaningful things that are the gentle ways of all Myopians. To many, Myopians are as much a legend as the unicorn or the vampire. Myopians believe their day was in the time of the destruction of the Dark King and the unmaking of the staff of power. They never asked for, nor did they seek, to be involved in the world outside of their borders. To live and let live, that is what they say. Keep your nose out of other people's business or expect them to be in yours. This is what Myopians believe; even those who understand the power of history and what it can, and will, achieve!

ONE

The Long Awaited Journey Begins

The sun shone brightly this early February morning as Burton Brew hustled about the kitchen, cleaning up what was left from his early morning breakfast. Today was a very special day indeed. Today, he would begin his month-long, highly anticipated journey to Fallquint to join in the celebration of the destruction of the Great Staff of Power. He had received his invitation several weeks ago and looked forward to attending the event now being held for its fifth time. Every five hundred years the Elves gathered the descendants of those who played a major role in support of the downfall of Porttia and the destruction of his evil empire. They remembered them in song and bestowed great honors on the races of that handful of great, yet humble, leaders who freed all the lands and brought about the defeat of the Dark Wizard.

Burton knew that he was the last in the long line of those who had actually carried the Great Staff, but, still, he could not help but wonder at how those times must have been.

"What a great adventure," he thought to himself, as he finished washing the plates that had recently been full of bacon, eggs, sausage, pancakes, toast, jam, and jelly. He had always been filled with the thought of what was beyond the borders of Myopia. In his younger days, his mentor Tordin, a Ranger from a faraway land, took him to all corners of Myopia. There he would teach him of the days gone by and the ways of all creatures, great and small, good and evil. Tordin had always thought there was special something in Burton that very few others saw, something that reminded him of the teachings of the elders of his kind. But most Myopians believed this constant wandering about, here and there, was a curse that was placed upon the Brews and Pecks because of their roles in the unwanted events of the past. Yet, they also knew there was something different in Burton. He had been seen out and about the land ever since he could walk. Seldom was he seen outside of the house without Tordin, his constant companion. And while Myopians were never patient in the ways of the world, detesting upheaval or things being out of place, they somehow understood that this young Myopian was a Myopian of rare breeding. And while not a popular though Burton was different in a good way.

As Burton wiped down the table and prepared to put away his dishes, there was a rap on the front door. Burton knew this knock. It was his lifelong friend and companion, Tordin of the Rangers. As he raced towards the door he suddenly remembered his training and the last visit of his friend.

"Always think about the unobvious when dealing with the obvious," he thought, and with that thought still ringing in his head, he wheeled quickly about and threw open the back door just off the kitchen pantry. There stood Tordin.

"Well done." exclaimed Tordin. "I thought I had you this time".

The last time Tordin had tried this, Burton was doused with a pail of water at the front door as Tordin silently made entrance to the house through some other port of access.

"I almost fell for it," said Burton. "But I remembered what we talked about last time you were here. And I also remember how cold the water was that you so kindly set above the door. But enough about all that, are you ready to go?"

A slight smile crossed Tordin's otherwise stoic face. Tordin stood tall and was very slender, almost Elf-like in appearance. Burton had always noticed the dark grey eyes, and when he asked about them, Tordin's response was that it was just a family trait, that there was really nothing special about them. Burton thought this was a very evasive answer, but he had learned long ago to never press or pressure Tordin, who had a temperament about him that was a little foreboding. He was much older the Burton, maybe ten or fifteen years. Burton had never given thought to this, and they never discussed it. It was just one of those things that you didn't question, especially between friends.

"I am ready. Are you?" asked Tordin.

"Yes, I am. Let's go. I have been waiting for this moment for many weeks and can't wait to start the journey." Said Burton as he started towards the front door.

Tordin began to laugh and said, "That's fine Burton, but don't you think you should take your traveling pack and pick up the supply bundles for the pony? It will be a very long and difficult trip without food and supplies."

It was then that Burton noticed he had left these most valuable assets sitting on one of the tables in the main hall. With a slight shrug, he took a deep breath and threw the packages over his shoulders. Burton was very strong for a Myopian; a fact that did not go unnoticed by Tordin.

"I am sorry about that" he stated. "I had completely forgotten about my pack and supplies. I am just so excited to go to Fallquint and visit with Lord Mindeloria and his people. It has been many years since I have seen him."

Mindeloria had once visited the Myopia upon the death of Burton's father, Gustov, many years ago. A bond instantly formed between them, and Mindeloria presented him with a small diamond pin that had a gold center. Burton never took it off and placed it on everything that he ever wore. As a matter of fact, he was wearing it in the corner of his tan walking cloak as he left his house. And so he placed the bags on the grey horse that was tied up to the fence outside of his house, next to the front gate.

He noticed two large saddle bags were already on the back of the great beast.

"You are not traveling very light this time" he said and stared to open one of the bags. "What have you brought with you? Anything good to eat?"

Tordin was on him in a moment.

"Don't you worry about these, boy." And he gently, but firmly pushed Burton's hand away from the bag.

"Personal stuff in here, nothing for you to worry about," he said as he cinched the ties tighter on both bags. "Just a few things we'll need for the celebration."

So Tordin untied the horse from the fence, and the journey that Burton had so impatiently anticipated began.

As the two travelers walked down the road, they were greeted by many of the locals, who waved and said Good Morning to both. As I said before, this was not a big thing to the Myopians of this time as Burton and Tordin were a commonplace sight, and

Myopians love commonplace. It was almost as if all the walks and treks they had ever taken were culminating in this one journey, and a strange feeling came over Burton as they traveled further and further from his modest house in the country.

"Tordin," he asked. "How many times have you made this trip?"

"Let me think. I go to Fallquint at least three times a year if possible," he stated. "Why do you ask?"

"I was just thinking that something about this trip feels different; not at all like our past travels. It is like I am beginning a new chapter in my life and that a great adventure awaits me, and this journey is just beginning of something that has yet to be revealed." said Burton. "But it's probably because I am actually leaving Myopia this time and not just going to the border."

Tordin looked deeply at his companion, and then allowed his eyes to look towards the sky, as if searching for something.

"I think you are more than likely correct in your thoughts; but you never know. Nor do I have any insight into what the future holds. I have found that every day is the start of a great adventure, and it is up to each of us to accept this journey with open eyes and heart," he said. "My grandfather was a very powerful and great leader. He was always deep in thought, they say. My father and uncle taught me that he was truly a wonderful man who cared about those around him and loved life in a way few understand. I think he would tell you that you should embrace this chance and learn from the opportunities that life presents. This is just another opportunity for you to live Burton, nothing more. I think my father and my grandfather, and even my uncle, would be proud of you and wish you well on this, the most important journey of our lives."

It came to Burton that this was very different coming from Tordin and that he had never talked to him about his family before. Tordin had always been a deep thinker and wiser than anyone that Burton had ever met. Well, Mindeloria withstanding. But Mindeloria was an Elf, not a Man. As Men go, Tordin was by far the wisest and most intelligent Burton had ever met, and it was not his way to talk of personal things. As Myopians go, Burton was in a very elite category that is not described in the annals of Myopia. Between them, they were truly a pair to be reckoned with in both wisdom and education.

"I think this is the first time I have ever heard about your father or grandfather, or your family for that matter. Is your father still around?" he asked.

"No." responded Tordin "He passed a few years ago. He was very, very old for a Ranger, and I miss him very much. I learned much from him, and he was truly great in his own way. He was both my father and my friend. It was he who passed on the knowledge of the old world and taught me the history of my family, and in particular, my grandfather. I wish I could have known my grandfather. He was gone long before I was born, and I never had the chance to meet him. My uncle tells me I am very much like him. I have never thought about him as much as I have lately. I don't know why, but for some reason I wish I could talk to him for just an hour or two. It's a very strange feeling I have never had before. It makes me a little uneasy. Like something is happening inside me that I can't explain."

The two walked in silence for many an hour after that, both lost deeply in their own thoughts. Each was caught in the kind of penetrating thought that brightens the mind and cleans the soul. Only an occasional word passed between them and a kind of eeriness overcame them that was very odd for that time and place. They had long passed out of the populated areas of Myopia and were enjoying the calm of the lush green countryside, when Burton noticed something lying in the trail ahead.

"What is that?" he asked and pointed to the object in the road ahead. "Look there are two, no, three or four. Too many to tell," continued the somewhat excited Myopian.

He raced ahead of Tordin and found that many small birds lay dead in the roadway - twenty or thirty as near as he could tell. Maybe more off of the road and in the trees to the right. Each was missing its head.

"What do you see?" yelled Tordin.

"Birds! Dead birds. Too many to count," replied Burton. "But it's worse than that. They are missing their heads. And there is something else."

Tordin dropped the lead to the horse and joined Burton, his hand upon the hilt of the sword that hung at his side.

"What is it?" asked Tordin, as he looked around making sure that they were alone on the road and that someone or something was not hiding nearby in the brush, waiting to pounce on them like a great cat.

Kneeling down to get a closer look, Burton jumped up and staring at the face of his friend exclaiming "If I am reading this right, and have learned from your teachings, this is Orc sign."

"Yes, it is." replied Tordin.

It appeared to Burton that Tordin somehow looked different in this evening light. He had never seen him like this before. In all the time they had spent together, he had never noticed him to be more keenly aware of his surroundings, and he noticed a light glowed in and around him. Only once had Burton seen this kind of light before. It was in the Lord Mindeloria and those Elves of his party that had visited years ago. But Tordin was a Man of the woods, a Ranger, not even close to an Elf. Burton decided that it was his eyes playing tricks on him in this dusky hour and diminishing light.

"How these signs got here, and why now, is a mystery to me. There has not been Orc around here since the fall of the Dark Wizard." continued Tordin. "These signs are a few days old, but unless someone is playing a trick on us, we had best be alert when we make camp, which might not be a bad idea. There is a very good site about thirty minutes from here, just off the road in the woods to the left. Let's make haste."

With that, the two travelers made their way to a small clearing just off the road in the woods to the left. They laid out their site, unpacking the horse and lighting a small camp fire between them. Tordin placed his saddle bags beside him, with his sword laid across the bags, unsheathed. Burton, still somewhat excited by the recent event on the road, could not keep quiet as he settled into his sleeping quilt for the night.

"Have you ever seen an Orc before? I thought they were destroyed in the great battles that ended the Age of Darkness, the Age of Milton and Cyrus." he asked.

In Myopia, the Age of Darkness is known as the Age of Milton and Cyrus. They were the two Myopians who played the biggest part in the fall of Porttia.

"Yes, I have seen Orcs before, years ago and very far from here. Orcs and the armies of the Dark Wizard were all but destroyed in the Great War. But darkness and evil can never totally be banished. It is as it is, and will always exist" Tordin said in a sadly quiet, somewhat distant voice. "But worry not my young friend, there are those that are vigilant and knowledgeable in the ways of evil. Some have never forgotten the lessons from long ago and are ready for anyone, or anything that may walk these lands. But for now, it is time to rest. There is no danger near us. Sleep is our best defense against this unfathomable event we have stumbled upon. Sleep Burton, sleep and dream the dreams of solitude and hope."

With that, Burton fell into a deep slumber and dreamed as he had never dreamt before. His dreams were filled with swift running rivers and tall mountains. Never-ending fields with wheat as far as the eye could see and a golden sunrise that filled the sky with wonder. And birds, soaring, gliding birds. The most beautiful birds Burton could imagine. Large black birds, with great white heads, that flew in majesty and wonder. He had heard of these birds. Eagles, they were called. Eagles!

Two

The Road More Traveled

It had been nearly two weeks since Burton and Tordin came upon the Orc sign. They had traveled without any further incident and were well past densely populated areas, on their way to Fallquint. The conversation alternated between the Orcs and tales of the old days. Burton was extremely interested in the stories of Cyrus and Milton and their travels along the same path many, many years ago. It seemed to him that the perils of those Myopians must have been almost unbearable - to be hunted by trolls and orcs and almost caught, all the while not really knowing where they were or were going. They really were fortunate to have run into Lord Sinford and must have been greatly pleased to have him as their guide. Funny, how those things work out.

He also liked to listen to how Will and Tom were so innocent in those days and how they came to be great Myopians in their own right. Will and Tom, and their role in the Great War, was particularly entertaining conversation when told around a campfire. Many a young Myopian would pretend to be Will and break the spell that protected the Captain of the Mertain Army, allowing him to be defeated by the Prince Egan. Burton had never imagined that he would be in an adventure of his own with Orcs about and all.

It was almost dark, and Tordin had led them from the road in search of their next campsite. He had become abnormally quiet the past few hours, and Burton began to sense there was something strange, rather foreboding going on. They were in an unfamiliar, yet familiar area, and soon Burton began to realize where they were.

"We are in the Thunder Hills, are we not?" asked the young Myopian.

"Yes, we are," replied Tordin. "I intend to make camp on Thinryon, or High Mountain, as it is called in your tongue. We will be safe for the night and should be able to get a good night's sleep before setting out in the morning."

"High Mountain!" exclaimed Burton. Once again he was barely able to maintain his composure. After all the years, and all the stories, to get to spend the night in this wondrous place, what a great moment this would be.

"Yes, High Mountain. We should be there within the hour. We will come up the south slope. Do not go to the northern end of the ruins." he warned. "That is where Cyrus received his wound, and it is an unholy place."

"If it so unholy, why do we go up there?" asked Burton.

"Nothing, even the darkest of creatures will step upon this ground. The stench of the Dark Wizard still dwells there. We, however, will be safe as long as we keep to the southern end of the plateau," he replied.

"But Tordin, we have nothing to be on guard against," said Burton. "We have seen no Orc sign or heard any fell beast of the woods or anything since we first left Myopia and found the birds on the road."

"Yes, I believe you are right and there is nothing to be afraid of," he replied. "Yet, I am uneasy these past few hours, and although I have seen no immediate danger, there is something not right. I cannot put my finger on it, but I feel we had best stay alert and keep one eye on the road and one on the brush."

These words did not sit well with Burton. It was very foreboding and not at all what he wanted to hear as they went deeper into the woods and the sky gave way to the twinkling of the stars.

"Behold, Thinryon!" declared Tordin.

There before them stood a dark hill, much higher than the rest and less covered in foliage. The climb to the top should be easy enough, and against the night sky, Burton could make out the ruins of the tower that once stood watch over all lands. Even in decay and after thousands of years, this was a very impressive site indeed, much more so than he could ever have imagined. He could feel his heart pounding in his chest as if trying to escape.

"We should make the top in no time," Tordin continued. "I will lead the horse and you will follow. Take care where you step and pay attention to me go."

As they started up the hill, Burton couldn't help but notice how easy it was to follow Tordin in the dark. Once again he noticed the strange glow of soft light that surrounded him. He had seen this when they came upon the dead birds, too. At that moment, as they climbed up the steep slope, Burton realized that there was more to Tordin then met the eye. His lifelong friend had a secret or two after all. Burton made his mind up at that moment that when the opportunity presented itself, he would pursue this and get some answers.

The climb to the top was uneventful despite a couple of near falls that almost had Burton tumbling back down the hill. But somehow he managed to keep his balance and not fall. Burton found this a little amusing as he had always had a great sense of balance and even as a young lad was able to keep his feet in situations that had others falling all over the place. Once he even crossed a small river by walking across a fallen tree. Unheard of for a Myopian, but it seemed to be almost second nature to Burton.

They did not speak the entire climb, and once they got to the top, Tordin took the bags off the horse and began to set up camp. Once again the large saddle bags were placed in a direct line of Tordin's sight and he appeared to keep one eye on them as he moved about the area. Burton's attention was instantly fixed upon the north end of the ruins.

"Is that where it happened?" He asked.

"Yes," replied Tordin. "Remember do not go near that end of the ruins. There is an evil that is best left undisturbed. We shall stay at this end, and it will remain at that end. We will be able to live with this evil for a short time. It will not touch us, and we are safe."

With that they built a small fire. A very small fire. The smallest fire yet. This seemed odd to Burton because if they were in such a "protected" area, why the extra precaution? This was a fleeting thought as Tordin began to fix dinner. It had been at least three hours since Burton had eaten and he felt hunger pains in his stomach like he had never felt. This is no life for a Myopian, he thought. Never get enough time to eat and relax!

After dinner, Tordin lit his pipe, as was his practice, and sat with his back towards the north end of the ruins. It was obvious to Burton that Tordin was not really happy to be here. But, he concluded, there must be a good reason or we wouldn't be here in the first place.

Just then the horse let out a loud neigh, broke free from where if had been tied to a tree, and bolted down the hill into the darkness.

Tordin jumped up and kicked out the fire as he pulled his sword. Then there was nothing but darkness and silence. Several minutes passed as they stood in silence, just listening, trying to sense something, anything!

"What happened?" asked Burton as he broke the long silence. "I have never seen an animal act like that."

"I am not sure," replied Tordin. "I do not hear or sense anything, but animals are far more sensitive then I. Maybe he caught a scent on the wind. But never mind that, you need to rest, for tomorrow we speed up our journey. I think we need to make haste and get to Fallquint and speak to Lord Mindeloria. Now you go to sleep, and I will keep watch."

With that Tordin crept just outside of the ruins and sat in utter silence the rest of the night. If it were not for the glow of light, Burton would not have known he was there. Burton tried, but was unable to sleep deeply, and so he just dozed off a few times. Maybe it was this place, maybe it was the horse bolting off, or maybe it was the fact that Tordin was on edge as well. But whatever the reason, Burton wanted no more to do with High Mountain or its famous history. Morning couldn't get here fast enough for him.

When the sun finally began its rise into the morning sky, Burton noticed Tordin had not moved all night.

"Good morning," said Tordin, with his back to the stirring young Myopian.

"Good morning," replied Burton. "Is it time for breakfast?"

Tordin came back to the campsite and began to pack the belongings. "No time for breakfast today, Master Myopian. It is time for us to leave. Look." And Tordin pointed to the south.

There on the horizon Burton could make out three distinct lines of smoke rising from the ground and floating away into the air.

"Those are Orc fires. And there is another to the east. Directly in our path I fear. Time is against us Burton, and we must move swiftly and silently" continued Tordin.

"But with no horse, how are we to carry our supplies?" Burton asked.

"I will take some food and water, and the rest we must leave behind. We should have more than enough supplies, and we will cut our traveling time down if we travel night and day. We can be in Fallquint in ten days with luck," said Tordin. And he began to go through the supply bags, tossing out anything that was unnecessary. Finally, all was packed, except for the two large bags that had been on the pony from the start.

"And what of those?" pointed Burton.

A slight smile crossed Tordin's face. "Those were meant to be given to you at Fallquint, as part of the ceremony honoring the legends of those that destroyed the Staff of Power. But with this unfortunate change in events, I think now would be a better time."

He opened one bag and pulled out a green cloak with a bright green brooch attached at the collar. What a truly wonderful cloak indeed. Obviously Elf made.

"This cloak was once worn by Milton Brew of your line, during his journey to Mertain. I give it to you now in the hopes it will protect and serve you as it did him. The broach is from the Lady Elladoria herself and was presented to all the members of the Staff Party when they traveled through her lands."

Tordin presented the cloak to Burton with a touch of reverence that left Burton full of pride and wonder. He took off his old cloak and put of the new one. It felt wonderful, so lightweight. He then took the pin that had been presented to him by Mindeloria, from his old Myopian cloak and attached it to his new Elven cloak. A light from the gold in the center of the pin momentarily blinded him as it was placed next to the green brooch.

"What was that?" he exclaimed.

"We will have time to discuss that at a later time, my friend" said Tordin as he reached back into the saddle bag. There he pulled out a diamond shirt. White diamond, the very rarest, and the shirt was trimmed in gold and silver.

"Cyrus' shirt," exclaimed Burton.

"Yes, Cyrus and Harry's diamond shirt. Made by the Dwarves of old," said Tordin. "We do not have time for you to put in on now but the next time we stop, please do so. It has served its past masters well and deflected many a fatal blow from finding its mark."

As Burton carefully folded the shirt and placed it in his small back pack, Tordin reached into the other saddle bag and pulled out a small bundle of rags. Or at least what appeared to be rags. He then placed it on the ground and unrolled the bundle. There, inside, was a sword in a leather sheath on a leather belt. Burton's heart almost stopped. This could be only one thing. "Warlight!" he thought.

Tordin gently lifted the belt and sheath and handed it to Burton.

"I present to you the blade Curfinalas, the Night Star. This blade has been handed down through those of my house, and we have been its guardian. It was once carried by the Myopians of your past, and you are now assigned its keeping and may it safeguard you at all times. It is truly a great weapon and was made in the Beginning Age by the most skilled Elven craftsmen of the time," said Tordin.

"This is Warlight, is it not?" asked Burton.

"You call it Warlight, and there are still other names, but its original name is Curfinalas" Replied Tordin. "Some say it is a dagger, but it is truly a short sword that was carried by the Elf Lord Angron, one of the greatest Elves of all times. The Lady Elladoria and Lord Mindeloria are of his line. It is said that it does much more than give a light if enemies are near. It is said to have a magical quality that has yet to be seen by Man or Dwarf."

Burton put the belt around his waist and buckled it securely into place. He could not help but pull out the mighty weapon and look at it. He pulled it from its sheath and began to look at the beautiful Elvish runes etched upon the blade. The silver of the blade shone in the bright sunlight. He could not imagine how old this sword was. Possibly as old as time itself. Warlight! The great blade, and he was carrying it. A great swell of pride built up inside him, and he felt bigger and stronger than he had ever felt before.

It must have been very obvious to Tordin that this had had a great effect on him.

"My friend, I know this is truly wondrous and exciting moment in your life," said Tordin. "And I wish it could have taken place in the setting and ceremony it so richly deserves. But now is not the time to get caught up in the moment. Our enemies grow closer every minute, and there is much going on I do not understand. We must hurry on our way and get counsel. We must go now."

With that they started down the hill. However, Burton could not resist taking a quick glance at the north end of the ruins. There in the midst of the lush green grass was a blackened patch of earth. Almost as if it had been burned and nothing could grow there. The very spot where the Captain of Mertain fell upon

Cyrus and with one savage thrust almost ended the life of one of the greatest Myopians to ever live. A shiver ran down Burton's spine, and he felt a cold breeze blow across the back of his neck.

"We must go now!" cried Tordin.

With that Burton turned and started down the hill, back toward the road and his journey to Fallquint.

THREE

MILO AND SILO

As the two adventurers walked towards their destination, Tordin informed Burton that they were only a couple days from Fallquint and their journey was almost over. However, he continued to point out Orc sign as they got closer to their destination. Orcs, it seems, are not very clean beings. Burton began to see the signs as well. He noticed tracks that would weave back and forth across the road. Never in the same pattern, but Orc sign just the same. Burton was very impressed with Tordin's tracking skills. He had never had the chance to see a Ranger work up close, and he couldn't help but notice that not a sign was overlooked. No matter how small. Even on a day like today, a cold and cloudy day, which had them seeking shelter from the downpours that burst from the clouds. As they approached a slight bend in the road, a pungent odor caught Burton's attention.

"What is that horrible smell?" he asked.

"That is the smell of death." replied Tordin.

They saw the source of their unpleasantness as they turned the corner. Hanging from a tree limb just north of the trail was the rotting carcass of some sort of animal. It had been all but picked clean of meat and left as a sign to anyone traveling in the area. This was the first time Burton had come face to face with the horror of death, and the sight of it made him feel ill.

"I think that we have found what happened to our horse," said Tordin. With that he pulled his sword and cut the poor beast from the tree. "I assume he must have caught the scent of the Orcs the night he disappeared and was attempting to get back to familiar territory."

"I see no sign of a fire," said Burton.

"Orcs do not cook their meat. They eat it raw." Tordin stated. "Come, we must go."

For the previous few days, Tordin would go off on his own into the forest as if attempting to catch the Orcs off guard. The trips started as short two or three minute excursions, but had grown in length as they traveled on. A couple of times he was gone for over an hour. This really did not bother Burton until now. He was beginning to realize that they were in danger, and the danger was growing stronger as they got closer to Fallquint. The past two times, Burton had the distinct feeling that he was being watched. He had written this feeling off as nerves and was not really concerned with it until now. This time he knew he was being watched as Tordin once again strode off into the woods.

Burton's first instinct was to pull Warlight and see if it were Orcs. As he pulled the blade he noticed there was no light. This made him feel a little better, but he still had that gnawing thought that something was watching him. A couple of times he ducked into the woods himself, as if he were playing a game of hide and seek. But this was no game, he thought to himself. Try as he might, he was unable to get a glimmer of whatever or whoever was watching him.

He continued on his way for a good half hour, always looking this way and that, always on the alert to his left and to his right, always watching for movement ahead or to either side. He had been taught well and he was pleased with how his training was paying off.

Then the unthinkable occurred. He had been so intent on what was ahead of him, he forgot to look behind. He could hear the running Orcs as they approached him. Nowhere to go, Burton Brew, he thought to himself. Might as well face the music.

With that he turned to face his attackers.

He didn't have time to count them but noticed five or six large Orcs and several smaller Goblins bearing down on him. They got to within a few feet of him when they pulled up and addressed him.

"What have we here?" said the biggest of the bunch. "One of those nasty, dirty Myopians, I think, and all alone in the middle of nowhere. What a shame for him, huh boys?"

This was the first time Burton had ever seen a Goblin or an Orc for that matter. What disgusting creatures, he thought. They each had short swords and wore leather armor. Not at all what he thought they would look like. In a way, he thought they would be bigger. Much more to his surprise, was the fact that they were speaking in his tongue, and not the tongue of the Orc.

"I think you will make a nice snack," said the leader, who took a couple of more steps towards Burton.

In the blink of an eye, Burton tossed back his cloak and drew Warlight from it sheath. It burned bright and now looked as if it were four feet long. The Orcs all reeled back a few steps and began to hiss and bunch together, as if they were drawing strength from each other.

"I think you will find this Myopian more than you can handle," cried Burton.

Just then a figure flew past Burton and fell upon the dismayed Orcs. It was Tordin, with his sword in one hand and a dagger in the other. He was in full fury and the slight light that surrounded him in times of danger burned brighter and stronger than ever before. His attack was so sudden that the Orcs did not even have a chance to even defend themselves. Two, then three, were down before Burton had even reacted to the situation. Then realizing he had to attack; he did. He struck swiftly and with a stab of his sword the great Orc went down with a look of astonishment on his face. The others turned to run but before they could their retreat was blocked.

From each side of the road sprung forth two Great Timber Wolves. One was grey, the other black. They stood at least four feet tall at the shoulders and their eyes glowed red as fire. They were very muscular and yet quick and graceful. They pounced on the Goblins who had already thrown away their weapons and made quick work of them.

In all the battle lasted less than two minutes.

It took a few seconds for Burton to realize what had happened. It was his first taste of combat, and he was shocked at the speed at which this had occurred. He was trying to comprehend the furious action and remember his every move. Try as he might, all he could remember was thrusting Warlight into the throat of the Orc nearest to him. After that, everything began to run together. He looked at the dead bodies lying about him and then began to look at himself for wounds.

"Don't worry. They didn't touch you." said Tordin. Burton looked in his direction and noticed he was kneeling with a wolf on each side of him. And he was petting them as if they were family pets. "Let me introduce you." he continued.

He patted the grey wolf on the head. "This is Milo," he said. And then he patted the other on the head. "And this is Silo. They belong to a friend of yours."

"A friend?" asked Burton. "I have no friends with animals such as these."

"You have more friends than you think," replied Tordin. "These are the companions of Erideous the Wizard. They have been with us for many days now and were sent to insure we did not have any difficulties as we neared the end of our journey."

"I thought Erideous was a legend. I had no idea he still existed," said Burton.

"He awaits us in Fallquint. As do many others," Tordin replied. "I have had many a conversation with those of my kind the past days and not all the news is good. There has been an uprising in the north and a great hoard of Trolls have laid siege to Rolling Hills. Bands of Orcs, far greater then these, are afoot throughout the lands. Myopia has been attacked and only through the valiant efforts of a handful of Rangers and the townsfolk, was the town spared. There has been a great loss of life these past few days, not only here but throughout Hatu. A great war appears to be upon us. The Orcs have become more aggressive, as if someone were spurring them on."

Burton thought for a moment and then asked, "Tordin, this was my first taste of war. Is it always like this?"

"How do you mean that?" queried Tordin.

"I froze in the heat of the battle. It all happened so fast that everything ran together. I remember thrusting my blade into the first Orc and then it was over. If you and these wonderful beasts hadn't come along, I don't think I would be here talking to you."

"One thrust? Is that all? My dear Myopian, look again. It was not I, nor was it our new companions who slew the enemy. It was you."

Burton looked again at the fallen Orcs and realized that many of the wounds were caused by Warlight. How could this be? He did not remember causing this much devastation. Is it possible? Yet, there it was.

Tordin motioned for Milo and Silo to return to the woods on both sides. They disappeared as quickly as they had first appeared in the battle.

"I would like to say that you will never have another experience like this again, but I cannot." sighed Tordin. "It is obvious that there is much wrong and that a conflict unforeseen and unforetold has arisen. This is a sad day indeed." A thoughtful look crossed Tordin's face, and it appeared that he was miles away. It was as if his mind had left his body (but only for a moment) and then the light returned to his eyes.

"But today we can celebrate a great victory against our enemies. You should be proud, Master Brew. This was truly the first great deed of many to come, I am sure."

Burton and Tordin started back down the road leaving the Orcs behind them.

Still, for some reason, Burton was anything but proud. He was confused as to what really had happened. What did he do that was so great, and why couldn't he remember it?

As the two neared their destination, these thoughts left Burton and he started to concern himself with the other happening in the world. How strange he thought. Dwarves were in trouble and Myopia had been attacked. How strange that bands of marauding Orcs traveled freely throughout the land. Truly, strange times indeed!

FOUR

Destinations of Dreams

At last, they came to the Ford of The Great River and the way to Fallquint. The past few days had been very uneventful. Since the encounter with the band of Orcs, Burton wanted to be in Fallquint almost as much as he wanted to be in Myopia, near his quiet little house. He thought heavily about what Tordin had told him concerning the attacks, and wanted all of his friends to be safe and well. Somehow he knew they were, but still his attention and thoughts had wandered to them. But now he was focused on something else, just beyond the river was the great Elf city of Fallquint, the last haven of the High Elves, the ancestral home to King Nuldoria and those who came after him, all of his sons and daughters, and of course, Mindeloria. But what he saw did not meet his expectations.

Across the ford he saw no path, no trail, no guards, nothing but thick, heavy unapproachable woods and thickets. The way was blocked and impassable.

"Tordin, do my eyes deceive me?" he asked. "There is no way across."

"Worry not, Burton," replied Tordin. "All is not as it appears. Lord Mindeloria, while mighty in his way, is not King Nuldoria. His powers do not control water and matter to that level. He has other, in some ways, deadlier powers. This is a moment of faith and trust. Not something our Orc friends possess or understand. Please follow and trust."

With that said Tordin stepped into the water and began to cross the river. Milo and Silo appeared and stayed to each side of Burton. It was as if they wanted to give him the strength and courage to perform this very daunting task. Their presence did reassure him somewhat, and he too, stepped into the water and waded into whatever was in store for him.

As the small party reached the other side it was as if through magic the woods and underbrush seemed to part and then close in behind them. It was allowing them to go where they could not. Elf magic! That is what this was. Burton had heard of these things, but this was the first time he ever experienced it to this level. It made magic swords and diamond pins look like a card trick. Burton was in awe.

Finally, they reached the other side, and to his surprise, there was a large wall built around the city. Banners flew from every tower and pinnacle. He could see guards along the top of the walls. Suddenly, trumpets sounded, and the large gates to the city opened. A dozen Elven Guards approached the party. They were led by an Elf who was obviously of great importance. He was dressed in traditional Elven armor with a great helmet upon his head. The silver of the helmet gleamed in the sunlight. Milo and

Silo shot past the guards and entered the city before the travelers got within distance to speak to the Captain of the Guard. Burton knew the great wolves were home.

"Hail, Master Brew and Lord Tordin. Welcome to Fallquint. I am Wendil, Captain of the Guard of the City, personal aide to Lord Mindeloria. He sends his greetings and regrets he is unable to meet you himself. There is a feast planned in your honor this evening and he will join you in the Great Hall."

And then Wendil turned back to the city and raised his sword into the sky. A voice from the wall exclaimed, "Hail the arrival of Burton Brew, last descendant of the Great Staff Bearers." Then the trumpets sounded again. "And hail Lord Tordin, son of Lurdin and Grandson of Nuldoria, Lord and King of Fallquint." Another blast of the trumpets was sounded.

The guards formed a line on both sides of the astonished Myopian and his companion. Tordin was the Grandson to Nuldoria, the great half-Elf of days gone by. Burton had never imagined that this was the secret his lifelong friend had kept from him all these years. Yet it explained so much. Tordin had Elf blood in his veins.

Wendil turned to Tordin. "My Lord, welcome. Will you please give us the honor of escorting you into the city?" he asked.

Tordin bowed low and replied, "We thank you for the honor and look forward to the hospitality of the realm. We have much to tell and many questions to ask. But this is not the time. I await your orders."

With that they went into the city. Such grandeur and beauty. Elves, Dwarves, and Men lined the streets and tossed flowers as the party made its way through the throng of well-wishers. Burton was quite taken by this. He had no idea that his arrival was such a big deal.

"Hail the Myopian. Hail Brew." they shouted. "Hail the heir of Nuldoria." A great Dwarf made his way to the line and shouted "To the memory of the Dwarf Kings who dwelt under the mountain." The attention was almost more than Burton could stand. He wished they had made their way into the city with no pomp and circumstance such as this. Tordin must have noticed how uneasy Burton was becoming.

He leaned over to the overwhelmed Myopian and whispered, "Did I not tell you of the great honor that was in store. You are the last of a great line that defeated the Dark King and set Hatu free. There will be many such demonstrations in your stay here. You represent the hope and freedom that all beings in Hatu desire. But rest assured, our departure will be quite different."

Burton wondered what that meant and made a mental note to ask later.

At last they made their way to a smaller gate, which led to a large house on the hill. Burton assumed this was the house of Mindeloria. They opened the gate and started up the hill towards the house.

"Lord Mindeloria will meet with you later. Right now he is in council and asks that I show you to your rooms." said Wendil. "You will find appropriate attire for this evening's dinner."

With that, they opened the door to the building. Inside the rooms were much simpler than Burton imagined they would be. Wendil motioned them to the right, through an archway that led down a hall with many doors.

"Lord Tordin, this first door is your room. Master Brew, you are just across the hall," said Wendil. He then bowed to both, turned, and left with the honor guard, leaving Burton and Tordin standing in the middle of the hallway.

"What do we do now?" asked Burton.

"Now we do as we have been asked and retire to our rooms until Lord Mindeloria calls us to dinner." replied Tordin as he opened his door and entered his room.

"I suggest you get some rest and enjoy the hospitality of our host. There is a very busy evening in store for you tonight," said Tordin, closing the door behind him and leaving a somewhat puzzled Burton standing in the hallway.

Burton shrugged his shoulders, turned to open his room door and entered.

The room was pleasantly decorated, although a little small, even for a Myopian. There was one window, which looked out over Fallquint. A very beautiful view indeed.

On the dresser was a basket of fresh fruit. This was a great sight for Burton. He opened the basket and began to eat an apple, and then a pear.

Soon he found he was tired and lay down on the bed. Soft and cozy, it was, covered in Elven silk and much fancier then Burton had ever seen before. Before long he fell into a deep slumber. Once again the familiar dreams of peaceful fields and tall mountains filled his head. Then there were those eagles again, flying high and free, riding the very wind itself. Graceful birds of majesty and beauty. Each time he dreamed of them they became more beautiful and clearer. It was as if he were flying with them, almost as if he were an eagle himself.

He was roused from his dreams with a loud rap on the door.

He jumped up and opened the door. It was Tordin.

"It is time my young friend," he said. "Lord Mindeloria has sent for us and expects to meet us within the hour. I suggest you wash your face and put on some clean clothes before your audience with the Leader of Fallquint. I will come for you in a short time."

Again, he turned and left. Burton thought how odd it was that everyone was barking orders and going about their business in such a rude manner. Elves had never seemed to him as being so rude before. They were pleasant and easygoing. And for Tordin to act so, was totally out of character as well. Maybe this is how it is before a big meeting. If this is how big meetings are, Burton thought, he did not want to be a part of them in the future.

He closed the door and went over to the cleaning bowl located on a table in the corner. Above it was a mirror. He looked in the mirror and thought, "Oh my, what a mess." For the first time since he left Myopia he realized that traveling was a very messy business in deed. He washed up and looked in the dresser for a change of clothes. He found a fine Elven silk shirt and a clean cloak. He quickly dressed and thought about putting on Warlight. He struggled with this for a few seconds and thought, "under the circumstances, I think they will be pleased to see the old sword of Harry and Cyrus." So he strapped it on and opened the door.

There in the hallway were Tordin and Wendil. They looked at Burton and Wendil said, "Master Brew, you look well rested. It is time to meet with my Lord."

"Thank you, Captain Wendil," he replied.

They then started to walk back in the direction they originally came in from.

"Tordin, can I ask you a question?" asked Burton.

"And what would that be?" replied Tordin.

"I have noticed that everyone, including you, appears to be preoccupied." said Burton. "Is there something going on?"

"Yes, my friend," said Tordin. "There is much going on in the world. Much has happened since we left Myopia."

"I'm sure it means something about the Orcs. Is there more? Is it serious?" continued Burton.

"Orcs are always serious Burton. And yes, there is more. But it is not my place to give you this information. I am sure Lord Mindeloria will tell you all you need to know." said Tordin.

They crossed the main hallway in the building to a set of great oak doors. Sitting by the door was a very old man, dressed in dirty brown clothes. He carried a large walking stick and wore a pointed hat with a large brim that hid much of his face.

"Master Brew," said Wendil "Allow me to introduce you to Erideous the Wizard. He will act as your host the rest of the way. I have very important business to tend to. Please accept my deepest apologies, but I must go and will not be able to join you this evening"

The old man rose and put his hand out.

"It is I who am honored." said Erideous, as he put out his hand.

"It is very nice to meet you" he said as he shook the old wizard's hand. Later he thought about his greeting and wished he had more to say.

"Hello, Erideous." said Tordin.

"It is great to see you again, my old friend." replied Erideous. "But I wish the times were better for such a reunion."

"As do I." replied Tordin.

It became clear to Burton that these two knew each other. He couldn't help but notice how alike they were. Although Erideous was obviously much older, they had the same kind of mystic power about them.

"Please follow me." said Erideous as he opened the large doors before them.

Burton could not believe his eyes as he looked into the room. It was a festive hall, decorated all about with banners and flags. There were flags for Ancintron and Forlosha, the Dwarfs of the Mystic Mountains and Rolling Hills. There were flags and pennants for all of the Northern tribes of Men and Elves, and so many others that Burton could not identify them all. Down the middle of the room, was a gigantic dining table. It could seat thirty or forty easily. Burton could only imagine the meals that taken place in this room.

At the far end of the room, at the head of the table was a single seat, more of a throne, really. It was adorned with gold, diamonds, and so many other precious stoness that it almost took Burton's breath away to look at it. Behind the throne was a banner that Burton knew. It was the banner of the House of Angron. Burton knew this was the throne of Lord Mindeloria. At this time Burton noticed that the three of them were the only ones in the room.

"Where is everyone?" asked Burton.

"They will join us shortly" replied Erideous. "I have been asked to show you to your seats. "Please follow me."

The walked to the far end of the table.

"Lord Tordin, please sit here." said Erideous as he pointed.

Tordin took the second seat to the right.

"Master Brew, you will sit here." said Erideous.

He pointed to a specially designed Myopian seat that included a small ladder so that Burton would be sitting at the same height as everyone else. He was seated immediately to the right of the throne – truly a place of honor.

Erideous went to the left of the table and sat in the second chair.

Just then the doors opened at the far end of the room. A small group entered.

Two Men were big, strong men, dressed in full battle armor. One was from Forlosha and the other from Ancintron. Two Dwarves with long beards also entered. They appeared strong, and they, too, were dressed for battle. There was one woman, an Elf. Beautiful she was, and tall and slender. The traditional glow of Elven power flowed around her and she glided as she walked. This was the first female Elf Burton had ever seen, and he was struck by her long golden hair and piercing blue eyes. Her entire demeanor was suggested power and elegance.

She was the first to walk up to Burton.

"Welcome to Fallquint, Master Brew. I am Lindeloria, Princess of Fallquint. It is very nice of you to join us. We are sorry for your perilous journey this past month, but we are happy you were able to join us for this celebration." said the stunning Elf Princess.

"Thank you," replied Burton.

A smile crossed Tordin's, face and Burton realized how he must appear in such presence. Not only was he out of place, but he hadn't had much practice in these kinds of social events.

"I am Derfer, and this is Zander" said one of the Dwarves. "We are from the Rolling Hills, and it is our pleasure to meet the last of the line of the staff bearers."

"I am Battlehelm, Captain of the Capital Guard of Ancintron," said one of the men. "Welcome."

"And I am Handil, Lieutenant of the Kings Guard of Forlosha, I greet you on behalf of our King." said the other man.

"If you will all be seated please, my father will be here shortly." said Lindeloria.

She sat across from Burton, to the left of the great chair and to the right of Erideous. Battlehelm sat next to Tordin, with Handil next to him. Across from them sat the two Dwarves.

"I heard you had a great battle with Orcs on your way here?" asked Zander.

"Yes, we did have a run-in with a handful of Orcs on the way here. However, I would not call it a great battle." replied Tordin.

"That is not way it is told here." said Derfer. "It is said that the Myopian fought like a Dwarf warrior of old."

"Too many dead to count." said Zander.

"And only the two of you. That is a great victory indeed" followed Derfer.

"And Milo and Silo." said Burton.

With that Erideous and Lindeloria let out a laugh and a smile crossed the lips of Tordin. However, the rest of the guests were not amused.

"Wizard business and great wolves as pets is not the way of Men." stated Battlehelm.

"And sometimes, the way of men is wrong" replied Erideous.

"Be quiet old fool. We did not come all this way to be amused by your tricks." roared back Battlehelm.

"Nor us to listen to the rambling of men," interrupted Zander.

A voice spoke from the back of the room. However, it was so clear and powerful Burton thought it was right behind him.

"There is a time for such debate and conversation. However, this is not it," said the voice. "We are here to break bread as friends and allies. There is a great fight ahead of us. We will not resolve any issues now. Therefore, I ask you to put aside your differences and let us meet in celebration and remembrance."

There at the far end of the room stood Mindeloria, Lord of Fallquint. He was tall and powerful, bathed in a golden light, just as Burton remembered him from their past meeting in the Myopia.

Mindeloria made his way to Tordin and spoke to him in a low tone.

Even though Burton was right next to them he could not hear a word they spoke.

Mindeloria then turned to Burton. "It is good to see you again, my young Myopian. I see that time has treated you well and you are fit. I welcome you to my humble home and look forward to the opportunity to sit with you later."

"Thank you, my Lord" replied Burton. "It is truly a pleasure to attend such a lavish event. I am honored to be in the presence of such greatness and renown."

"The Myopian does better with the Lord than the Princess" laughed Zander.

With that, everyone laughed and Mindeloria made his way to his seat. Burton glanced over at Lindeloria, who was watching him as if she were looking through him, a smile on her face.

Mindeloria remained standing. He picked up his glass and raised it. "All hail to the last of the line of the staff bearers, Burton Brew of Myopia," he said.

The others raised their glasses in toast. As they put the glasses to their lips, trumpets throughtout the city sounded as if on cue.

"Let the celebration begin."

Mindeloria sat down and food came from every direction of the great hall, through doors that Burton had never noticed. They feasted as Burton had never feasted before. And for a Myopian, that says a lot.

FIVE

THE WORLD TURNS

I f there was a dish invented, it was brought to the table. They had ham and turkey, potatoes and corn, water lilies and sea plums, food of all kinds, fried, baked, baked twice, broiled, and even grilled. Soon everyone had their fill, and the small group retired to a room off the main dining area. There they smoked some of the finest tobacco Burton had ever had. And drank ale until almost sun up. Most of the conversation centered on the exploits of the Great War and the roles each had played. Mindeloria made it a point to keep the conversation away from the most recent events. It soon became clear to Burton that the Dwarves were not very happy to be in the same room with the men, especially Handil. Burton assumed that dated back to the dispute over the diamond mines in the days after the Great War. Dwarves have long memories, it seems.

Burton was particularly fascinated by Handil. Handil said very little, yet he seemed to be extremely attentive to all conversation. He did nothing to antagonize the Dwarves and ignored any remarks they made. It was as if he didn't hear them. However, it was much different with Battlehelm. It was very obvious that he did not like nor respect the Dwarves. He often took up the arguments that were directed at Handil. This was particularly irritating to Zander, who used any excuse he could to insult all men, but in particular Ancintron and Forlosha.

They were in the middle of one of these exchanges when Wendil entered the room and approached Mindeloria. He whispered in his ear and then left the room.

"My friends," said Mindeloria. "I have just received some terrible news. Captain Wendil informs me that the Troll siege of the Rolling Hills has ended."

A sorrowful look passed over Mindeloria's face.

"Zander and Derfer, it is with great sadness I must inform you that the Rolling Hills have fallen."

Zander stood, gripping his axe handle, staring at Battlehelm. Derfer looked at Lord Mindeloria, as if he were inviting the great Elf to read his mind.

"Where are your precious armies now, Battlehelm," asked Zander. "Who was standing at our side in our hour of need, I ask?"

Battlehelm stood and put his hand on his sword. "Do not speak to me in that tone, Dwarf," said Battlehelm. "The armies of Ancintron have long protected your kind. We cannot be everywhere at once. And since when do Dwarves ask for or need the help of anyone?"

Zander was about to answer when Derfer interrupted, his gaze still locked on the eyes of Mindeloria.

"Zander, this is not the time. I ask Lord Mindeloria to hold council before we return to our homeland so that plans can be made," said Derfer. "There are other Dwarf colonies and cities to defend. This war is just starting, my brother."

"I will send word that we will meet as the sun reaches its peak in the sky," said Mindeloria. "For now I beg all of you to return to your apartments and rest. I fear we have lost much time this evening, and time is no longer a luxury we have. There will be time for further celebration after this conflict has been resolved."

Mindeloria then reached up and pulled a rope from behind his chair. By the time his hand had left the line, the room was full of Elves. To his side reappeared Captain Windel. He and Mindeloria began to have a conversation as another Elf rolled open a map on a nearby table. Burton found all this fascinating. He had never seen so many move so fast and with such purpose. It was almost as if they followed a single consciousness. He felt a hand settle softly on his shoulder.

"Come Master Myopian, this is the work of warriors and thinkers, not such as us."

Burton looked up and found the hand on his shoulder and the voice he heard was that of Lindeloria.

"It is time we took leave." she continued.

They left the room and made their way back to the hallway and the apartment door. There Lady Lindeloria said something that Burton would never forget.

Before she left him she said, "I can see why you are here and I know what you must do. The bloodline you possess will soon come back to life. You must be alert, as there are others who are aware of your existence as well. They will leave no stone unturned to stop the quest you are about to begin. Even here you are not safe. Beware Master Brew and be careful."

She then turned and was gone before he had a chance to ask any questions. A million thoughts swirled in his head. "What did she mean?" he thought. "And watch out for whom?"

And so he went to his room and tried to rest. There were no sweet dreams this time. As a matter of fact, Burton didn't know if he were sleeping or not, half the time. He thought about the foreboding statement Lindeloria made. He thought about Myopia and his home. Somehow he knew that there was a great adventure to come. He knew that he was about to be called on for something. But what? Tordin made no mention of such things. But he knew that Tordin was aware of something. What was it that Tordin knew? Could all of this be an accident or was it by some grand design? And if it was a grand design, where did he fit in? Was he supposed to be here, at this time and place? Never had so many thoughts filled his head.

Suddenly he jumped up and opened his door.

There, about to knock on it, was Wendil.

"I see you have strange senses for a Myopian. How did you know I was here?" asked Wendil.

"I did not," replied Burton. "And yet I did. I do not know for sure."

"It does not matter right now, young Myopian. All others have assembled, and I was sent to get you to join us. Please follow me."

They walked out of the building and through several narrow streets. As they made the last turn, they began to walk downhill towards the entrance to a cave. The entrance was guarded with two of the biggest Elves Burton had ever seen. They were Dark Elves. Burton had heard of these, but never had seen one. Legend had it that they were outcast during the early days and suffered long at the hands of their enemies. Dark Elves carried large, heavy battle weapons. They were the warriors of the Elf world. There was no doubt about that.

They looked hard at Burton, almost as if they had never seen a Myopian. Burton thought for sure they were going to attack him. He was quite ill at ease with these two.

As they passed the guards, heaviness came over him. He had never felt this before and had to overcome a sudden urge to turn and run. Wendil must have seen this.

"This is the power of the Lord Mindeloria," said Wendil. "It is his magic and will keep all unwelcome visitors out. It works three times as well on those with a wicked heart. It will pass soon."

After a few hundred feet, the feeling did leave.

"I am surprised we are meeting underground," said Burton.

"I am sure" replied Wendil. "Lord Mindeloria has said that the time for Elves to pass freely throughout the land is coming to an end. Soon we will have to hide in places such as this or leave Hatu altogether."

"I did not think that Elves passed freely these days anyway." replied Burton.

"Just because we are not seen, do not be so vain as to think we are not there. We have developed new ways to pass amongst our friends. Remember, Master Brew, not all is as it appears." said Wendil.

They reached a large door. Burton could not make out all of the materials it was made of, but he did notice steel and iron. There were two more Dark Elves stationed there. One of them opened the door.

The room beyond the door was a large round room with a round table in the middle. There were no windows, nor could he see any other doors.

One way in! One way out!

At the table sat Tordin, Lindeloria, Derfer, Zander, Battlehelm, and Erideous. Burton noticed that Handil was not yet there. There were other Elves that he did not know. Some were Dark Elves, and some were Elves that wore steel helms with the wings of birds on them. Burton knew these were Elves from the sea ports to the west of Myopia. There was also another Ranger sitting at the table besides Tordin. Burton noticed that the Ranger was wounded, as he had his left arm in a sling.

At the far end of the room was Mindeloria. He did not sit at the table, but was in a loft overlooking the entire room. Burton took this to indicate there was no question as to who was in charge here!

"Please be seated, Master Brew," said Mindeloria. "We are just about to begin. And before you ask, Handil has been sent on an errand and will not return for this council."

Burton took his seat next to Lindeloria. He had developed a fondness for her and knew that she would be there for him almost as much as Tordin.

Again, Lindeloria just looked at Burton and simply smiled.

"As you are aware, the Rolling Hills have fallen and Myopia has been attacked." said Mindeloria. "Our first concern is for the well-being of our Dwarf allies. What word have we?"

One of the Dark Elves stood.

"My Lord," He said. "A great horde of Trolls and Orcs came from the east and laid siege to the Rolling Hills. Several attempts to break out were attempted, but all failed. The evil army outnumbered the Dwarves five to one."

"Five to one is no match for a Dwarf," exclaimed Zander.

"Please, allow him to continue," Mindeloria asked quietly.

"The Trolls were smarter than any we have ever run into before. They were well armed and armored. They carried a new sword that struck fear into all who looked upon it" said the Elf. "It was made from a material we have never seen and could cut through the Dwarven armor as if it were butter. Only diamond armor stood against it. Alas, the Dwarves had little."

"We would have had more had the lowly horse soldiers honored their agreement from days of old," said Zander.

"Why should they have to honor a contract that was made when Dwarves were less greedy and did not pillage the land?" questioned Battlehelm.

"A contract is a contract." said Derfer. "We had rights to the mines, and we exercised those rights within the framework of our agreement. It was the horsemen who lied and cheated, not us."

"We are not here to discuss that." said Mindeloria. "This is a council of war, not of contracts. Lieutenant, please continue."

"The Orcs attacked in the middle of the day. They fell upon the defense like water to the shore. The Dwarf defenders slaughtered thousands; but still they came and were mowed down. Soon the Trolls joined the fight, and with these terrible swords they cut their way through the might fortress."

"What of survivors?" asked Mindeloria.

"Some escaped through secret tunnels and have made their way to the Mystic Mountains. However, most did not and the Troll army took no prisoners," said the lieutenant.

"Who led this attack?" asked Zander. "Surely, you do not expect me to believe a leaderless rabble of Orcs and Trolls were able to defeat the fortress at the Rolling Hills?"

"If there was any leader, it was not seen." replied the Dark Elf.

"An army such as that does not fight without someone giving the orders" said Tordin. "I think we must find that someone or something before it is too late."

"I agree," said Battlehelm. "But where do we look?"

"Why does a man care anyway?" blurted Zander. "It was Dwarves that felt the pain of this army, not man. Why don't you just go back to Ancintron and wait for this battle to come to you."

"I go where I please, Dwarf," replied Battlehelm. "And if we were present, there would not have been a defeat such as this. A leaderless army of Trolls and Orcs attacking in midday? Have the Dwarves become so weak?"

"Open your mouth again, man-child, and I will show you how weak the Dwarves are," said Zander, as both he and Derfer stood up. Zander pulled a short sword from his tunic.

Just then a blinding light hit Zander in the chest and drove him back from the table.

"I will not tolerate actions such as this in my council. Do you not understand? It was the voice of Mindeloria. The light had come from his hand and hit Zander squarely in the chest. Burton had no idea there was this kind of power in the world, let alone from someone as peaceful looking as Mindeloria.

"There is no time for your bickering. A war is on us from an unknown source," he said. "The Rolling Hills are gone, and Myopia is in danger. I cannot see where this evil is coming from, but it is here just the same. Now is the time for unity, not this. We must find a way to defeat this evil or we will all fall. One at a time, but we will fall just the same."

As Zander picked himself up off of the floor, Erideous spoke.

"My Lord, my animals tell me that a great army of men is coming from the east. It is led by someone, but I know not who. I am attempting to find out, but the creatures that are small enough to go unnoticed to gain such information, are also very slow when it comes to traveling," he said.

"Men," said Zander, however quietly. "Isn't that the way it always is." He glared at Battlehelm. Burton could feel the loathing between them.

"My Lord, it is time we go," It was Derfer speaking. "My brother and I must return to the Rolling Hills and try to help our people."

"My dear Derfer, I doubt there is much you can do," replied Mindeloria. Burton couldn't help but notice the pained look upon Mindeloria's face. Derfer noticed it too.

"Lord Mindeloria, I know you feel our pain, but you must understand that this is what we must do." stated Derfer. "Our place is with our people, not here."

"I understand Derfer, as I would do no different myself," answered Mindeloria. "Please accept my deepest thanks for your presence here. I hope we meet again under better circumstances."

"Master Brew, Lord Tordin, it has been the deepest honor for me and my brother to meet with you and break bread," said Derfer. "I hope that all goes well with whatever journeys you take,"

With that Zander and Derfer started to leave the room. As they got to the door, Zander turned and defiantly said, "Let me make this clear to all men of Hatu. No matter what evil befalls you and your kind, you will get no help or assistance from a single Dwarf as long as I live. This I swear on my ancestors, and my ancestors' ancestors."

He then turned and left the room with the door slamming behind him.

A silence fell over the room. Burton looked at Lindeloria, who no longer had a smile on her face.

"I declare this meeting adjourned," stated Mindeloria.

Everyone started to get up from their chairs to leave.

"Master Brew, will you please stay and talk for a while?" said the Elf Lord.

Burton looked at Tordin.

"It is time you learn why you are truly here, my friend," said Tordin. "I will meet you in your room later."

"I too will see you later, Master Myopian," said Lindeloria. "Enjoy your talk with my father."

With that, she smiled and left the room empty except for a young Myopian with a great Elf Lord from days gone by.

Six

The Story Unfolds

Burton had a million questions and did not know where to begin. But then where does one begin when addressing the most powerful Elf in Hatu. Before Burton had a chance to say a word, Mindeloria spoke as he descended from his loft.

"I had hoped we would have time to sit and talk of days gone by and I would have the chance to answer all of your questions," he began. "But much has happened in the past few weeks and much must occur in the weeks ahead. I have a special task for you Master Brew."

Burton knew this was the moment he had been waiting for ever since he left the Myopia weeks ago.

"I need you to go to the Mystic Mountains and deliver this message for me." said Mindeloria. He reached under his cloak and pulled out a small cylinder. "In here lies the only hope we have to defeat this new evil. I need you to accompany Lindeloria and Tordin to the Mystic Mountains and find the Dwarves that live in that land. Deliver the message and return with an answer."

"Why me?" asked Burton.

"Did you not see the animosity that was displayed here this evening?" asked Mindeloria. "You are a Myopian and not involved in the disputes that have taken place in the past. These problems between Dwarves and men must be settled before we can form an alliance to defeat this new enemy. The Dwarves respect you, Master Brew. They believe in their past and pay homage to their ancestry. In you they remember the glory days of the great Dwarven kings that lived before them. It is up to you to deliver this. In short, they trust you."

"But I am not a warrior. I have no experience in such things." pleaded Burton.

"A warrior you are," replied Mindeloria. "A great warrior in deed. Possibly the greatest warrior to ever have lived. Have you not suspected so?"

Burton thought for a minute before he answered. He had always picked up on Tordin's teaching very quickly and had begun to notice his ability to anticipate actions before they happened. Like Wendil about to knock on his door this very day.

"I am not Harry or Cyrus, or even Milton. They were great warriors" stated Burton.

"That is true. They were great warriors, but they did not possess your abilities," replied Mindeloria. "Allow me to show you. I notice you are wearing the pin I presented to you and the brooch of Elladoria. Clear your mind and hold both together in your left hand. Think of nothing."

Burton placed his left hand on the items firmly attached to his cloak. He gripped them tightly and started to look down.

"Do not look down Master Brew. Look straight ahead," said Mindeloria. "Do you feel anything?"

"My hand is warm," replied Burton.

"Is that all?" asked Mindeloria.

"Yes, that is all," said Burton. "Should there be more?"

"You tell me," replied Mindeloria. "Hold your right hand straight out and concentrate on the chair at the other end of the room."

Burton did as he was asked, and a white light shot from his hand and the chair blew a part. This was the same type of light that Mindeloria had used on Zander earlier in the evening. Burton released the grip on the brooch and pin and the light stopped immediately.

"Tell me, Burton, do you think that Milton or Cyrus could have accomplished such a feat?" a smiling Mindeloria asked.

"I do not know," said a frightened Burton. "If they had Elf magic items such as these, they might."

"Don't forget they both had brooches, my young friend" said Mindeloria. "No, I think neither could have accomplished what you just did. I think you must learn the power is within you. The pin and brooch are but conduits that channel the energy you already possess. No, Master Brew, I think you must learn to understand that you are quite unique, whether you want to accept it or not. The force you possess will stop any Orc or Troll and has a terrifying effect on many other creatures."

"And what do I do with this power? How do I use it?" asked Burton.

"You have already begun to use it. The battle with the Orcs, the sudden intuition that you have exhibited," replied Mindeloria.

"But I do not understand it. What if I misuse it or do not know when to use it and my friends get hurt because of it? I do not want this responsibility," pleaded Burton.

"As I said," started Mindeloria. "Whether you want it or not, it is yours. You will learn how and when to use it and when not to, just as all Elves have. That is why Lindeloria will accompany you on this journey. She is skilled in the ways of such power, and her tutelage will prove invaluable to you. Tordin, as you are now aware, also possesses such skills. They will provide you all of the guidance and assistance you will need on this journey."

"Has Tordin known this?" asked Burton.

"He is aware of your power, but does not know how powerful you can become. No one knows that, Master Burton, not even I. But rest assured that we will all have answers to these questions by the time this war is over," said Mindeloria.

With that he handed the cylinder over to Burton, who tucked it safely in his shirt.

"For the past few months I have been negotiating with Dwarves and Forlosha to put their feud to rest. It has gone on far too long. I have long seen an evil coming, but have been unable to find out where and when this evil would strike. Our foe has picked the weakest link in our already fragile alliances. Yesterday, I asked Handil to return to Forlosha with a similar offer. He left unnoticed and unannounced, as you will. The offer is simple: Forlosha has agreed to honor all past contracts and reopen the mines around Moewirth Lake. In addition, they will agree to form a combined army designed to react to any community under attack or siege. While it is too late for the Rolling Hills, it may save what is left of the Dwarven race as they are making their last stand in the Mystic Mountains," said Mindeloria. "That is why I need you to get there ahead of the invading army."

"Invading army?" inquired Burton.

"Yes, Master Brew" replied Mindeloria. "The army that destroyed the Rolling Hills is on its way to the Mystic Mountains to finish the task. If they get there before you, there is no hope for the Dwarves. You must get there before the enemy force or all hope is lost. With the Dwarves destroyed, they will attack either the Elven sea ports, cutting off all escape from Hatu, or Myopia, destroying the Rangers and Myopians at the same time. And as you already know, the Myopia is fending off marauding Orcs as we speak."

The thought of an Orc and Troll army tramping through Myopia was almost unbearable for Burton. He wanted to ask Mindeloria permission to forsake this task and return home to defend his friends. However, Burton knew deep down inside that the only way to help his friends and even have a chance to save the Myopia was to fulfill his mission.

"When do we leave?" asked Burton.

"Within the next few days, my friend," said Mindeloria. "There is much preparation to take place. I have already sent word to the Rangers to be on the alert for anything strange and watch for your arrival."

"Then I guess all that is left is to pack provisions and be on my way," said Burton.

Suddenly, there was a sound of trumpets coming from the walls and one of the Dark Elves entered the room.

"My Lord," he said. "Two of our Guards are dead. Their bodies were found hidden in a stable. Captain Wendil has sounded the alarm."

"Please, have the Captain report to me. Double the guard and form search parties immediately," replied Mindeloria.

"It has already been done my Lord. Captain Wendil will be here soon," replied the Guard.

"Thank you and return to your post," commanded Mindeloria.

The guard saluted Lord Mindeloria and left the room, shutting the heavy door behind him. Burton could hear the turn of a lock and knew they were locked in until Wendil arrived or Mindeloria wanted to leave.

"Well, my dear friend, it appears that once again we have run out of time," said Mindeloria. "Whoever or whatever is orchestrating this turn of events has obviously thought long and hard about setting things in motion. I suggest we leave here and start your little party on its way."

Burton was about to reply when he heard the lock click and the door opened. It was Wendil.

"My Lord," Wendil said, addressing Mindeloria. "Two of our men are dead and it appears to be the work of spirits."

"I thought Dark Spirits were a myth." Burton said.

How could anything have gotten through defenses such as these? thought Burton.

"They are very real, Master Brew," replied Wendil.

Burton could swear he heard, no felt, a distant rumble. Almost like subdued thunder. He looked at Mindeloria and it was obvious that he had felt, or sensed it, too. As did Wendil.

Both Mindeloria and Wendil drew their swords. Mindeloria had a beautiful weapon that was burning a bright red. Never had Burton seen such a sword. It was at least six feet long and looked as if it were on fire. Wendil's sword was also a magnificent weapon that glowed with a white light.

"Elven blades," thought Burton. "How beautiful and mighty they were."

Burton then pulled out Warlight.

"My young Myopian, you questioned me about your being a warrior earlier," said Mindeloria. "I think you are about to find out much more than you wanted to know. Stay behind us as much as you can, but protect yourself at all costs. This is no beginners' task you are thrust into today."

Burton could hear the sound of battle just outside the door. Whatever was out there had already defeated the outside guards and was about to make short work of the inside guards.

He also noticed how bright the room had become. His vision saw Mindeloria and Wendil clearly, but everything else was bathed in a white light. It struck him that this was the first time he saw things like this. Normally, the Elves glowed white and all else was clear. But there was no time to think of this any further as the door blew open and in came five Dark Spirits.

Three fell upon Wendil and two went down with a single stroke. And then Wendil fell. Burton could see the light from him diminish until he was gone from his sight. He knew he was dead.

The other two made their way towards Mindeloria. It was obvious they knew he possessed great power, as they did not attack him as they did Wendil. Rather they tried to circle.

For the first time in his life, Burton saw the true power of an Elf Lord. Mindeloria did not strike with his sword, but reached out as if he had entered one of the spirits. The Dark Spirit exploded and was gone. He then turned his attention to the second one. Once again, he simply raised his hand and white light shot out, hitting the spirit squarely in the chest. It drove him up against the wall, and with a final shriek, he, too, exploded and was gone.

That left but one Dark Spirit.

After it had killed Wendil, it turned towards Burton. While Mindeloria had made quick work of two of these creatures, this one pressed in on Burton. It was the very one that had killed Wendil, Captain of the Guard of Fallquint.

Burton noticed the dark foreboding shadow that the spirit possessed. The undead, that is what this was.

The spirit struck a blow at Burton, who easily avoided it. Burton then thrust at the target that deflected his blow as well.

Once more it came at him, more intensely then before, as if this was the target of the entire attack. Burton once again easily avoided the blow. He struck back.

Warlight found its mark. With a howl of a wolf the spirit dropped to its knees. Burton quickly withdrew his blade and struck the vile creature in the chest.

The Dark Spirit dropped, lifeless, and then faded away leaving just old bones, dust, and rusted armor behind.

"Come Burton," urged Mindeloria. "It is time we go. I fear our enemy has grown far more powerful than we had first imagined. This is not the work of a mindless rabble."

Just then Erideous, Tordin, and Lindeloria came into the room. Tordin and Lindeloria had swords drawn.

"Are you alright, Father," asked Lindeloria.

"Yes, I am Princess. But I fear we have lost a good friend and confidant."

They looked over at the lifeless body of Wendil. Burton had not known him for long, but he liked him.

"I will send someone to take care of him later," continued Mindeloria. "But now we must look to the living. I think you must leave within the hour. The enemy knows of this place. For them to get this far undetected and unchallenged does not bode well. Please gather up your belonging and meet back here quickly."

They started up the long hallway towards the cave entrance. Burton saw the dead door guards and thought how they must have fought to defend their Elf Lord. At the entrance to the cave were four more dead Elves. The carnage made Burton's stomach turn.

"Are you alright, Master Brew?" asked Tordin.

"I am fine, Tordin," replied Burton. "Much has happened today, but I am fine."

"Do you still question your abilities as a warrior, Master Myopian?" asked Mindeloria. " It was no mindless Orc you struck down today, my friend. That was a Dark Spirit of great renown, a Captain of Men from the old days. It was not by chance that he came for you. Not by chance at all"

Burton now wondered if there was a master plan in all of this or was he just in the wrong place at the wrong time. All he knew for sure was that he was heading home. Maybe not directly home, but at least farther away from armies and Dark Spirits.

Or so he thought.

Seven

To The North and Beyond

Much of the time Burton spent in Fallquint had deeply impressed him, and these last few days showed him a side of Hatu he did not understand. As a Myopian, he led a quiet, peaceful existence. The world of men and Dwarves and even Elves was new to him, at least as far as this side of things. The hatred and pain of these races was truly sad. Thinking about it made Burton homesick and made him want to just return to his own humble home. If he was so powerful, surely his presence in Myopia would be enough to save his small, peaceful corner of the world.

The small party assembled towards the northern end of the city. Here it was remote and there were few to be seen. Only the occasional Elf patrol as had been order by Lord Mindeloria earlier in the day. Here they met Tordin, Lindeloria, and Milo and Silo. Also with them was the young Ranger who had been at the meeting in the cave. His name was Warrant.

"Young, Master Myopian, I am glad you survived your encounter with the enemy today," said Warrant.

"As are we all," chimed in Tordin. "Word has already spread throughout Fallquint of a great Myopian warrior arising to join the fight against the enemy in our great hour of need."

Burton could not help but notice the slight smile on Tordin's face.

Milo moved directly to Burton's side.

"Erideous has directed that one of these beasts is to be with you at all times," said Mindeloria. "They will walk and sleep with you and protect you throughout your journey".

Burton patted Milo on the side and the great beast looked at Burton as if the two had known each other for years, instead of weeks.

Silo looked at Lindeloria and ran ahead. Burton already understood that one of the wolves would be his constant companion and one would act as the scout for their small band as they travel to the Mystic Mountains.

"We will make our way to the north along the base of the mountains. There is a small encampment of Rangers located near the Northern Moors," said Tordin. "There, Warrant will rejoin his command, and we will rest for a short time. Once we leave there we will make our way further north until we come to the edge of the West River, at the western corner of the Northern Wasteland. Then we will turn southwest and travel to Cye, the Lost Kingdom. Once again, we will meet with Rangers there who will provide us rest and shelter."

"Once you leave Cye, your dangers will truly grow," said Mindeloria. "There are no more Ranger outposts or places to seek shelter until you reach the Mystic Mountains and find the Dwarf settlement."

"That is why we will no longer travel west but will once again turn north to the Great Ice Bay, keeping between the bay and the low hills. We will follow the shoreline of the bay until it runs into the northernmost ridge of the Mystic Mountains," said Tordin.

Then he turned to Burton.

"Did I not tell you our way from Fallquint would be far different from our arrival," he said.

"I pray you speed and safety along the way," said Mindeloria. He looked at Lindeloria, and Burton could see the love between father and daughter.

Lindeloria looked at Mindeloria and simply smiled.

Then a small patrol of Dark Elves appeared with a package and presented it to Mindeloria. He took the package and unwrapped it. It was the sword of Wendil. He handed the sword to Tordin.

"My friend, I give you this sword in service to the free peoples of Hatu. May it serve you in the struggles to come as it served its past master," said Mindeloria, as he handed the great blade over.

"I thank you, my Lord," replied Tordin.

He then took his old sword out and replaced it with this new blade.

"Does it have a name?" asked Burton.

"Yes, but I will not say it now" replied Mindeloria. "For then you would want a history and might even want to know who made it, my inquisitive Myopian."

Burton knew that he had asked one too many questions and felt it was time to move on.

"Come, we must begin our journey" said Lindeloria.

"I wish you well and shall see you upon your return," stated Mindeloria. With that, he turned and walked away.

Lindeloria looked at Burton as if she were reading his mind.

"Worry not, Master Burton, we will return once our task is complete. And fear not for my father, he has been through much in his life and there are none alive that can harm him. Not in this realm or the next. He has traveled roads far more perilous than ours and has battled creatures from the deepest, darkest parts of the world," she said.

"He is as Elves were meant to be," she continued. "He is from before time and has walked the Halls of Life. He is one of the first and one of the mightiest ever to have lived. No, Master Burton, make no mistake. My father is here at the right time and in the right place, and he will be safe."

As she said that, she picked up her pack and the party began to depart Fallquint.

"Stay close to me, Master Brew" said Tordin. "The way from Fallquint will be very difficult this time."

The path they took was winding and at times very narrow. They passed though many magic doors and hidden entrances. Some filled Burton with terror, while others left him confused and disoriented.

Tordin led the way, with Burton behind him, and then Lindeloria and Warrant. That's if you don't count Silo, who was not in sight of the small band. And then, of course, there was Milo.

Milo had strict orders and stayed by Burton's side no matter what. In some of the tighter places, Burton and Milo had such a hard time staying together that the great wolf would snatch Burton and tossed him on his back. There Burton would sit until Milo decided it was time for him to walk again. Then a slight shake, like a dog that had just come out of the rain, and Burton would go sprawling to the ground. This brought many a smile to Lindeloria and Warrant as they could see the action take place. Burton marveled at how such a giant animal could be so graceful and quick. After the first few times, Burton began to land on his feet whenever the animal tossed him. Soon it became a game between the two, as Burton would try to anticipate the snatch and toss. Of course, we all know about Great Wolves and how playful they are.

The two were so caught up in the game that Burton had not even noticed how far they had traveled and that the terrain was now smooth, with woods to the left and the mountains to the right.

He soon was in awe of the majesty and height of the mountains.

"Tordin, have you ever been in the mountains?" he asked.

"Yes, many times," replied Tordin.

"They are so big," said Burton.

Burton had never seen a mountain before. While he was in Fallquint, he had noticed them, but there was so much going on that he never really looked at them until now.

"Yes, they are big and beautiful, are they not?" asked Lindeloria.

"Yes, they are," replied Burton. "Have you been in the mountains before? Mountains as big as these?"

"Yes, and bigger," said Lindeloria.

"Bigger?" exclaimed Burton.

"Much bigger, my young Myopian" stated Lindeloria. "I have spent weeks if not months in the mountains. When I was younger, my father would take me to visit the Dwarves in the Rolling Hills."

Burton noticed how her face saddened as she spoke. Her eyes looked to the mountains as if she were reliving all of her trips and remembering each face and event as if it happened yesterday.

"The Dwarves back then did not hate as they do now," she continued. "They were more like Derfer, whom you met in Fallquint. Kinder and gentler. That is as Dwarves go."

A smile crossed her lips.

"We rest here for a while," said Tordin, as he placed his things on the ground beside him. "How is the arm, Warrant?"

Burton had not noticed that Warrant had removed the sling several hours earlier.

"It is fine, my Captain," replied Warrant.

Burton and the others removed his pack, and they all sat down. As they did, Milo was so close that he almost sat on Burton as he let his great mass settle to the ground beside him.

"It seems the Great Wolf takes his duties to heart," laughed Warrant.

Burton liked Warrant. He was like Tordin, and yet not like him. Burton knew that there was no Elf blood in Warrant's veins, but still he was tall and sturdy and somehow noble. Burton's opportunities to visit with men such as these had been very limited. He liked the few that he had met, but he did not understand most. He thought this might be a good time to get to know one better.

"Excuse me, Warrant, but I have not known many men such as yourself. Would you mind if I asked a few questions?" asked Burton.

"Ask away, Master Myopian," replied Warrant.

"I can't help but notice how different you all are. Handil of Forlosha was quiet and appeared to want to learn, while Battlehelm of Ancintron was antagonistic and seemed to hate every race but his own. And yet, is it Forlosha that has the grievance with the Dwarves and not Ancintron. Why is this? Are all men thus?"

"The Myopian is wiser that you said, Captain," said Warrant in the direction of Tordin.

"I will try to answer your question, but the answer is far more complicated than the question I fear," said Warrant.

"No, not all men are thus and yet they are." started Warrant, began.

"In Myopia," he said, "do you not have different families and different views? Do you not want different things and yet you want what is best for Myopia at the same time? It is this way with other men, too. Our many races are like families. We want unique things for our families and our friends, and yet we want the same thing for all. Do you understand?"

"Not really," said Burton shaking his head. "How can you want the same thing for all races and yet hate so? I do not understand."

"I think all races do want the same thing. And that thing is to live in peace and live the way we want to live. Without other people dictating how we do it. In Forlosha, there is peace and joy, and the people are happy. They have their problems with the Dwarves and in time there is no doubt they will work those problems out," said Warrant.

"The world of other men is not a bad world," said Lindeloria. "They are much like Myopians."

"Men are not at all like Myopians." said Burton.

"Are they not?" asked Tordin. "Do they not want to live in peace and be left alone from outside troubles and strife? Do they not care when the rest of Hatu is hurting and it is beyond their control? Do they not fear, and, yes, even hate things or situations they do not understand? I think they are more like Myopians than you would care to admit, my young friend."

"Myopians do not hate so!" commanded Burton.

"Do they not?" said Lindeloria softly. "Yet you do not love the Orc or the Troll?"

"But those are evil things. They were put here to destroy and kill. They do not wish peace unless it is on their terms, unless they are the masters and we are the slaves. No, I think I shall never understand or love such thinking as this." replied Burton.

"As some men do not understand Myopians, or Elves and even Dwarves?" asked Warrant.

Warrant continued. "I do not love the Orc or Troll, and there are members of other races, other cultures I do not like either. Not because I do not understand them, but because I do. There will always be evil, Master Brew. Evil in all forms, the outward evil of the Troll and Orc, the evil of Men and Dwarf breaking their word to one another, and the evil of plague and famine. But not all Men hate such as you believe Battlehelm and the Dwarf Zander do. They stand for their people and simply wish to protect them from things that will harm them and things they do not understand."

"Much like Myopians, Master Brew" said Tordin.

A black shadow appeared from the trees. It was Silo. He approached Tordin.

"It is time to move now. Silo has been many miles ahead. There is no danger in front of us," said Tordin. "But I fear the longer we delay, the greater it will grow. Come."

With that they all got up and picked up their belongings and started on their way North. Silo shot ahead and was soon lost in the thickets again.

Burton mulled over the conversation and tried to make sense of what he had heard. In some way he felt more self-assured and not as distrustful of other Men as he had been. Much of what was said did make sense to him, as he thought about it. He did not fully agree with the comparisons of other Men and Myopians, but he did understand how much both races simply wanted to live a peaceful, quiet life. His thoughts wandered back to Myopia and his friends as the small band came to a stop for the night.

EIGHT

A New Day

Ten days had passed since Burton and his party left the safety of Fallquint and the house of Mindeloria. The time had passed very quickly and was uneventful. Burton had the chance to have many conversations with Warrant and began to get a better understanding of how things worked outside of Myopia. While he didn't agree with all of it, he found that his way of thinking, and his attitude towards others was slowly changing. He was beginning to understand more and more about the world as it was seen through the eyes of others. He also had a few opportunities to "practice" many of his newly discovered powers.

It became apparent to Burton that he could channel the energy from his brain through to his hand. Not really channel, but think it through. He merely grasped the brooch and pin in one hand, concentrated, and a white light would shoot from the other hand towards a target. The light was not nearly as powerful as the one he had seen Mindeloria produce, but it could still move objects such as large boulders and break small trees. He might never be able to kill anyone with this magic, but they would know he was there. He became quite proficient with his ability to hit a small target and was learning now how to spread it out from a pinpoint beam to a wide beam. Of course, the wider the beam, the less potent the strike. This was something that Burton did not really want to know, but Lindeloria insisted he learn how to use a wide beam.

On this day they had camped beside a large river, the largest river Burton had ever seen. At first, he thought it was a lake, but then he realized he could see the other side. The river was just over a mile wide and had very little current. Tordin informed him this was the most northern branch of the Great River. And that they would have to cross it in order to get to the Ranger camp in the Northern Moors beyond.

Warrant took off to the west once they arrived at this spot.

In the last few days, Warrant began to take more and more solo trips into the woods and surrounding countryside. It was clear to Burton that this was his ground, and he knew his way around.

"Where has Warrant gotten off to this time?" asked Burton.

Tordin replied, "He has gone to get us a boat so that we may cross the river and camp with my kinsfolk in just a couple of days."

A boat, thought Burton. How grand! He had never been in a boat, and this would be another one of those great adventures just like Milton had experienced a long time ago. Burton could hardly wait. And as we know, Burton did not have the fear of water that most Myopians do.

Soon a small sail appeared near the shoreline and came toward the party. At the helm of the boat was Warrant.

The boat was not very big, and Burton wondered how the small party would fit into it. Of course, he already knew that he and Milo could fit into spaces smaller than this, but he was not so sure about the rest.

Warrant guided the little craft to the shore.

"We must hurry," he exclaimed. "There are Orc about."

The party packed their belongings and were ready to get into the boat when Silo appeared and jumped in ahead of them. As soon as Burton started in, so did Milo. Burton noticed that the animals were not comfortable, and he began to think they might capsize the craft in the middle of the river. Since Burton did not know how to swim, this thought bothered him very much.

Lindeloria got into the boat and went up to each of the wolves and sang softly in their ears. They both fell fast asleep, first Silo and then Milo. Before he slept, Milo gave Burton one more look, as if to say "I am not supposed to sleep right now." And then despite a valiant effort to stay awake, he fell fast asleep.

Finally, Tordin got into the boat and pushed it away from the shore.

Warrant deftly maneuvered the craft and soon they were making their way across the great river.

Just then Burton heard a sound that he had never heard before. A whizzing sound going right past them. He began to look around when Tordin pushed him to the floor.

"Orc arrows! Stay down," commanded Tordin.

Being a Myopian with a natural curiosity, Burton had to peek over the back of the boat. What he saw amazed and frightened him.

These were the biggest Orcs he had ever seen. They dwarfed the Orcs he had encountered on the road to Fallquint. Heavily armored from head to toe, with each carrying a huge shield, that was covered in red with a back orb in the middle. There were at least fifty of them, and they were firing arrows as fast as they could. The boat had moved out of direct firing range, so the Orcs were lobbing the arrows in as if trying to rain down upon them. At times the sky was so full of arrows that Burton was sure they would be hit. However, no one was, and soon the Orcs gave up. There they were, a band of Orcs standing on the shore screaming and hollering at the top of their lungs. The sound was so shrill and heavy that it seemed to crawl up Burton's spine. Right now, all he wanted was to get to the opposite shore and dry land.

Just as the craft reached the opposite shore, Tordin jumped out, followed by Lindeloria and Warrant. Burton was just about to get out of the boat when the same cry he heard from the opposite shore came from the woods ahead.

"Stay in the boat!" commanded Tordin.

Just then over twenty Orcs came from the woods ahead. They were dressed in the same attire as those on the other side of the river. Burton could hear the cries of approval from the Orcs on the south bank. It was a trap!

All three of his companions drew their swords and faced the oncoming Orcs. The Orcs must have been surprised to see three such as these, and they hesitated. When they did, Tordin gave the boat a strong push from the shore and sent Burton and his two sleeping wolves down the river to the west.

"Stay to the shore. I will find you later," said Tordin who turned to face the onrushing Orcs.

As the little boat drifted the into the center channel, Burton was amazed at how the current picked up. So did the wind. Burton looked back at his companions and saw that Warrant and Tordin were heavily engaged in the battle and the Lindeloria was facing the river with her sword shining brightly in the sun. With a copper hue to the magnificent weapon, she was standing with her arms outstretched and was looking to the sky as if praying. Burton understood. It was she who was strengthening the current and causing the wind to pick up. More of that Elf magic!

Try as Burton might, he could not get the craft to turn back. Burton knew that if he was to do anything to help his friends, it had to be now.

With that he grasped his brooch and pin and held his hand out, aiming at one of the largest Orcs in the battle. The distance grew and Burton let forth a pinpoint stream of light that hit the largest Orc right in the eye. Burton had never heard such a scream in his life. The other Orcs appeared to grow confused and almost began to fight with each other in an effort to make sense of what had just happened.

Burton took one last look and saw a smile from Lindeloria as she turned to join the battle. Her golden hair burned hot white and the copper sword looked as if had grown to a length of at least twelve feet. As she jumped into the fray, Burton could not help but almost have pity for what he knew was about to befall the Orcs and suddenly noticed how quiet it had gotten.

The small boat drifted under the strong current and swift breeze for many miles. Burton knew that there was not a man or beast in Hatu that could keep up with the speed he was no approaching.

Then the current stopped and the wind died. Suddenly and without warning the boat drifted back to the northern bank.

Burton was tense as he reached the riverbank and pulled Warlight from its sheath. It glowed with a very faint light. That meant there were Orc about, but they were not very close. The problem was that Burton had never been alone like this, with the threat of an Orc attack. How close was close? Or not close, for that matter! Regardless, his guard was up as he jumped from boat and onto shore. It seemed that the small boat had drifted for hours. He wondered how many miles had he traveled, and how far away he was from his companions. Did they win the battle and were they still alive? A myriad of thoughts raced through Burton's head as he tried to gain his bearings.

Then his two sleeping guards awoke and leapt straight to his side. It was as if they were supposed to do so as soon as Burton stepped back on dry ground. Burton was happy to see them, and they appeared to be happy to see him as well. Once again Milo, took up his usual position at his side, and Silo bounded off into the woods.

Burton gathered his things and thought about where to go next. His first thought was to go back the way he had come and hope that he would find a Ranger or his party. He knew that Tordin would travel west along the river and if he went east, they would have to meet in the middle.

However, Milo had other thoughts. Every time Burton attempted to go east, Milo blocked his way and pushed him north. While this frustrated Burton, he soon realized that maybe the wolf knew something that he did not.

Finally, Burton stood face to shoulder with the great beast and said; "If you will not let me go the way I want, then point me in the direction I should go. Tordin told me to stay close to the river and follow the shore."

The Great Wolf Milo then crouched as low as he could go, almost as if bowing to Burton. He then snatched Burton by the cloak and tossed him on his back, as he done during their departure of Fallquint, and leaped into the woods, leaving the river behind and once again going north.

NINE

NEW WAYS AND NEW FRIENDS

Milo and Burton went deeper and deeper into the forest. Many times Burton had to cut his way through the thick underbrush. At times he felt as if he were suffocating and the forest was closing in around him. Never had he been so scared and so alone. Alone except for the great wolf.

Milo did as command and stayed by his side. Just like in Fallquint, Milo would pick up Burton, let him ride awhile, and then toss him when he saw fit. But Burton noticed that the rides were getting farther and farther apart. Another thing he noticed was that Silo was staying a lot closer than before the party had split up and went their separate ways. Burton thought this was because of the thickness of the brush and density of the forest.

Burton found himself thinking more and more about all of the conversations he had with Warrant since their departure from

Fallquint. He liked this Ranger. He knew that Warrant was a kind, gentle soul, and yet he was s great a warrior in the defense of his realm. He and his kind had kept a watchful eye on Myopia for thousands of years. Surely, he was a better example of man than others. Burton was pondering this thought when they came to a small clearing at the edge of the woods.

In the clearing was a very old house. Burton was sure no one lived here, as the house was run down and dilapidated. It was overgrown with weeds and vines, and where there was once a fence, there was now just broken timber that was sticking up here and there. There was once a chimney on the house as well, but most of the stone work had long given up its shape and collapsed into ruin. There were numerous holes in the roof, and the front door was half off its hinges.

"What a fine house this must have been at one time," thought Burton. "We should be very careful," he said to the wolves.

Silo once again took the lead as they approached the main structure of the house. Burton pulled Warlight.

It glowed brightly in the afternoon sun. Orcs were very close.

Just then Milo spun around and looked behind them. Burton had learned from his trip to Fallquint to be extra careful when something or someone might be behind them. He quickly decided to hide in the house. If there was a back door, they could slip out through it if they needed to.

"Come," he said to Milo.

And they both raced into the house and found there was indeed a back door. "Milo, go get Silo and stay on the edge of the woods," commanded Burton. He was sure Milo did not want to go, but he added in as stern voice as he could muster, " Do as I command."

Milo reluctantly obeyed, quietly leaving through the back door and disappeared into the woods behind the crumbled shack. Burton looked around and found there was a second room off the main room he was in. He decided that he would hide in there, just in case the Orcs came into the house. With his sword drawn, he crawled into what appeared to be one of the bed chambers of the old house. There were old mattresses, rotten clothes, and linen everywhere. Whoever lived here had left in a hurry.

Burton found an old pile of linen and crawled under it, making sure he could see the door he had just come through. He was not going to put himself in a position that he could not at least see what was coming his way.

As he finally got settled, at least two, maybe three, Orcs entered the main room. They were dressed in the same battle armor as the others who had attacked them hours ago. Burton lay silent as one of the Orcs spoke.

"My feet are killing me," he said.

"Mine, too." replied the other.

"How long before we get off this lousy patrol?" inquired the first Orc.

"It will not be long now," said the second Orc. "The wizard and his army will be here within a fortnight, I'm told."

Wizard! What wizard? thought Burton. Why would Erideous be out here and in league with Orcs? It's not possible.

"Well, it can't be soon enough if you ask me" said the first Orc. "With that stinkin' Myopian and his Elf friends comin' this way, it can't be soon enough."

"They'll never make it past the river" said the second Orc. "Raznic and his boys will stop them for sure. Eighty against a handful. Should be no contest."

"Yah, but what if they sneak by or fight their way through. You know how them stinkin' Elves are," said the first.

"Even if they do, they'll get no help from those blasted Rangers." said a new voice.

There were three, not two. This made Burton's heart heavy. He knew now that if he were discovered, he was done for.

"We got them good, didn't we, boys?" said the first. "Found that camp they called a stronghold and took care of business straight away. They'll not be givin' no help to no Myopian and his Elf friends that's for sure."

Burton knew what this meant. The Orcs had found and destroyed the Ranger camp in the Northern Moors. So even if Tordin, Warrant, and Lindeloria did survive, there was no longer anywhere for them to go. He started to regret not staying close to the river as Tordin had directed. What a bad string of luck this was. How would he find his friends, that is, if they were still alive?

"Well, come on, you goldbrick. Let's get back to work. There may still be one or two of those pesky Rangers running around." said the third Orc.

"Don't worry, they won't be around for long." said the first.

"Get your gear and let's get a move on." said the third.

Relief came over Burton. He now felt confident that he would not be found. He could hear the three leave when one of them said something that made his breath stop.

"Should we search the house?" Inquired the second Orc.

"Nah," replied the third. "Just set a torch to it"

A few seconds later, Burton heard the sound of something thrown into the front room and caught the unmistakable smell of smoke.

The house was on fire.

Afraid to move, Burton stayed buried under the pile as long as he could stand it. One more look at Warlight showed his enemies had moved on, and it was safe to come out.

He tossed the pile from himself and began to look for a way out. The smoke was so thick he could not make out a single shape in the room. He could find neither door nor window. He was lost in this hellish place and began to feel his way along the floor, trying, no sensing, how to stay away from the heat. Burton was trapped, and although there were ways out, he could not find them. He began to feel helpless and felt a panic building up inside of him.

Just then he heard the howl of a wolf to his left. Milo! Maybe Silo! Either way it was like a light in the darkness. Light! That's what he needed. He grasped his brooch and pin and held his hand up. A wide beam of white light burst forth. But light is no match for smoke, he thought. As a matter of fact, he noticed how the light actually reflected from the smoke and created a kaleidoscope of colors. Even though he was in a fight for his life, Burton could not help but notice the beauty of the smoke as it caught the light from his hand.

Just then a great figure reached down and gripped him. Placing him under his arm, the massive giant burst through the thin wall of the shack and carried him to the safety of the woods.

As his eyes cleared, Burton could focus on the shape that had rescued him. It was a Dwarf.

Derfer as a matter of fact.

"And how is my young Myopian today?" asked Derfer.

"Okay, I think." replied Burton, standing up and brushing the filth from his body. "What are you doing here?"

"I am on my way to Doubblegate to have council with my kinsmen." said Derfer.

"Where is your brother?" asked Burton.

"He is gathering those that are left of my people and will find his way to Doubblegate in a short time." said Derfer. "I do not know how many he will have with him, for not all of my people were taken or killed in the siege. Some escaped."

Burton noticed how proud Derfer was of the fact that some of the Dwarves had escaped the massacre of the Rolling Hills and the ruin of his people.

"Tell me, Master Brew, how is it I find you here alone in the wilderness?" said Derfer.

"We were on our way to a Ranger camp near the Northern Moors when we were ambushed by Orcs. Tordin kept me in a boat and set it afloat just before the battle began. The Lady Lindeloria called upon the water and wind to push me down river and here I am." said Burton.

"So where is the rest of your party?" Asked Derfer.

"I do not know." replied Burton sadly. "The last thing I saw was the Lady Lindeloria turn, and join the battle, and then all got quiet. After that, I know nothing else. I did overhear some orcs and they said that the Ranger camp we were heading to was destroyed. That and some talk of a wizard."

"Yes, the Ranger camp was found and razed." stated Derfer. "I got there too late to help and I don't think there was any left alive. As for a wizard, that, too, is true, I am afraid."

"But the only wizard left in Hatu is Erideous. Surely he is not with the enemy?" exclaimed Burton.

"No, No." replied Derfer. "Remember your history, Master Brew. There were four wizards who came to Hatu to fight the Dark King. There was Quickfoot, Erideous, and two other wizards who went into the eastern lands. It is one of them who has raised the army and incited the Orc and Troll that now hound us. I have discovered that his symbol is a black orb on a red field. A Crystal Stone, I think. He is Maloneous, and he is a master of manipulation and guile. It is said that he has spent all these past years living with the men of the east as a high king. His rule is absolute, and he has been waiting for a time to conquer the rest of Hatu and make this his own realm.

One of the Holy Wizards, thought Burton. "Why now?" he asked.

"It has been said," replied Derfer "that he was in league with Porttia during the dark days of his reign. Many believe that he was in possession of a Crystal Stone, and it was because of his involvement that the armies of the east came to Porttia's aid, bringing a massive army of eastern men to his arsenal. With the defeat of Porttia, he simply faded away and was forgotten about until now."

"But I thought the King of the easterners was King Bulclius? Is it not he who has brokered the peace with Ancintron these many years?" asked Burton.

"No, Master Burton, it was not he who orchestrated peace with Ancintron." replied Derfer. "For it seems the real power in the eastern realm has been behind the throne in the shape of Maloneous, and until Maloneous recently decided to step forth and take control of the kingdom, there was a false peace. It is he who has planning this war for many hundreds of years. His hated of the people that destroyed the staff of power has festered for twenty-five hundred years, and it is now that has he chosen to exact his revenge. He believes that he can exact that revenge by eliminating and enslaving the races one at a time. He has started his attacks with us Dwarves as we are an isolated people, and he believes that when we are defeated, the rest of Hatu will be destroyed one by one."

"I know that the Dwarves are the most highly trained warriors in Hatu, but surely he cannot believe that by destroying them the rest will so easily succumb to his tyranny?" asked Burton.

"Master Myopian, if the Dwarves in the Mystic Mountains fall, he can easily sweep down upon the Elf sea ports and cut off any hope of escape. He then will march through Myopia to the very doorstep of Fallquint. With the fall of Fallquint, the Elves will have been defeated, and he can go south to destroy Forlosha, where it is said he will construct a fortress and take it as his home. All the while, his massive army of Men will pour in from the east and lay siege to Ancintron and its people. With the fall of Forlosha, he will crush Ancintron between two great armies and his conquest of Hatu will be complete. If he succeeds, Master Brew, he will have his revenge."

"Surely, he cannot have a big enough army to accomplish such a feat? inquired Burton.

"Neither one, nor two, but three such armies, I'm afraid," replied a sullen Derfer. "The army of Orcs and Trolls that defeated my people in the Rolling Hills numbers in the range of fifty thousand and has begun its march towards Doubblegate, the Great Dwarf city of the Mystic Mountains. A second army of Men, of about the same number will follow within weeks and support the great Orc hoard in its quest to devour the western world of Hatu.

"Fifty Thousand Men and Orcs against one city, surely there is no hope!" thought Burton.

"Another army of men, another fifty thousand strong is poised to encircle Ancintron and lay siege to their mightiest city," continued Derfer. "I'm afraid the future for them is very bleak, indeed."

"So what are we to do?" asked a shocked Burton.

"We must continue our quest and resume our duties Master Brew. That is what we must do," said a suddenly confident Derfer. "I will go to the great city and provide every assistance I can. With luck my brother Zander will gather enough of our people that the Dwarves will make a stand that will rival that of those who defended Mipore and Tresdin."

Both of those cities were great Dwarf cities from long ago, and both cities lay in ruin to this very day. Great defeats in Dwarven history, but heroic stands nonetheless, recalled Burton.

"If we can take enough sting out of the enemy, we may slow them down so that there will be time for song and remembrance of the Last Stand of the Dwarves!" exclaimed Derfer.

Burton noticed how much pride and courage swelled in Derfer as he made this statement. It stirred an ember of hope within him, and he no longer felt that defeat was inevitable, although he did admit to himself, winning was very unlikely!

"Master Dwarf," said Burton. "I must travel to the Great Dwarven city as well as you. Will you please allow me to travel with you? That is me and my companions."

It was the first time that Burton noticed that Milo and Silo had not returned.

"I thought you said that you were separated from your companions?" asked Derfer.

"I meant Milo and Silo," stated Burton, as he looked around.

"If you mean the Great Wolves that were with you," replied Derfer, "they have gone. I found them, or should I say they found me, and I gave them new instructions from Erideous. He has given them orders, and they are on their way."

"Will I see them again?" asked Burton.

"I think so, Master Brew," replied Derfer. "They have been sent to the Elf sea port to deliver a message to the Elf King who dwells there. It is because of the knowledge passed to me from the creatures on the road that I know as much as I do. The wizard Erideous and his animals are hard at work."

"What of Tordin and Lindeloria?" inquired Burton.

"I would not worry about those two if I were you," laughed Derfer. "They are far better off than we are. They are of great lineage, and I think it would take the whole Orc army to give those two any trouble. No, I think we had best just look to ourselves and take care of own business."

"Well, Derfer, where do we go from here?" asked Burton.

"Straight into the fire, Master Brew. Straight into the fire," replied Derfer.

Ten

A Good Night's Sleep?

It had been eight days since Burton met Derfer at the old house and they had begun their journey north through the forest. They came across many Orc sign, but no Orcs. This made Burton very happy, as he was not sure what he would do if they came across a large band of Orcs in the middle of this vast wilderness. So far his taste of battle had not been very sweet. He longed to be back in Myopia, or with his friend Tordin and the others. Burton often wondered what became of them after the fight on the shore. Derfer's words had given him some encouragement, but he wanted answers just the same. The talk of a wizard being involved in this war made him uneasy as well. In the Great War against the Dark King, there were plenty of wizards to go around. Sure, they had Erideous on their side, but he was old and no one had ever seen him perform great feats of magic. His strength was his ability to communicate and correspond with animals. Granted, all wizards have some degree of magical abilities, but Erideous kept any powers he had very close to the vest. Burton's thoughts also turned to Milo and Silo, and what was the great part they had to play in things. They were told to stay with him at all times, and yet something of importance must have occurred for them to be given new orders. But what? Burton wondered if he would ever see any of his friends again.

Burton and Derfer had many conversations about the siege and fall of the Dwarves in the east. Derfer informed him that the siege had lasted many weeks and only when the wizard Maloneous arrived did they actually attack and destroy the besieged Dwarves. He said the battle was glorious, and the Dwarves put up a valiant struggle. But the result was inevitable. Burton asked him of the tomb of Tindron, the Great Dwarf King. Derfer told him the grave had been dug up and desecrated by the Orcs. He did say that the great axe, Smelter, was saved and, he thought spirited away. Smelter was the mighty axe that was placed upon Tindrons tomb when he was buried. It made Burton feel better to know the axe was safe, but still he could not help but feel pity for the Dwarves and the pain they had suffered.

Dwarves had suffered through the ages and had been the target of every evil being to inhabit Hatu. Still, they were a hardy people and despite the constant harassment and ridicule, had done quite right for themselves. It was said that the city of Doubblegate, Burton's current destination, was very beautiful and rivaled that of the Rolling Hills. After the defeat of the Dark King, the Dwarves constructed this city in the hopes that they would have one place to call home and that it would serve as the capital for all Dwarves. Many attempts had been made to move back into other Dwarf habitats, but there still existed an evil living in those places. After several attempts to reclaim them, the Dwarves gave up and looked to rebuild their other realms. That is why the loss of the Rolling Hills was so painful and could prove to be the costliest loss the Dwarves had ever known. Derfer believed that army of Maloneous would travel north through mountain passes far north of the Great River. If that was the route they traveled, then they would pass just north of the Northern Moors and the distance between his friends and Maloneous' army would not be very great at all. This increased the concern Burton had for his friends, a point he brought up to Derfer probably more than he should have.

Derfer was very gentle and kindly towards Burton, especially for a Dwarf. He and his brother Zander were both what would be Princes in other realms, but in the Dwarf world they were called Commanders. Because of the warrior nature of Dwarves, their social structure was more along the lines of a military unit. They had Kings, Dukes, Commanders and Generals. Each line of Dwarves had its own king. There was a king in the Rolling Hills and a King in the Mystic Mountains. They were all direct descendants of the great Dwarf kings of old. If the line was broken, such as the case of the Dwarves of the Rolling Hills, then the purest bloodline that could be established took over the role of King.

Dukes were those relatives of the king who were not direct descendants of the King, but could show some sort of lineage. A duke, it seemed, was more of a thinker or builder in the Dwarven realm. They were the ones who ran the fires and produced the weapons and armor needed to supply a Dwarf kingdom. Commanders were the battlefield representatives of either a living or a past king. Derfer and Zander were just that, descendants of a past king who was dethroned during one of the many Dwarf civil wars. Dwarves, it seems, will fight each other as often as they fight someone else, especially when there is no true enemy to be found. As direct descendants of a past king, they received privilege and title accordingly.

Burton found Derfer to be a very intelligent Dwarf who was very rich in knowledge of Dwarven and Elven history. Derfer told Burton that when he and Zander were young, they journeyed into the forbidden realm of Mertain. He said they wanted to see the remains of that foul place firsthand, to experience the seat of power that Hatu had once been under. Derfer was often lost in thought when the conversation came to Mertain, and was very reluctant to talk about it. Burton made it a point to stay away from the subject as much as possible. To be honest, just thinking about Mertain, the Dark King, and those evil days made Burton uneasy.

It was almost dark when the two settled in for the night. As was their practice, they found a cave or thick underbrush, which was out of the way, where they could sleep. There was never a fire, and Burton longed for a hot meal with tea every time they settled in. However, he knew that there would be no fire until they were safe. Safe somewhere, but where? Burton had assumed that they would go to Cye, as this was Tordin's plan. But the constant travel north made him wonder if this was truly where they were going.

"Is it your plan to travel to Cye or to try to find the Rangers?" inquired Burton.

"I have thought long on this, my young Myopian friend" replied Derfer. "There is a greater risk of being found the closer we get to any populated place. Therefore, I believe that if we go north of Cye and turn west, our chances of getting through undetected will increase tenfold. I do not wish to be found by an Orc patrol now, Master Burton. We have traveled, far but we still have a long way to go."

"Do you still plan to find the Great Ice Bay?" continued Burton.

"Yes, I think that will be our best way," replied Derfer. "Once we pass the Great Bay, we can turn south, at the base of the Mystic Mountains, and we should be able to make it safely the rest of the way. Of course, there is always the chance of an Orc patrol, but it will be far easier to avoid them in the mountains than out here in the open."

The open he calls this, thought Burton. They were surrounded by trees and brush so thick that one could almost choke on it.

"I expect that the great army is not far behind now," said Derfer. "We must get some rest. Tomorrow we will have to pick up the pace."

With that, Burton wrapped his Elven cloak around him and nodded off to sleep.

Sleep was becoming easier and easier to Burton these past few nights. When he first started his journey, he was lucky if he could get two or three hours of sleep on any given night. His once peaceful dreams of Myopia and eagles had long faded into dark despairing dreams of blood and death. For a while Burton was almost afraid to sleep, as he thought those dreams would consume him in a hell that from which he would not be able to awaken. But tonight was different, and once again he dreamed of his home.

Burton was sitting at his breakfast table in his house, having coffee and reading the daily paper that was just delivered by the messenger service. Burton always liked reading the paper after breakfast and catching up on all the local news and gossip.

Today was the day that the farmer's market was to open. A new and extravagant place with row upon row of produce as far as the Myopian eye could see. And Myopians have very good sight.

There were all his neighbors with their shop tables full of corn and apples, berries and pears. What a site to behold, thought Burton, as he turned the page.

Oh my, he thought, a sale of gardening equipment at the local shop. Hoes and shovels and wheel barrows, all marked half-price. What a savings! He could save many a farthing this day.

Burton noticed the smell of a freshly baked pie wafting through the kitchen window. Birds were singing beautiful songs, and there was a touch of dew on the grass glistening in the early morning sun. The sweet, unmistakable smell of freshly brewed coffee. What a grand day to be alive, he thought.

Then there was a tap on the front door. Burton got up from his table and went down the hall to open it.

"Who could it be at this hour?" he said softly to himself.

He opened the door, and there stood a Myopian and an Elf.

"May we come in, Master Burton Brew" asked the Elf.

"Why, of course" replied Burton. "Please do come in and join me for a spot of tea."

"That would be wonderful" said the Myopian.

"Please, this way to the kitchen," said Burton, as he led them back down the hall.

"Oh, I know the way very well," said the Myopian.

"You have been here before?" inquired Burton. "Strange, I do not remember you being here before. However, you do look familiar, in an all too unfamiliar way."

"I have spent many hours at this very table, but it was a long time ago, and you were not here then," replied the Myopian.

"However, this is my first time here," said the Elf.

Burton took a moment to notice that the Elf did look familiar. He was tall and had grey eyes. He looked a lot like Tordin, but more Elf than Man. But Burton knew there was Man in there somewhere.

"Please, have a seat," said Burton as he placed the tea service before the two. "Would you like anything else?" he continued, as he poured his visitors their tea. "And what may I do for you today?" he asked.

"It is what we can do for you," replied the Elf. "We come to give you strength in your hour of need."

"My hour of need?" inquired Burton "What hour of need?"

"It is a perilous journey you have begun, Master Brew," said the Elf. "There is much danger ahead for you and your companions. It awaits you at every turn. You must remember your training and reach deep within yourself for the strength to do what must be done."

"I, too, have traveled many roads such as the one you are on," said the Myopian. "I have seen war and death and destruction such as the world has not known for thousands of years. My courage was tested, as yours will be. I know the doubts that trouble you and the worries of such a great responsibility that you and you alone carry. The fate of Hatu may very well rest in your hands before this war is through."

"I did not ask for such a burden, and I do not wish it now!" exclaimed Burton.

"Yet it is already yours," the Elf quietly replied. "Once again the hopes and dreams of all Free Peoples rest in the actions of a single Myopian. Truly a remarkable people!"

"What is it I must do?" asked Burton. "I am only delivering a message for my Lord Mindeloria to the Dwarves. Surely, this is not such an important task that all of Hatu will fall should I not deliver it?"

"There is more to your task than that of a message service." said the Myopian.

"And what would that be?" inquired Burton.

"The answer will show itself in time, Burton," replied the Myopian.

"I am no adventurer," said Burton. "I am not like Will or Tom or Cyrus; nor am I like the Great Milton. I have no staff to unmake, and I do not wish to be a part of any such task that relies solely on me. I do not journey into the depths of Mertain. I neither accept nor am ready for such a responsibility. I do not want it!"

"As I have already said," softly replied the Elf, "The task is yours and yours alone. It is you. No other who bears the burden that has been ordained for you. And bear it you will. Make no mistake, Master Burton, the blood of the Great Milton Brew flows within you and you will undertake things you have never dreamed possible. No, Master Burton, there are many roads you must travel and many obstacles to overcome. But remember. You are not alone. Your companions are always with you, even when they are not. Even now old friends are making their way to a great meeting. The enemy has stirred the fire and more than embers are making their way into the air. Look to your dreams for guidance, Master Burton, it is there you will find us"

"But I do not know who you are?" a confused Burton said.

"Do not be so sure of that," laughed the Myopian. "Just because you have never met us, it does not mean that you do not know who we are. You know our names and you may look for us in your dreams."

Suddenly, Burton woke up. He woke up so fast that he forgot that he was nestled down in a thicket of thorns. He made such noise that it must have been heard for miles, he thought.

"What is it?" exclaimed Derfer, coming forth with his great axe drawn.

"A dream." replied Burton.

"Just a dream?" relaxed Derfer. "What kind of dream would make you act so? Do you not mean a nightmare?"

"No, it was the strangest dream. I was home talking to an Elf and a Myopian. I had never met them before, but they knew me. They told me that I was on some great quest and that I must prevail or all of Hatu will fall."

"And what did these dream-crashers look like?" an unbelieving Derfer asked.

"The Elf was tall and had grey eyes and was obviously powerful, but he was not just an Elf, I think he was half Man" said Burton. "He looked a lot like Tordin."

"And the Myopian?" continued Derfer. "What did he look like?

"I don't know, just a Myopian I guess," replied Burton. "But he was very familiar to me, like I'd seen him before."

"Have you seen him before?" inquired Derfer. He was no longer laughing or disgusted, but was much more interested in what Burton had to say than when he first approached him after he awoke from his slumber.

"I don't think so, but I thought he looked a lot like me, or rather I looked like him," said Burton.

"Strange, how very strange indeed. I have heard of visions before, but I have never had one," said the now studious Dwarf. "It is said that those who possess the gift will get messages from the past and sometimes the future. I believe that you have had one of those visions, Master Brew. Although that is more Elf magic than any kind of magic we Dwarves possess. Gnomes are the only Dwarven race that has the gift of visions. You are very lucky, indeed. I have never heard of this in a Myopian."

"But who were these visitors to my slumber?" inquired Burton. "What does it mean?"

"I do not know," replied Derfer. "But whoever they are. you must have a past tie to them somehow or they could not meet you in the night. This is very strange, Master Myopian. But we will not master this riddle now and I suggest we get on our way and proceed to our destination."

With that they gathered up and started their trek towards the north of Cye and the Great Ice Bay.

Burton could not shake his uneasy feeling until almost noon. He went over and over the dream until it faded away the longer he stayed awake. Before long, all he could remember was that they would be there in his dreams when he needed them and that he must have courage.

And he was about to learn just how important that courage would be!

ELEVEN

THE LAND OF CYE

Burton and Derfer had just finished lunch when a wind began to blow in from the north and the temperatures began to drop. The grey clouds turned to black as if a downpour would burst forth at any moment. Burton and Derfer frantically looked for a place to hide until the impending storm blew over. They happened upon a small cave just as the skies opened up. The thunder was like the sound of cannon and the lightning so frequent Burton thought that it was one steady stream. Never had either of them had ever seen such a storm.

"I wonder how long this will last?" asked Burton.

"I do not know," replied Derfer. "This is the type of storm that I have read about in the ancient text."

"What ancient text would that be?" inquired Burton.

"In the first age, there were many such storms," said Derfer. "It is said that this was a sign the ancients were in battle against one another. Dwarves have never recorded such events because we live underground and the thunder and lightning means little to us. But the rain. The rain is another matter."

"What do you mean? I do not see where rain can matter to Dwarves," said Burton.

"The rain must go somewhere, Master Brew," scoffed Derfer. "It either goes into rivers, which lead to the sea, or it goes to ground. Any ground, you see. Even Dwarf mining colonies. Does that make it any clearer?"

Burton could tell that this conversation was bothering Derfer, but he failed to understand why. So he changed the subject.

Looking back toward the rear of the small cavern, he asked "How far back do you think this goes, and how deep underground?"

Derfer looked to the rear of the cave as well. "I do not know" he replied. "Could be feet, might be miles. No way to know for sure."

"Can we explore?" asked Burton.

"We can look," was Derfer's response. "But I did not think that Myopians liked caves and digging in the dirt"

"We love to garden." said Burton.

"Gardening?" laughed Derfer. "You call that digging in the dirt? That is chicken scratching to a Dwarf, Master Brew. Come with me and I will show you digging in the dirt."

Derfer made a torch out of a part of his tunic and a rather large stick. In the light of the darkness, Burton could see that the cave was quite a bit larger than he expected. There were many corridors and paths leading in all directions in the very rear of the cavern. Some went up, but most went down.

"Which path shall we take?" asked Derfer.

Burton pulled out Warlight and went to the opening of each path, looking for any sign of Orcs. The blade did not change, so he was confident there were no Orcs.

"I think this one." pointed Burton. He had chosen one of the paths that appeared to lead up.

Derfer stuck his head in the doorway as if searching for something.

"I do not like the smell of this one, my young Myopian. Too wet." he said. "I recommend you choose another."

Burton then picked one that went slightly down.

"How about this one?" he asked.

Derfer stuck his head in.

"Much better choice, quite dry in here," was Derfer's reply.

"Then, let's go," a confident Burton said.

And the two started down the tunnel.

It was narrow, and even with the light of the torch they could not see very far. Burton was taken with many of the crystal formations and liked to see the fire from the torch reflect in the many colorful rocks and gems. There were clear stones, and blue stones, and red stones, stones of every color. The light of the torch enhanced their beauty and made colors that danced and shimmered in every direction. Burton was quite taken with the glorious hue that each stone possessed as it was bathed in the light of the torch.

"What kind of stones are these?" he inquired.

"Just some rubies, a few some emeralds, nothing of real value. Those are sapphires." Derfer said, as he pointed to three stones that were at least six inches around. "All virtually worthless."

"Worthless?" exclaimed Burton. "With a handful of these I would be the richest Myopian in Hatu."

"True, but to a Dwarf these are mere trinkets. Give me gold and diamonds any day. That would make you a rich Myopian, indeed." said Derfer.

Just then there was a low rumble from behind them. Burton whirled about with Warlight pulled. The sword showed no change.

"What is that?" asked Burton.

"As I told you Master Myopian water must go somewhere, and I fear it has chosen the same path we have. Run! It is a flood"

So the two explorers took off at a dead run down the tunnel while the sound of the rushing water grew louder and louder. Burton looked anywhere and everywhere for a path out but could find none. He was sure the water would overtake them.

As they rounded a corner of the tunnel path, there was a small path to the right.

Derfer yelled, "Go to the right. The path rises here. Hurry!"

Burton turned to the right and after a hundred feet or so he found himself on a ledge with a sheer drop of a distance he could not imagine, let alone estimate. The opening provided a small ledge on each side of the tunnel they had just emerged from. Burton pinned himself to one side against the wall, and Derfer pinned himself to the other.

They no sooner found this small isle of safety when a great cascade of water poured from the tunnel and spilled into the abyss before them. Never had Burton heard so much noise. The sound was deafening. The water poured straight out twenty feet before it dropped into the cavern. The sheer force of this flash flood was beyond belief.

It lasted about five minutes before it slowed to a small stream and then a trickle before dying out altogether.

"Are you okay, Master Brew?" asked a concerned Derfer.

"Yes, yes I think so," replied Burton, gathering himself and taking inventory as if to see if he was all in one piece. "Is that a common occurrence in caves and underground dwellings?"

"No my friend, it is not," replied Derfer. " That was quite unnatural"

"What do you think caused it?" continued Burton.

"I do not know, but I think we had best move on before something else happens" was Derfer's response. "I suggest we back track and find our way out of these caverns."

So the two went back the way they had come. Many of the beautiful stones were gone and gaping holes were left in their place. Some of the holes were so massive that Burton could almost walk into them.

Since the flood Burton, kept Warlight out and in front of him. He was sure that the evil that befell them in the shape of water was caused by something that was after them, and he was going to be ready.

They at last came to the corridor they had traveled in and turned back onto their original path. The gem stones were once again back where they belonged in the walls of the tunnel. That meant the water had to turn after them and travel up hill in order to try to sweep them into the deep, dark cavern below. This fact was extremely bothersome to Burton, as it meant that someone or something actually tried to direct the water in pursuit. Derfer was right; this was no natural event.

Once again the two came to an opening that offered several choices. After several minutes of debate, Burton gave in and the two took the path to the far left. This path went steeply up hill and it was obvious it had not been used in many, many years. There were no longer any gemstones, but Burton thought he could see notches in the side walls, as if there had once been torches placed at distinct intervals. There were no torches or any other ornaments, but the walls were smooth and, it was clear, manmade. Well, maybe not manmade but not natural just the same.

At last they came to a door. Burton looked at Warlight, and it shone brightly.

"Derfer," he whispered. "There are Orcs on the other side of this door."

Derfer pulled his mighty battle axe from the sling that carried it across his back.

"Good, my axe is ready and my hand is strong," growled the Dwarf.

Burton had never seen a Dwarf ready for battle before. Just the look on Derfer's face; the confidence and disdain; made Burton shudder.

"But I don't know how many," said Burton quietly.

Burton knew that he was about to face an enemy that could kill him, and he was not sure if he was ready for combat.

"Master Brew," scolded Derfer. "We cannot go back. That means our only options are to attack or sit here like children waiting for the rain to stop. Any second they could open that door, and we are in battle nonetheless. I am ready for them, and I will take the fight to them; be the one or one hundred."

With that, Derfer forced open the wooden door and entered the room with his axe swinging.

The light from the room blinded Burton for an instant as all he had experienced for the last few hours was the flickering light from the homemade torch that guided them through the tunnels. There was little time to look around and adjust his eyes.

Derfer threw the torch towards one of the Orcs, hitting him the chest. A second Orc fell under one crushing blow from the might axe. Two other Orcs were sitting in the corner and were so surprised by the sudden onslaught that one of them actually fell backwards in his chair. The other fumbled for his sword, and he was struck dead by a stroke of the axe before his metal blade ever cleared the sheath.

Burton found that his agility was far greater than even he knew. He was able to leap and jump about the room like a gazelle or a mighty mountain lion. He struck down two Orcs with such rapid succession that they almost hit the ground simultaneously. A third was in his sight when he felt an urge to turn and look behind him towards the tunnel they had just come from. Four Orcs appeared in the doorway. Derfer was right, they would have been trapped!

Derfer turned to meet this new threat just as Burton felt the air from the scimitar of the Orc that was directly behind him. A miss! Still far too close for Burton's liking. Burton turned to face his attacker.

This was the first time that Burton stood face to face with one of the large Orcs of Maloneous. He was a huge brute, with armor that covered most of his ugly, hairy body. Burton noticed the stench for the first time. Vile creatures, he thought. With that he launched into a series of stabs and thrusts so violent that they drove the great Orc backwards as he tried to defend himself against Burton Brew of Myopia. Burton felt energy radiate throughout his body and creep into his hand until it became one with the sword. Then Warlight changed color. It turned into a dark grey light and began to grow in length. Soon Burton, too, felt that he was growing. Bigger, taller, and stronger than he had ever felt before. His attack was so intense that he felt he could look the great Orc squarely in the eye. Finally, with one savage thrust, the great Orc fell from a blow that rent armor in two and cut straight to the evil beast's vital organs. The Great Orc was dead before he hit the ground.

Burton felt immediate relief, and Warlight, the might Elf sword, turned back into a silver short sword just about the right size for an average Myopian. It no longer shone with light or looked grey. Burton felt exhausted as he turned to face Derfer.

There was Derfer, staring directly at Burton with a look of shock upon his bearded face.

"What is it?" inquired Burton.

"I have seen Elf magic this day," replied Derfer. "But not from an Elf."

"What do you mean, Derfer" asked Burton.

"Do you not know?" replied the still surprised Dwarf. "You grew Master Brew. As the battle went on, you grew until you were almost the size of a most men. You were bigger than any of these Orcs. As soon as your blade changed to that dark grey, your body became larger and larger. The instant you struck down your foe, you returned to your normal size. Never have I heard of such magic as this. Yet I have seen it with my own eyes. Still, I find it unbelievable. Had I not seen if, I would never believe it. Did you not feel it?"

"I did feel it Derfer, yet I did not know it was happening," said the studious Myopian. "I could feel the energy build, and it released through my sword as I fought."

"Master Burton, there is truly more to you than meets the eye," said Derfer, as he looked upon the Myopian with a new sense of respect. "I would love to know more about this magic, but I think we had best be on our way."

For the first time, Burton looked around the room. They had entered some sort of weapons armory. Rack upon rack of various battle weapons lined the walls. There were pikes and spears, long and short swords, ash longbows and iron crossbows, shields with large and small battle helms. The shields and battle helms were unmistakably Ranger and Ancintron in fashion. He also noticed the dead Orcs. All nine of them.

"These weapons are Ranger, are they not?" said Burton. He had been trained in the history of many cultures and was familiar with most markings and designs of weapons and armor.

"And some fine Dwarf battle gear," said Derfer, as he pawed through a pile in the corner. "I think we have stumbled upon an Orc weapons hoard. Judging by the size of this cache, we must be farther south than I had planned. I believe we are in Cye."

"Cye? Then the Orc army has traveled faster and farther than we thought." replied Burton.

"No, this is no army here, Master Brew. Had we stumbled into an army, they would have descended upon us like flies to sugar. No, I think this is simply an advance party. But I still... what is this?"

Derfer pulled a battle axe from the bottom of the pile. The axe was slightly larger than his, but the way Derfer handled it made Burton think it must be very light, indeed. Derfer swung the weapon back and forth in a figure-eight motion. It actually sounded as if it were singing as it danced under the hand of the mighty Dwarf.

"A grand weapon, indeed," said a delighted Derfer. "Weapons such as this have not been seen in many, many years, Master Brew. This is a weapon from the glory days. Days when we Dwarves were masters of fire, skilled in the making of weapons and other great, magical things. This magnificent axe has seen the beginning, and it will see the end. I know not where it came from or by whose hand it has been seized, but I claim it now in my name. It will once again sing in battle"

Burton knew this was a weapon of great importance to the Dwarf. Derfer was mesmerized by its beauty. It was difficult for him to take his eyes off of it.

"Come, Derfer, I think you are right. It is time we depart," said Burton.

"I agree," said Derfer, and he went forward to the door. "Are there Orc about, Master Myopian?"

Burton looked at Warlight, which was gave no response and did not show any form of light.

"We are safe for now," he said.

Derfer opened the door and Burton could see that they were in what appeared to be a city. Burton had never really seen a city, but this must be what one looked like. There were buildings and more buildings. Some larger than mountains, others small and quaint. But no people. Where were the people? he wondered.

"Welcome to Cye, Master Myopian," said Derfer as he looked right and left. "Home to great kings and ancestral home of the Rangers, protectors of mankind"

Burton could not help but notice the sarcasm in Derfer's voice as he introduced him to the city, home to the men of old, he thought, the home of the Rangers.

Twelve

The Lure of Yesteryear

B urton and Derfer entered the city and began to make their way through its twisting, winding streets. They knew that this was once a great city, but they knew neither the name nor the exact location of where they were. All they knew is that they were in the land of Cye. Their time in the tunnels had gotten them turned around, and they did not know how long they were in the mighty labyrinth or how far they had traveled. Burton figured that they must have departed Fallquint about three months ago now. He knew that they had traveled north and west, but how far he could not begin to fathom. All he knew for sure was that the farther they got from Fallquint, the more perilous his journey had become. Even now in a great city of men, he was not safe and he knew it. He and Derfer spent many hours making their way through the city, being very careful to avoid any unpleasantness with the local Orc population.

After the destruction of the Staff of Power and the downfall of Baldortor, King Sinford ordered the realm of Cye to be reopened and made safe for the return of men. He had hoped that the country would prosper and the greatness of the Rangers be returned to the glory of past days. For a very short time, life did return to this once mighty land. For several hundred years a great population grew and enjoyed prosperity under the watchful eye of the King. After his death, the lands once again fell into decay, and the people moved from the great cities. Many retuned to Ancintron and began life anew within the protective gates of the great capital. Only the Rangers were left in this great realm, and from the looks of things, they, too, had moved on.

The two travelers had several opportunities to engage the Orcs that roamed freely about the street. Burton thought there must be at least a hundred Orcs in the area as they ran across patrol after patrol. Derfer's main concern was that the Orcs they slaughtered in the weapons room would be found and the alarm sounded. If this were to happen before they made their way out of the city, Derfer was sure that they would be doomed. But their luck held, and they at last came to the outer edge of the great city. Here they found that the city was once surrounded by a great wall that encircled as far as the eye could see. But now, that wall was in as much decay as the rest of the city was. It would be dark soon, and Derfer decided they should find a place to hide until after dark. Then they would make their way across the three or four hundred yards that would get them safely back into the woods and away from this hive of danger. The two found a small gate house that had been vacant for centuries and hunkered down to wait out the last couple of hours of light.

"This was once a great city, was it not?" asked Burton. "Do you know the name of it?"

"No, I do not," replied Derfer. "Nor do I care. There are many such cities throughout the land of Cye, and they are much the same as this. It seems that men have no love for their history; nor do they believe in the power of learning from those that have traveled before them."

"Why do you say that?" inquired Burton. "I have met few men, other than Myopians, but they do not seem to be as uncaring or undisciplined as you say they are."

"I do not think that all men are bad," said Derfer. "I just think that as a whole, they allow too many of their bad leaders to guide them with unwise advice and therefore they repeat many of the mistakes they have made since the beginning times. Many times I have been in council with men, and we Dwarves and the Elves have attempted to get them to watch their own borders. We Dwarves understand greed, and too many times have I seen this greed in men. It is that greed and arrogance that has us in this position today. If their great and mighty kings would have listened many, many years ago, this evil that is on us today would not be here."

"What do you mean by that Derfer?" asked Burton. It was obvious that there was more going on here than he had realized. If there had been council given years ago, why did someone not do something about it sooner? That made a lot of sense to Burton.

"Orcs have been seen in the farther reaches of Hatu for going on five hundred years now," continued Derfer. "They have been raiding the Dwarf colonies of the Rolling Hills and the furthest outposts of Ancintron, becoming bolder and bolder with each passing year. Many types of council have been held, Master Brew, and only a few such as the Elf Lord Mindeloria, have paid heed to these troubling events."

"I cannot believe that he is the only one who has heard what the Dwarves have said," replied a defiant Burton.

"Nor do I," said Derfer. "However, there are those, such as my brother, that do not trust Men or Elves; especially when it is not they that are under attack and have very little to lose. We Dwarves are a dwindling number, Master Brew. Time has taken a toll on us, and we are not as mighty as we once were."

Burton could not help but see the sadness that came over Derfer's face as he spoke.

"There was a time that our might equaled any that lived in Hatu. Our armies were strong, and our hand was willing," continued Derfer. "I do not blame our fate on any one race, my young Myopian, but it is the treachery of man that has been our undoing, and it is because of man that we face the fall of my race"

"Surely, there is more to it than that." said Burton "You cannot believe that one race can affect another one thusly? That they and they alone are responsible for all of this? I think not, friend Dwarf, I think that we all share equally for what has befallen us. It is because of our distrust and our unwillingness to forget and forgive that we are in this war. Man did not make the Orc, nor did he invent evil. That, Derfer, has been here before the arrival of Man or Dwarf or Elf. Even we Myopians have our bad eggs. You cannot hold an entire race responsible for the shortcomings of a few. That, I think Master Dwarf, would be the greatest threat of all to our survival, not a rabble of Orcs or a wizard led army. There is still good in this world, even in Men, I think you will see it before this great conflict is over. That is what I believe, Commander."

"You never cease to amaze me, Master Brew," said Derfer. "You show a wisdom that has not been seen in many years."

"I have had a very good teacher these last many years," said Burton "Tordin has taught me much in the ways of all races:

Elf, Man and Dwarf even Orc and Troll. Much of what you call wisdom I have learned from a simple man who has protected my people from much of the evil that you have described. Because of him, and others like him, much evil has been kept away from our doorsteps, and we have been allowed to live our peaceful existence, away from the troubles and concerns that now haunt and threaten our very way of life. No, I cannot feel the same way that you do about men. It is man who has protected us. It is he who has built the great libraries and cities of the west. It is under his hand that this evil has been kept from us. Maybe not through open war, as some would counsel, but through vigilance and perseverance. All is not lost, and as I said, I think the race of man plays a more important part in the good of Hatu than either of us knows."

Derfer and Burton continued this conversation until well after dark. It was around midnight when they felt it would be safe to make their way to the woods and get back on the quest they had undertaken.

Slowly, quietly, they crawled across the open ground. Burton was so tense that he felt that if he were to breathe it would give them away. Of course, he knew differently, but many thoughts ran through his head as he made his way to the safety of the woods. Burton looked behind him a couple of times and could see the light from the torches of the Orc patrols as they made their way through the city. He knew that he and his companion were never in any real danger as long as there was no reason for the Orcs to come out of the city and into the open.

A few more yards and they would be safe, thought Burton. A slight relief came over him as he could barely make out the tree line that was directly in front of him.

Suddenly, a loud horn blast came from the city. Followed by another and then another. Great monstrous flares were sent into the night that exploded when they hit their zenith.

"Run, Master Brew, I think they have found that their weapons hoard has had visitors." said Derfer, as he got to his feet and headed for the trees.

The dead Orcs! They must have found them, thought Burton, as he, too, got to his feet and ran for the trees. He was sure that they would be found as the great flares from the city lit the country side as if it were midday.

The two ran as fast and as far as they could. Finally, they stopped to see if they could get their bearings and to see if they were being pursued. Fortunately, there was no sign of pursuit. They continued to walk and once again turned back on their northern path.

It had taken several hours for them to advance hand over hand through the field and daybreak was right around the corner when they decided to stop and rest for a bit. Burton looked at Warlight and confirmed that they could stop as the blade remained its normal hue.

"It took them much longer to find their friends than I thought it would," said a rather proud Derfer.

"I am just happy we were able to get away," sighed a relieved Burton. "Never have I seen such light as I saw tonight."

Obviously, he was referring to the flares that were launched in his general direction a few hours earlier.

"There is much I have not seen before that I have seen lately," replied Derfer. "But I think we had best rest a bit before we go on. I think it wise that we travel less conspicuously in the days ahead, Master Brew."

This made sense to Burton as he, too, realized that things were far worse than he had anticipated. That was no small troop of Orc that they had just escaped from. Judging by the patrols they dodged and the response to the discovery of the dead Orcs, there must have been several hundred in this party. Burton thought the main army of Orcs might be much closer than he had thought.

At any rate, he and Derfer found a small thicket to crawl into and got some needed and well deserved sleep. Now, when Burton slept, he kept Warlight out and near at hand. His times of feeling safe and warm were far behind him. If nothing else, the last few days had taught him that this war was no longer a distant threat, but one that was right at his very feet. He was determined not to be caught unprepared ever again.

The sun rose high in the sky, and it was well after noon when the two weary travelers woke from their slumber. They had a quick meal of bread and Dwarf hardtack and were on their way. The terrain was level and brushy, with large patches of dead earth scattered along the way. Derfer said that these patches were signs from battles that had taken place a long time ago, probably from the great wars of the first and second times, he thought. In the distance they could see a mountain range that rose in majesty against the horizon. Derfer said they would travel to the base of these mountains and then turn northwest towards the Great Ice Bay. Once, they passed the Ice Bay they, would be at the base of the Mystic Mountains and almost at their destination.

It took almost a day and a half for Derfer and Burton to reach the base of the mountains that stood before them. It was dusk when they finally reached the foothills of the great mountain range. They reached the hills they turned northwest and followed the outline that loomed about them. There was a full moon this night, so they stayed as close to the shadows of the mountains as was possible. Derfer wanted to make up as much time as they could tonight. Burton could not help but notice the urgency with which Derfer had picked up the pace in the last ten hours. It was as if Derfer knew they were being pursued and that danger was close at hand. Burton kept a close eye on Warlight, but there was no change. He, too, began to feel as though someone, or something, was closing in on them. He knew that they were being followed. But by who or what? wondered the Myopian.

They came to a clearing that gave them two options: a path straight ahead or a path that took a sharp right turn leading up into the mountains.

"I do not wish to go into the mountains this evening, but I feel that is our safer path," said an agitated Derfer.

"I think we had best go forward, and soon," replied Burton. "I fear we are being followed."

"As do I, Master Brew," said Derfer. "It is no Orc that pursues us, but pursued we are. We have a choice to make, Master Burton. Do we continue away from our pursuers or do we stand and fight? If we continue on, we must do so quickly. If we fight, we know not what we will be up against. What say you?"

Burton did not like the idea of fighting something he could not see. But he knew that if they continued on, they may be overtaken and the choice of battleground would no longer be theirs.

"We fight," said Burton. "While I do not know what hounds us this night, I know that we must choose the ground on which to fight. I say here and now!"

"Good," exclaimed Derfer, as he pulled his mighty axe from across his back. In his zest for battle he had forgotten that this new axe had magical qualities, and he swung it in the same figure-eight as he has before. The great axe let forth a beautiful sound that filled the night air with song.

"Well, so much for surprise," said Burton.

"Let them come!" replied Derfer. "I fear not that which I cannot see. Let them know I am here and that my hand awaits them!"

Once again he swung the great axe. This time faster and harder than he had before. The great song filled the forest and echoed in the mountains. Never had Burton heard such wonderful music. He was fascinated by the melodious songs that reverberated from hill to hill. Soon he came to realize that whatever was pursuing them was close at hand, just outside of the light to the east. Burton could make out three figures. All very tall and all very familiar. Derfer stopped swinging the axe and prepared to meet his foes head on.

"What a wonderful sound this Dwarf makes," said a voice.

Burton knew the voice in an instant. It was Lindeloria.

Into the moonlight stepped Lindeloria, Tordin, and Warrant. They had survived their ordeal at the river and had found them in the wilderness.

"Tordin, it is good to see you," exclaimed Burton as he went forth to meet his lifelong friend.

"It is good to see you as well, Master Myopian," replied Tordin. "I am glad we find you well,"

Burton wanted to ask a million questions and find out where they have been and what news they had. He had begun to ask Warrant about the Ranger camp in the Moors when Lindeloria interrupted.

"Master Brew, I am sure there will be time to talk soon, but I fear this is neither the time nor place," she said. "I'm afraid that we have already brought far too much attention to our presence and we must be on our way."

Lindeloria looked at Derfer, who sheepishly looked away. However, once again she just smiled and carried on with her conversation.

"It was good that our friend unleashed the sounds from his mighty weapon as we did not know if you were friend or foe," she continued. "It was at that moment we knew it was not Orc or Troll that we followed."

Derfer perked up at this and felt vindicated for his childish behavior. But Burton knew that the Elf was simply trying the let Derfer off the hook for what could have been a very deadly mistake.

"But now we must be on our way," said Lindeloria once again. "We are not far from safety, such as it may be, and the longer we delay, the more our peril grows."

With that the five companions marched off into the darkness toward their next destination. Burton felt more comfortable than he had in a long while. His friend was alive and back at his side, as he has been for many years. His new allies, Warrant and Derfer, made him feel far less alone and not as vulnerable as before. And, of course, with the Elf Princess in their party, surely they would be safe and sound.

Yes, Burton Brew could even find the time to look to the heavens and admire the view, full of gleaming stars that danced and shimmered in the night sky. The light of the moon was bright, and Burton was filled with faith and the hope of a bright new tomorrow.

THIRTEEN

THE GREAT ICE BAY

I n the next several days that followed Burton's unexpected meeting with his old companions, the small troupe spent much of their time filling each other in on the events that had unfurled in the time they were separated.

After the encounter with the Orcs at the river crossing, Tordin, Warrant, and Lindeloria decided to follow the trail upriver to the Ranger encampment and enlist the aid of Warrant's people in tracking down their Myopian companion. They had several more encounters with roving bands of Orcs, and when they came upon the encampment, they found that Orc raiders had destroyed it. Warrant was able to see sign that several dozens of his people were able to escape, and he insisted they follow the trail to Cye in an attempt to find them. Tordin said that they had, in fact, run across some Ranger patrols, but the main body they were looking for had eluded them. Again, after serious consideration, they decided that their best course of action would be to turn their attention to the trail north by northwest and head for the Great Ice Bay. Tordin had determined that if he knew Burton, and he did, that Burton would get back on track at all cost. That is how they happened upon them in the wilderness at the base of the great mountain range.

Derfer spent much of his time conversing with Warrant and telling him all about their journey through the underground passage and the great city they came upon. Derfer had always thought that this city was Fornel, the great Ranger capital located at the north end of Green Lake that ran through the east of Myopia. However, Warrant informed him that this was not the great city and that they were much farther north and west then Derfer had thought. This was the city of Isnel. Isnel served as more of an outpost for the realm of Cye and was once home to the mightiest army the Rangers had ever known. It was never reestablished after the fall of the Dark King, as there were not enough Rangers left to garrison this really unimportant city. The fact that so many Orcs had taken up residence in this post was a fact that made both Lindeloria and Warrant very uneasy.

Burton discussed with everyone the news he had received from Derfer about the Orc army, the Man army and the wizard Maloneous. Lindeloria in particular did not like word of the involvement of a wizard in this war.

"The Elves are not who we once were," she said, "and a wizard is not someone that can be taken lightly." But the really bad news came from Tordin. He informed both Burton and Derfer that the size of the army, was in fact, much larger than they had anticipated. The Orc army alone was over 200,000 strong. The only good news was that the army, in fact was moving somewhat slower than Tordin had thought.

"I guess it takes longer to move that many Orcs," thought Burton.

When asked how the army could grow so large without being detected, Warrant replied, "This is the result of the folly of some who bury their head in the sand while the world turns around them."

Burton understood exactly what Warrant meant, and Derfer, while saying nothing, nodded in approval.

Soon the conversation turned to Burton and his battle in the armory. Derfer talked in wonder as he told Tordin, Warrant, and Lindeloria of the astonishing feats the Myopian had performed. Lindeloria just looked at Burton with that shy, half-knowing smile that he had come to love so well. Warrant was full of a thousand questions that no one could seem to answer. Why had this power to grow not shown itself when either Harry or Cyrus had used the sword? Or, for that matter Milton, who had the same lineage as Burton. And why now did the blade come to life?

These and many more questions remained unanswered, and all that Tordin could say was, "There is a time and place for everything. While we may not understand it all, we must have faith and allow events to unfold as they are intended."

Warrant was particularly interested in the axe that Derfer found in the weapons hoard. He and Derfer spent hours looking at the great axe in hopes of finding a clue as to who made it or who once owned it and how it came to Isnel in the first place. The one thing they did know was that this was not Tyrindus' axe. But Warrant suspected that it may have been made around the time of the mighty Dwarf king and that someone close to the great Dwarf leader may have carried it. Derfer was quite taken with Warrant and his knowledge of all the races of Hatu.

The two spent much of their time talking about the past history of Dwarves and Men, and it appeared to Burton that they were becoming rather agreeable with each other.

Tordin, on the other hand, was not as talkative as he had been before. Burton was not sure what was going on, but it was obvious to him that Tordin had something pressing on his mind. Burton tried many times to talk to him about this, but each time Tordin would change the subject or go off on a scouting mission. Burton was a little worried about his friend, but he found comfort in talking with Lindeloria, who told him not to worry, that this would pass in time. She assured Burton that everything was alright.

The band of travelers was now traveling mostly by night. The presence of the Orcs dwindled, and soon there was no sign of their enemy anywhere. Burton assumed that this was probably because it was getting colder as they traveled further north. Orcs, it seems, do not like the cold and will do all they can to avoid it. Burton's Elven cloak provided almost all the comfort he needed. It was surprisingly warm, and he found he could bundle up in it very easily. Tordin informed them that would reach a small Ranger outpost tomorrow at first light. The outpost was long ago abandoned, but he expected to find a few bear furs there that they could wear in the few weeks they would be traveling the shore of the Great Ice Bay. It sounded to Burton as if it might get a little colder yet.

The moon was covered in the fog of nighttime and Burton thought it must be almost midnight when Tordin, who had been leading the way, fell back to his side.

"My young friend," started Tordin. "I fear I owe you an explanation. As a young boy, much of my learning from my father was in the ways of the Rangers. I fear for their safety. My father and I made our home in Isnel. It was there that he taught me much of what I now know. It was there that he made me the man who walks beside you. In the weeks that have passed, I have seen much, and it sorrows my heart. Many of the boyhood places I knew have been destroyed by this evil that plagues us."

So that was it. Burton had all but forgotten that Tordin grew up in this northern land. He was so caught up in his own worries that he completely misunderstood the mood of his lifelong friend.

"I am sorry for that," replied Burton. "I had forgotten that this was once your home."

"I completely understand," said Tordin. "The last few months have not been easy for you, I am sure. It is just a shame that neither of us will see the former glory of this once great realm."

"We may yet, Tordin," said Burton, trying to pick up his friend. "I have learned much these last few weeks. I am not the same lad who once played hide and seek through the foothills of Myopia. I have seen much that I do not understand, but I do know that there is still a power out there that protects and guides us."

"You still amaze me, my young friend," replied Tordin.

"Did you think it was chance that Derfer and Burton found themselves in the caves?" inquired Lindeloria, who was now walking beside them. "They did not find themselves lost did they? And if it were not for the caves, and the water that chased them down, they would not have found the weapons room. Burton would not know of the power of Warlight and what is within him. And the musical axe that Derfer now carries would still be lost."

"I have not lost faith, princess," Tordin replied sternly. "There is much going on that we do not yet understand. Our young Myopian has visitors in his dreams and this does not make sense to me. Only a wizard can control water as was done to our friends. Is his power so strong? No, I have not lost faith. I only question our circumstances"

"And I do not question your faith, Master Tordin" replied Lindeloria softly. "I too do not understand what is unraveling around us. But I know that all will be revealed in time."

The conversation carried on for several hours with questions abounding. Unfortunately, there were very few answers.

Just before dawn they came upon a small entrance to an underground facility. Warrant informed them that this was the outpost they were searching for. He opened the cover and found a ladder heading straight down.

"And I thought only us Dwarves liked the bowels of Hatu," laughed Derfer.

"As you have seen," replied Warrant. "Trying times led to trying solutions." With that he started to climb down the ladder.

One after the other they climbed onto the ladder, with Lindeloria being last. Burton heard the closing of the cover and for an instant it was as dark as dark could be. Then the light of Lindeloria filled the ladder chamber, and soon his eyes adjusted to the light of the Elf princess.

They climb was long, or so it seemed, and they soon found themselves at the bottom. Warrant found a torch and led the way into a room that was full of furs and stores. He reached and pulled a large bear fur from the pile.

"I suggest we move quickly," he said. "Someone find a bear cub fur for Master Burton. I will cut down this one for Derfer"

He pulled out his short sword and made quick work of a fur, then handed it to Derfer.

"I hope this will meet your needs, my friend," he said.

"Yes, I think this will do just fine, my Ranger friend," replied Derfer, as he placed the fur in his backpack. "I will get it out when we reach the lake"

"But I think I, too, need some help" said Burton.

Everyone turned and laughed as they looked at the Myopian who was wearing the smallest fur he could find. Obviously, it was still too big. The small man looked as if he were a large pile of bear fur.

"I will see what I can do," laughed Warrant, who took the fur and began to trim it to size.

Soon the company was outfitted and ready to go. Warrant took them further into the tunnels of the underground facility, informing them that they would make up lost time and cover far more miles underground then above. This was a wonderful time for Derfer, who like all Dwarves, loved being underground.

Burton did not account for how much time they spent in the tunnels. It could have been days or hours, but he was more than ready to exit when they at last came to another ladder leading up.

"I suggest you put your furs on now," said Warrant, as he wrapped himself.

It had been very pleasant underground, Burton came to realize, and they had stored their bear furs as they were not needed.

They all wrapped themselves and began the climb up the ladder.

Warrant came to the top landing and pushed open the cover.

Snow fell in on the party, and they could feel the bone-chilling wind hit them as the lid was removed and revealed the light of day.

Warrant crawled onto the snow as did Tordin. The two motioned for the others to wait and moved away from the opening.

This was the first time Burton had experienced anything like this. Snow! And tons of it. It was not snowing now, but he could not wait to see it. He wanted to look out and see this new and exciting land. The cold pushed against his face, and he did all he could to cover himself until only his eyes could be seen. Surely, from a distance he must look like a bear, he thought.

Soon the two scouts came back and motioned for the others to come out. Burton's first look at this land took his breath away.

Straight ahead was a frozen white plain, with snow as far as the eye could see. With the sun glaring down, the blinding light was almost more than he could stand. Burton looked at the sun and thought it must be about 4:00 p.m., or late afternoon. He looked to his left and to his right and saw nothing but the same white field that first greeted his underground exit. Finally, he turned around, and what he saw he could never have imagined.

White mountains were scattered around a blue lake. Some were so high they almost reached the sky. Others were small, just floating as if suspended on a string. Far off in the distance he could make out a white line that stretched from east to west as far as he could see in either direction. It was magnificent sight, and Burton stood is awe of its beauty.

"That is the Great Ice Bay," said Tordin. "We are at its southwestern end. We will travel the shore line for five days. Then we will see the Mystic Mountains straight before us. We will travel day and night, Master Brew. The temperature will drop when the sun sets, and you will feel cold as you have never felt it."

"What are those mountains?" inquired the stunned Myopian.

"Those are no mountains, Master Burton" replied Tordin. "Those are huge piles of floating ice. They break off from the white shelf you see in the distance and float from one end of the lake to the other. It is said that what you see is just a tip of the ice float and that what lies under the water is far greater and grander. Eventually, they will melt and will be replaced with pieces from the far shelf"

"It is so cold. Why does the water not freeze?" asked Burton.

"No one knows." replied Tordin. "It just is as it is."

"It is time we turn west and start this last leg of our journey before we get to the home of my kinfolk." interrupted Derfer.

"I do not think we will see much along the way," said Warrant. "All life from this plain died many, many years ago. It is said there are not even fish in these waters."

"Then I think we will find neither Orc nor Troll, Master Brew," said Derfer, slapping Burton on the back and almost knocking him over.

Warrant and Derfer took the lead with Lindeloria, Burton and Tordin, right behind.

Burton watched the floating ice mountains and could not help but be impressed with their size and grandeur. He wondered how old the small floating ice might be. If they all started as the big ones, some of the small ones could be hundreds, if not thousands of years old, he surmised. He was entranced with their beauty and found himself walking aimlessly to the sound of the water as it gently lapped against the shore. Burton found a peace here. The cold did not bother him and his mind was cleared of all thought. In a way, he wanted this walk to last forever.

FOURTEEN

FOOTHILLS

The sun had risen and set for the fifth time, and far ahead in the distance, Burton could see the mountains, just as had he had been told. The ground was beginning to poke through the snow, and he could feel the temperature warm on his frozen face. They had left the Great Ice Bay behind only a few hours ago. Now were turning slightly south as they approached the mountain range that had been the object of their journey. Their trip had been uneventful and they had spoken little, because of the cold. Breathing was difficult enough, without trying to talk.

Burton would miss the great lake and hoped that someday he would get to see it again. He enjoyed the quiet gentle sea and the majesty of the floating Ice Mountains. Much of the time Burton spent in the solitude of his own thought. Twice, as they traveled the snowy fields, he was visited in his dreams. The party traveled night and day, as they said they would. But even the heartiest travelers need rest. Twice a day they would sleep for a couple of hours before picking up and pushing on. The dreams were much the same as the first one. A message of hope and faith, but Burton still did not know who the visitors in his nocturnal world were. However, still he was comforted by them and almost looked forward to sleeping just to have conversations with them.

Warrant said that they were less than a day or two away from reaching the very foothills of the Mystic Mountains. He was not sure what they could expect, but he felt confident that they had reached their target long before any Orcs had.

Almost immediately Burton, Warrant, and Tordin noticed an increase in Ranger sign. Tordin remarked that he thought the Rangers who had escaped the massacre in the moors might have made their way through the frozen north just had they had done. Because of the snow and ice, it would have been impossible to notice, or leave any sign for that matter. The spirits of the weary band picked up immediately, and Burton felt a renewed confidence that they were doing the right thing. He was satisfied that in a little while they would find some allies and their worries would be over.

Just then they heard a loud horn in the distance. It came from straight ahead of them.

Tordin immediately drew his sword, as did the rest of the band.

"That is an Orc horn," said Tordin, as he pressed forward, making sure that he was between the sound and Burton.

Burton pulled Warlight, which did not burn brightly.

"Warlight says we are safe," said Burton.

"It does not take an Orc to blow an Orc horn, Master Myopian. It is possible something, or someone, has learned the magic of your blade and can mask itself from it," replied Warrant.

There were few trees and bushes in this landscape, but still everyone managed to find a place of concealment.

Burton heard faint answer to the call far behind them.

"Master Tordin, there is an answer," said a slightly excited Burton.

"Master Brew, I have heard it. My guess is that we have not outdistanced our enemies as we had hoped," said Tordin. Burton noticed that Warrant had edged ahead. It was clear that he would scout to see what this sudden intrusion was.

Warrant crawled off in the direction of the sound.

Burton, and the others lay quietly for what seemed like an eternity.

Suddenly Warrant came running from the direction he had set out to investigate.

"TROLLS!" he exclaimed.

Burton could hear the clamor arise from behind Warrant, and it was obvious they would have to fight.

"How many?" asked Tordin. Burton noticed that Tordin and Lindeloria stood side by side and had begun to glow. He had seen this at other times, but this time he was close to it and for a split second, stood in awe at the power that was directly before him.

"I do not know," replied Warrant. I think eight or ten.

"Ten trolls!" exclaimed Derfer. "We have no power to fight ten trolls. But they will know that we were here!" With that said, Derfer began to swing the mighty axe he had found in Isnel. The axe reacted much differently this time. It still sung, but it was a much lower, deeper kind of music.

"I think your axe has a dislike for Trolls," said Warrant.

"As do I," replied Derfer.

Just then ten Trolls broke though the surrounding fauna. They were huge, ugly brutes to Burton. But then Burton had never seen a troll before. Each stood eight to nine feet tall and was covered in hair and armor. The stench of these foul creatures filled the air. They stunk much worse than any Orc. Burton knew right away that they could not sneak up on anyone based upon the impact his nostrils took with each breath. Each Troll carried a spear that was at least ten feet tall. The shaft was some form of metal, and the point of the spear was really much more like a double edged sword with ridges running from point to tail. The very thought of anyone being struck with such a weapon made Burton's skin crawl. On the end that touched the ground was a large metal ball, larger than the head of a Dwarf, and that was pretty large.

"Watch out for the ball on the end, Master Brew," said Warrant. "They mean to knock you down and then run you through with the business end"

"I have never seen such Trolls as these," said Derfer.

"They are Mountain Trolls, I think," replied Warrant.

"They look like no Mountain Troll I have ever seen" said Derfer.

"But it has been hundreds of years since Trolls have been seen at all, Master Dwarf," replied Lindeloria. Burton could only pause for a moment, but he could not help but notice how stunning the Elf princess looked in the glow of battle. Surely, such a sight would stop any Troll, Orc, or Army in its very tracks.

Derfer swung the mighty axe above his head and rushed into meet the foe.

"For the Rolling Hills and vengeance!" he cried as the sound of the mighty axe increased in volume. One swing and a Troll fell. Cut completely in half in one smooth stroke. Just as the axe found its mark a brilliant green light shot out and the axe became silent.

The other Trolls were so taken a back that three more fell before they could react.

The first took a direct stab in what Burton could only guess was its heart. Tordin had taken his Elf made sword and struck quickly and deeply. With the second, Warrant attacked high, while Burton attacked low. It may have taken several thrusts and cuts but the two were able to accomplish the task. The third fell at the blade of the mighty Elf princess revealed in her wrath. Her copper sword grew in length until it rivaled the weapon of the Troll. She swung it back and came forth like a whip, bringing it straight down upon her foe. The flash of light and power was amazing.

Soon the remaining Trolls regrouped and the attacked became the attackers. The Troll onslaught forced the companions into strictly a defensive fight. Burton found himself dodging both blade and ball, having very little time to press the fight to his enemy. Fortunately for him, he was a Myopian of quickness and speed. Derfer took the brunt of the attack. It would seem that the dislike between Dwarfs and Trolls had not lessened over the course of time. Several times he was struck by one of the mighty troll balls only to regain his feet in the nick of time. Twice, Warrant stepped in; deflecting what may have been a fatal blow from reaching the outmatched Dwarf.

Tordin and Lindeloria commanded much more respect from the Trolls, and they were not pursued in such a violent manner. A few of the Trolls circled them and swung and poked at them more than attacked. Burton thought it was like someone who was poking at an animal with a stick to see what it was. But this was no game and one "poke" could mean the end for him or his companions. Tordin had avoided several death blows, but still was bleeding from numerous flesh wounds. Lindeloria had received only one small scratch on the side of her left arm.

Another Troll fell. A flash of light from Lindeloria's hand and he was gone. Not just killed, but gone. He simply ceased to be!

It was becoming obvious that this fight was taking a toll on his friends and all would be lost if Burton did not do something and do it soon. At that moment he pressed in to an attack as hard as he had in the weapons room in Isnel. Warlight, the mighty short sword of old, sprang into action. It began to emit the grey coloring of before and Burton began to grow. He grew until he, too, was as tall and large as a Troll. He cut into his opponent until the Troll fell under the weight of this unexpected magic. But even with this victory, Burton knew that his band were in serious trouble unless something unexpected happened.

Just then hundreds of arrows flew from the surrounding brush.

"Down!" yelled Tordin. And the five valiant warriors hit the ground.

The arrows came from all direction and most found their marks. The remaining Trolls were all dead within seconds. Never had Burton seen such marksmanship as these mysterious archers possessed. Each Troll had to have at least fifty arrows in various parts of its body and armor. Still, the last Troll might not have gone down except for one last blow from the Axe of Derfer.

"Hail, brother," said a voice from the bush.

"Brother?" asked a stunned, but normal-size Burton.

"Yes, brother," replied Warrant.

Several dozens, if not hundreds of Rangers began to appear from the surrounding countryside.

"It is good to see you, brother," said one particular ranger as he approached Warrant.

"My friends, this is Tisiron, my brother," replied Warrant as he took his brother's hand. "It is very good to see you too. How is it you come here?"

"Across the Great Ice Plain," said Tisiron. "We have been gathering our people as they retreat from the north and east. There are over two thousands of us now. The main force is just ahead in the foothills of the Mystic Mountains."

"How is it these Trolls came to be here?" inquired Tordin.

"There are many such marauding bands of Orcs and Trolls about these days," replied Tisiron. Burton noticed for the first time how much the three looked alike. Tordin was as tall and hardy as the other two, but with just a hint of Elf characteristics or one would have thought all three were brothers. "You are fortunate that you have found such a small group."

"Small group?" exclaimed Burton. "I have never seen such monsters as these in my life."

"Usually they travel in groups of twenty or more," said Tisiron. Tisiron looked at Burton as he spoke. Burton could not help but feel that he was being scrutinized; as if Tisiron was trying to make his mind up as to whether Burton was friend or foe, a fact that did not go unnoticed by Tordin, who spoke rather abruptly.

"I doubt this is the first Myopian you have seen, Master Tisiron," said Tordin.

"I forget myself," said Warrant. "This is Burton Brew of Myopia," Burton bowed slightly. "And this is Lady Lindeloria, Princess of Fallquint." Lindeloria nodded as if to acknowledge the introduction. "You already know Captain Tordin." Tordin also nodded at Tisiron. "And this is Derfer, Dwarf Prince of the Rolling Hills, and a Lord of his realm." Derfer grunted and swung the axe into its sling on his back.

"It is very good to meet you," said Tisiron. "I apologize for my rudeness, but these are strange times. We are not sure of friend or foe. Had you not been traveling with my brother and Captain Tordin, I do not know that we would have been of any assistance."

"Then it is lucky for us we travel in the right company," said Lindeloria.

"But now we must go," said Tisiron. "And the rest of my company will travel with you to our camp, which lies ahead." He then let out a low whistle, waved his hand, and watched as the rest of the Rangers disappeared into the brush. "Let us be gone while we may. I heard the horn of this party call to the others. But I did not hear a return, so we may have time".

"I did." said Burton. "There was a call behind us not thirty seconds after the first."

"Then we must hurry," said Tisiron. "Trolls can travel twice as fast as we and the others may be very close"

The band of travelers and Rangers pressed forward and left the carnage behind. They must have had almost two dozen in their party now. They moved as quickly and as quietly as they could. Tisiron had never traveled with a Dwarf before and it showed. Dwarfs are the not the quietest creatures in the forest and many a glance was fired at Derfer for his noisiness. Warrant just smiled and had a low conversation with his brother. Soon a smile crossed the face of Tisiron, and he and Warrant were softly laughing and smiling as if they had not a care in the world.

"Master Brew," said Lindeloria quietly.

"Yes," replied Burton.

"I may now tell you that you have the magic of the ancients in you." she said. "It has been foretold that in our greatest hour of need, one would arise who has the magic of old. I have seen it this day."

Burton did not reply. He simply looked at the ground as he walked. He was deep in thought, and his mind wandered as if he were asleep and dreaming.

This time he found himself on a dock overlooking a great sea, far greater than the one he had just seen. It was blue and stretched to the west as far as he could see. Great white birds flew over the coast and the clouds were as fluffy as fresh pureberries from his garden.

Soon an old man came and sat beside him. This man looked as old as time and was dressed in the same fashion as Erideous. He had a long beard and carried a bent walking stick in his hand. The old man laid down his stick and took out an ancient pipe. He lit the pipe and began to smoke. He never said a word. He and Burton sat there for who knows how long, just looking out over the sea that lay before them.

As Burton came out of his daydream, he noticed that they had at last reached the foothills of the Mystic Mountains and the mighty mountains were right before him.

"Welcome back, Master Brew," said Lindeloria softly.

"I never left," replied Burton.

"I am not so sure," replied Lindeloria as she smiled. "We have walked many, many hours, and you have not said a word. Tordin and I could tell that your eyes were open, but they did not see."

"I was on a dock with an old man" said the young Myopian softly.

"Was he dressed as a wizard?" inquired Tordin.

"Yes, from head to toe with a long beard and hat. How did you know?" replied Burton. Once again the intuition of his Ranger friend amazed him.

"It is said that we all have ties to our past, Master Brew. That we are but one family and our line will never truly end," added a thoughtful Tordin. "I believe these visions are visitors from your past. I think these ties run strong in you. Although you have never met them, I think they are reaching out to help you."

"How can those who are dead in my past reach out to help me? That is impossible," said Burton.

"Not if those in your past are not truly dead," said Lindeloria. "You are the last of the Staff Bearers line. The Staff Bearers did not die, Master Burton. They left Hatu from our western shore and traveled to the faraway lands of our making and an undying life. And though they may never step foot in Hatu again, they may yet find ways to reach us and give us the strength and courage we need in our darkest hours"

"So who are these people?" said Burton. Tordin could tell by the sound of his voice that he was not as confused as before. The truth was slowly coming to him.

"Who would have an interest in your well-being?" inquired Lindeloria. "I think you know more than you are willing to accept. But accept it you must. It is your burden, Master Brew. A great task awaits you and its birth is closer everyday"

"Welcome to my humble home," said Tisiron in a loud voice. As if he were making an introduction to a grand ball in Myopia.

Before him Burton saw rows after row of green tents. Before each tent was a tripod of spears or bows. They had at last reached a Ranger camp.

"Please take advantage of our humble facilities," said Tisiron.

"Yes, we must get some rest," said Tordin, "for tomorrow we start for Doubblegate and deliver the message we have risked all for."

They were led to tents in the middle of the vast encampment. Derfer and Warrant went off to find food, for neither had eaten in days. Tordin found a grinding wheel and sharpened his mighty sword, in preparation for those things yet to come. Lindeloria and Burton crawled into their tents and fell fast asleep, each one hoping to catch a glimmer of solitude in the midst of a deep, deep slumber.

FIFTEEN

WINDS OF CHANGE

The morning brought with it a brisk breeze from the east as the fog clung to grass top. The camp was full of activity as the Rangers prepared to move out. Burton arose to the commotion and was the last of his party to do so. He stuck his head out of the tent and immediately caught the faint aroma of bacon cooking somewhere nearby. This was more than enough motivation to get a move on. Burton found the cooking site and was greeted by Lindeloria.

"Good morning, Master Brew, would you care to join me for some breakfast?" she inquired.

"It would be my pleasure," replied the Myopian as he sat at the small field table for a bite. There was all the food he had been missing for months now. Burton made quite the pig of himself as he filled his plate with all it could hold, not once, not twice, but three times.

"When you finish we have been summoned to a meeting" stated Lindeloria. As was her way, she stated this fact softly and gently. Burton took a second to acknowledge her as he wolfed down his last pancake.

"Where are we going this morning? I see the Rangers are pulling up camp," said Burton.

"That is why we are meeting soon," replied Lindeloria. "But it can keep until you have had your fill."

"I think I have had quite enough until lunch," he replied sheepishly.

"I am afraid there will be no more meals such as this for many days," said the sullen Elf Princess. Burton finally came out of his feeding frenzy enough to realize that something was not right this morning.

"They mean to go with us to the Dwarf city, do they not my lady?" asked Burton.

"I think it is time we got to the meeting," said Lindeloria as she rose.

Burton got up also, taking a breakfast biscuit with him, and the two made their way to a tent at the very back of the encampment. Burton followed Lindeloria who went into the tent. There they found Tordin, Warrant, Derfer, Tisiron, a Ranger Burton did not know, and Zander, Derfer's brother. Burton would later find out that Zander, had in fact, met up with several hundred survivors of the siege of the Rolling Hills, and they had made their way to the Dwarf city of Doubblegate. Zander had been sent for from Doubblegate in order to hold council with the Rangers. It was pure chance that he had arrived late the night before, only a few hours after his brother.

After "Good Mornings" were exchanged, and a few jokes were made about a late sleeping Myopian, the members of the meeting sat down and held council.

"I would like to introduce you to Borgon. He brings word from Mindeloria of Fallquint," said Tisiron.

"I bring word that the Orc army approaches from the east and is north of Myopia," said Borgon. "The army is moving somewhat slower and more cautiously than we had anticipated."

"Is Myopia alright?" interrupted Burton.

"Yes, the army is much farther north than we had first thought," replied Borgon. "They are not ransacking, as is Orc habit, but appear to be simply bypassing many minor outposts. They are moving slowly, but it is obvious they have a purpose and that purpose is Doubblegate."

"The Rangers have been asked to act as a screen between the Myopians and the advancing army," said Warrant. "We will leave immediately upon completion of this meeting. Our task will be to keep as many of us between the Myopians and the Orcs as possible."

"What if the army turns or goes in a direction we are unprepared for?" inquired Tisiron.

"I have been informed through a rider from Lord Mindeloria that the Elves will also be advancing on a parallel course with the main body of Maloneous Orc army." replied Tordin.

"I, too, have talked to my father's messenger," said Lindeloria. "I am to make my way to the Elf port city of Malquint with all possible speed."

"The horse he dispatched for you is in the west stable," said Tisiron. "It can be ready to leave forthwith."

All this planning and strategizing made little sense to Burton as he sat and listened to the comings and goings. What about him and his quest to deliver the message from Lord Mindeloria to the Dwarf King of the Mystic Mountains? Burton found himself worrying more about his task, and Myopia, than talks of armies and main bodies.

"And that brings us to you, Master Brew." said Tordin. The sound of his name, and the fact that all eyes turned to him, abruptly stopped Burton's daydream.

"As I was saying, Master Myopian," said an agitated Tordin. "That takes us to you."

"What about me?" asked Burton.

"I have spoken to Master Derfer. He and his brother will accompany you the rest of the way to the Dwarf city." said Warrant.

"But what of you, Tordin?" said Burton.

"My place is with the Rangers and performing my duties, Master Burton." replied Tordin. "There is naught for me to do with this part of your journey. But I leave you in the quite capable hands of these two hardy Dwarf Commanders. They will provide all the protection you will need on this leg of your journey."

"More likely he will protect us," said a laughing Derfer. This statement brought a laugh to all who sat at the table, except Zander.

Zander sat hard and quiet. Burton noticed that he had said nothing since the council started and did not appear to be the same confident, confrontational Dwarf he had first met in the meeting at Fallquint. Burton made a mental note that he would have to find time to talk to Zander on the trail to Doubblegate.

"Then it is settled. Lindeloria will proceed immediately to the Malquint. I, Tordin, and Tisiron will take the Rangers and screen the Myopians from the oncoming army should they suddenly change direction or a handful of Orcs get adventuresome and go looking for prey. And Lords Derfer and Zander will escort Master

Brew to Doubblegate to deliver Lord Mindeloria's message," said Warrant.

"I suggest we be on our way then," said Tordin.

As the council ended, the warriors took a few minutes to say their good-byes and make preparations to be off.

Warrant made it a point to say good-bye to Derfer. The two had become fairly close these last few weeks, and Burton was sure they would miss each other's company as they had spent hours in conversation along the trail.

"I shall see you again, Master Myopian," said Warrant to Burton. "You are in the greatest hands in all of Hatu. I am sure that Lord Derfer and Lord Zander will provide you all the protection you may need. I only wish I had two such warriors as these with me."

"There are many such warriors where we are going," replied Derfer. "We will send some your way when we get to Doubblegate."

"I rather think we will meet you at Doubblegate, my Dwarf friend," replied Warrant.

Lindeloria and Tordin spent several minutes talking alone in the tent before they found Burton.

"I will keep your home safe, my young friend," said Tordin.

"I wish you were going with me," said Burton. Deep down inside, Burton was still uneasy about all of this and longed to have his lifelong companion at his side.

"I must perform my duties as a Ranger, Master Myopian," replied Tordin. "There is much work to be done before we can all rest, my friend."

"Stop by my house and tell everyone I said hello, and that I am safe," said Burton.

"I will do that. But now I must be on my way. My company is the lead unit, and they are ready to move out" said Tordin. He hurried on his way. "I will see you again, Burton, fear not," he yelled as he raced to join his command.

Borgon then walked up leading the most beautiful white horse Burton had ever seen. It was as white as the field of the Great Ice Bay, with a silver and gold harness decorated in various gems and stones.

"My lady," said Borgon, as he handed the reins to Lindeloria. "Thank you," said Lindeloria, as she took the reins. "This is Laberador, of my father's stable."

"It is beautiful," said Burton.

"Yes, he is," replied Lindeloria. "But now, my young Master, I must bid you farewell and be on my way. I have miles and miles to go before my task is complete. I think you will complete your task with no trouble, Master Myopian. These are Dwarf lands and the Orc have not yet defiled it with his presence. Masters Derfer and Zander will be your guides and protectors. You will find your way and our paths may once again cross."

"I hope so my lady," said Burton with a low bow.

Lady Lindeloria laughed as she climbed on the back of the great white stallion. Burton was captivated by how beautiful she looked as she sat on Laberador, who let loose a mighty neigh and reared back on his hind legs. As his front hooves once again touched ground, he raced forward with such speed as Burton had never seen. Then he and Lindeloria were gone, and Burton was standing all alone. For the first time since he left his home in Myopia, Burton felt as if he were alone.

Derfer and Zander approached, carrying Burton's hiking gear and pack.

"I guess we had best be on our way too, Master Myopian" said Derfer, as he handed the backpack to Burton.

"Yes, it is time we go," said Zander. These were the first words he had spoken since Burton had seen him.

The three headed back into the foothills even further until they found a path that led both north and south.

"This is the Tyrindus Road," said Zander. "It will take us directly to the front door of Doubblegate. Come, we go south."

The three turned and headed south.

The road was difficult to make out. It was obvious to Burton that this was once a mighty highway that had led somewhere. But where? Maybe there were Dwarf cities farther north than Doubblegate at one time, he supposed. But at least he was on a road and not trekking through the wilderness or crossing frozen fields or walking in endless tunnels beneath the earth. While this was not the main street of his beloved hometown, it was a lot better than what he had been walking on.

Alone the way Burton noticed several broken-down buildings and debris. Derfer told him that this was once a great Dwarf realm and that these were small villages and defensive outpost that dated all the way back to the Beginning Days. Burton had never seen so much in such a short time. It boggled his imagination as to how great this realm must have been at one time. He passed columns that were made of marble and granite. Porcelain urns and broken pottery lay in ruins all over the ground.

"I thought that Dwarves lived underground." said Burton.

"That is true," replied Derfer. "These ruins are those of the race of men who lived in harmony with us when the world was young. They were our friends and allies until they were tempted with the lies and deceit of he who all but brought us to ruin."

"It must have been very beautiful," said Burton.

"Yes, it was. Very beautiful indeed," replied Derfer.

"But that was a different time and place," offered Zander. "There is no peace in Hatu now. Men lie. Orcs and Trolls run free and destroy at will. No, Master Myopian, the world is not a beautiful place at all."

"Tell me, Master Dwarf, how was your journey to the Rolling Hills?" said Burton, trying to direct the conversation a way from such evil thoughts.

"'Twas a journey, Master Brew," replied Zander. "When I got to the Rolling Hills, it had indeed fallen. I found some of my kinsfolk, who told me of the battle that took place. It was a fight for the ages, Master Myopian, but there were too many and we were ill-prepared. The mountains fell, and my people fled as best they could. Those that remain will join us in Doubblegate in a few days. There are less than six thousand, of us in all Master Myopian."

"I am sorry to about your losses, Zander" said a saddened Burton. That meant that over fifty thousand were killed in the siege of the Rolling Hills. What devastation!

"I am sure you are, Master Myopian," replied Zander. "I spent many hours talking with my brother when I arrived in camp last night, and he informed me of your great deeds in battle. It is good that you can kill your enemies face to face. I await my chance to do so." Zander adjusted the straps of the shield that hung over his back. Burton knew that this Dwarf was ready and willing to exact his revenge for the injustices inflicted upon his people.

The rest of the day passed in idle conversation among the three companions. At night fall they made a small camp, complete with fire, and enjoyed the peace of the mountains. Burton knew that they had little, if anything to fear here in the mountains. The army that approached had not yet reached its ugly arm out this far yet. The three would travel for four days and nights until they finally made their last camp less than a day from Doubblegate. The time passed swiftly, and Burton found the answers he had been looking for as he discussed events with Zander.

Burton had come to learn that Zander had, in, fact seen much more in his journey to the Rolling Hills. Twice, he had almost been captured on his way there. When he got there, he found the road leading to the Rolling Hills had been lined with posts. On each post there was the head of a Dwarf who had been killed in the battle. The marauding army had set fire to the towns and villages and the land had been burnt black. The great cities of the Dwarves had been systematically wiped out. The mighty gates and parapets that had protected the inhabitants for centuries were broken and destroyed. The devastation was so complete that the Orcs had no need to leave so much as a single scout behind. Zander could walk the streets and tunnels unafraid of being detected. There was no life left at all. Dwarves, animals, even plants and trees were destroyed. This explained much to Burton about the change that had overcome Zander. He could almost smell the need for revenge and the Dwarf's bloodlust that had taken hold of Zander. Burton knew that he did not want to be in the wrong place when this volcano exploded.

"Tomorrow we will reach the last Dwarf city left in Hatu. There we will make our stand," said Zander.

"But tonight we must rest and finish our journey tomorrow," said Derfer as he set up his small tent.

The others did the same. They set up camp, had a small meal, small by Myopian standards, that is. Then each crawled into his tent and settled in for a night's sleep.

Burton went to sleep knowing that the end of his task was at hand. Tomorrow he would deliver the message from Fallquint, and his part in all of this would be over. For Burton Brew, tomorrow could not get here soon enough.

Sixteen

Doubblegate

Burton awoke from the best night's sleep he had had in months. He was packed and ready to go in record time. He could not wait until his journey was over. Today he would reach his destination and he could deliver his charge to the Dwarf king and be on his way. Burton longed to get back to Myopia. With his newfound powers, he wanted to be there to defend his people and his homeland. If the Orcs would come, they would find much more than they had bargained for.

"You are ready to go early, I see," said Zander.

"Yes, I want to get my task completed and get home where I belong," replied Burton.

"At least you have a home to return to, Master Brew," said Zander. "Doubblegate is my new home now."

"It has been a long journey for all of us brother," said Derfer. "It is time we conclude this portion of our journey and make plans for the defense of our realm."

Once again the three headed to the south.

It was a matter of hours when they came across a small band of Dwarves who were acting as lookouts. They eyed the Myopian carefully as Burton and his companions made their way past them. Burton was sure this meant that the Dwarf city was close. Just after the outpost, the three entered a chasm that was barely wide enough for them to pass side by side. The faces of both walls were smooth, and Burton knew that this was the craftsmanship of the Dwarves. The path continued for more than a mile and then suddenly turned to the west. There, before Burton was a flat field more than two miles wide. On both sides were mountains as far as the eye could see. On the far side of the field, to the south, Burton could barely make out another opening like the one from which they had just emerged. On three sides were the mountains. Only the two small paths facing each other would permit entrance into this valley. On the other side of the field, facing west was a great wall. Burton could see Dwarves lining the parapets of the massive fortress. Hundreds, if not thousands, lined the upper walls with small openings, too numerous to count, scattered throughout the structure. Archers could fire their arrows through these openings and rain terror upon any who approached the great city. Across the top of the wall were plumes of smoke about every twenty feet. Burton could not even guess how many there were. Directly in the middle of the wall were a set of huge diamond gates.

"Welcome to the last Dwarf city in Hatu. I give you Doubblegate," said Derfer, as he swung his arm across in front of him. It seems that Dwarves had a flair for the dramatic.

The three approached the gates under the watchful eyes of the Dwarf guards. They were not challenged, but Burton knew that at least one hundred archers had a trained eye on them as they approached the city. When they got within range, a voice called from above.

"Who goes there?" inquired the voice.

"Lords Derfer and Zander from the Rolling Hills," Zander loudly replied.

"And who is that with you?" asked the voice.

"The Myopian Burton Brew, last of the Line Of The Staff Bearers, Elf friend, Dwarf friend, and Messenger of Lord Mindeloria of Fallquint. He brings word for the king," said Zander.

A horn blew and the gates slowly opened. Burton noticed several other small, almost undetectable gates at the base of the wall. He assumed these were for small parties to go in and out, unnoticed, of the massive Dwarf city. Burton and his companions stepped into the city. With the sound of the horn, the gates closed behind them. Four large, heavily armored Dwarves with battle shield and axe approached.

"We will take you to the king. Follow us," said the captain of the guard.

The group walked several hundred yards until they reached another gate. This gate was in the very front of the mountain. It, too, was large and made of diamonds and iron. The gates opened, and the party descended into the mountain. Burton noticed the ornate decorations and magnificent craftsmanship of the halls.

"Much of this city is underground, Master Brew." said Derfer. "We will go several miles under the mountain to get to the palace of the king"

"It is very grand indeed," said Burton, who stood in awe of the pillars and grandeur of the halls.

"Most of the living areas are in the corridors that you see on your left and on your right. The heart of the city is at the end of this corridor," said Zander.

"The corridors were actually like streets in other cities Burton had seen. There were shops and Dwarves everywhere. Many of the buildings were actually carved into the very stone of the mountain. This was unlike anything Burton had ever seen. And it was clear that many of the inhabitants had never seen a Myopian. All the glances and stares made Burton a little uncomfortable. However, one thing did stand out in Burton's mind. There were no Dwarf women.

"I do not see any women," stated Burton. He kept his voice down so that only those immediately around him could hear him.

"They are home with the children," replied Zander. "Is that not where your women would be?"

Burton knew that this was one of those political moments in his life. He took a few seconds before answering.

"Some are. But some are not," he finally replied.

"Some are not? What does that mean?" pressed Zander.

"We allow our women more freedom to come and go. Some work in the shops or actually run the shops on their own," said Burton. He knew that this conversation would lead to no good, but he could not find a way out of it.

"Your women work?" said a startled Zander. Derfer, who was a little wiser in the ways of Hatu, simply smiled and laughed to himself. It was clear to Burton that Derfer was rather enjoying this precarious position that Burton found himself in.

"In my world, they are considered equal, and we treat them that way," said Burton. He knew that this was not the way he wanted this conversation to go.

"Equal, you say?" laughed Zander. "Equal? Do they work in the mines and carry arms as well?"

Zander's attitude was beginning to get under Burton's skin. How was he going to carry on a conversation with someone who was so set in his ways? If he had a thousand years to try to explain this to Zander, he knew he would never get his point across to someone who was so set in the ways of the old world.

"I think you take the point to extremes," chimed in Derfer. "There is a large world out there, brother, and it is not up to us to pass judgment on how they live. Would you agree with me on that?"

"'Tis true, brother, but women being equal to men? I think I do not want that part of life in my world," replied Zander, shaking his head. "Women, equal to men, humph."

Derfer just laughed and gave Burton a slight nudge. Burton was so thankful that Derfer was getting involved in the conversation that he could not help but smile at the mighty Dwarf.

"Wait here," said the captain of the guard. He went ahead.

The small party at last reached the middle of the mighty Dwarf realm. The palace of the king stood before them. It was a large granite castle that was cut from the very heart of the mountain. It was surrounded by a parapet, much the same as the outside wall and manned with several dozen guards. Soon the captain returned.

"My Lord has instructed me to take you to his audience chamber, where he will join you soon. You stated you have a message for him. Give it to me, and I will take it to him," said the captain as he put out his hand for the scroll.

"I am sorry, my lord, but my orders are to give this to the Dwarf king and no one else. I must obey my Lord Mindeloria's orders" Burton said defiantly.

"And I, too, have my orders," said the captain as he pulled his axe from its sheath.

Immediately the other guards placed their weapons on ready, as did Burton, Derfer, and Zander.

"I would think twice before I take my duties to my grave," said Zander. "I am a Commander of the Rolling Hills, Lord of my realm. This is my brother, and he would now be prince. This is Burton of Myopia, and he is under our protection. He is our ally and friend. If he is to give a message to your king, then it is his duty and we will see it through."

"My lord, I meant no disrespect," said the captain, putting his axe away. He also motioned for his men to do the same. He then gave a sign to the Dwarves manning the wall to stand down as well. "These are trying times. My king bid me test you with this ruse. If you simply handed over the parchment, then you may have been under the spells of the wizard. We must be sure, my Lord."

"I understand," said Derfer who was far more relaxed then Zander. Burton could still see the fire in Zander's eye's as he reluctantly put his axe away.

The Dwarf captain noticed Derfer's axe and could not take his eye off the great blade.

"Please follow me." said the captain, and they headed into the palace.

The palace was, simply put, the most extravagant place Burton had ever seen. Pictures and tapestries hung on every wall. The furniture was made from the finest wood, all hand crafted. There were decorations from every culture. Some must have dated to the dawn of Hatu. Silk drapes adorned the walls, and the doors were made of mahogany. In the hall that led to the meeting room, there were pictures of the Dwarf kings of old. The first picture was that of the great Dwarf King Tyrindus. He was standing on a mountain top looking into the distance and leaning on a mighty axe. Burton could not help but stop to admire the portrait. Tyrindus, the greatest Dwarf of all time. Burton also noticed how much the axe the in the portrait looked like the axe that was now in the possession of Derfer.

Derfer noticed, too.

"As I said, Master Brew, this is not the same blade." said Derfer.

"But they look so much a like" said Burton still engrossed in the painting.

"That they do. But believe me, Master Brew, as powerful as this weapon is, it pales in comparison to the Great Axe," said Derfer.

"He must have been a wise and just leader," said Burton, almost in reverence.

"You are a Dwarf friend, indeed" said the captain of the guard. "But my king awaits. We must be off"

The party continued on their way until the end of the corridor. They then turned left and entered a room much like the other halls, but with a large table at its center. At the far end was a great throne with a large, ornate anvil above it.

"Please be seated. The king will be with you shortly," said the captain. He turned and left the room.

The three sat down.

"I am not well-versed in the ways of Dwarves, so I hope your king will forgive me if I do not observe the proper protocols," said Burton.

"He is not my king," said an agitated Zander.

"But he is the king here, brother," replied Derfer. "And we must be respectful in these times."

"It will not be I who causes strife or dissension, my brother," said Zander.

"Long have our two realms spat at each other," continued Derfer. "This is the realm of the Mystic Mountains. This is the last seat of the Great Dwarf kings, of whom Tyrindus was our greatest. It is said that the truest line of Dwarf blood exists in this realm and this realm alone. There are many, to include myself and my brother, that do not agree with that line of thought. We do not believe that anyone line, that of Tyrindus or any other, is higher or purer than the others."

"Even in this place, there are those who question such folly," said Zander.

"But nonetheless we are guests, and we will follow the rules of this house," Derfer sternly said, staring at his brother.

Zander, who did not reply, just looked down at the table.

A voice from a side window loudly announced, "All rise for King Thuron, King of the Mystic Mountains, Lord of Doubblegate and descendant of Tyrindus, King of the Dwarves."

The three stood up, Zander rather reluctantly as King Thuron entered through a door directly behind the throne.

"Please be seated my friends," said the king.

King Thuron was extremely old, even for a Dwarf. He wore a blue silk cape that covered his gold and silver battle armor. On the front of the chest plate was a gold anvil, much the same as the one that was above his throne. He carried no weapon, which was odd for a Dwarf, even one of advanced years. He sat on his throne and looked directly at Burton.

"You have a message for me?" inquired the king.

"I have a message from Lord Mindeloria of Fallquint," replied Burton as he got up from his chair and walked over to the king. The scroll had been in Burton's shirt these many months and was quite the worse for wear.

"I see you have been on a long journey with this," said the king as he opened it and began to read it.

"Yes, my lord," replied Burton, as he took his seat again.

"We have faced many perils to fulfill this task," said Derfer.

King Thuron looked long and hard at the message. A look of disbelief crossed his weathered face.

"Do you know what this says?" asked the king.

"No, sir, I was simply to deliver this to you and thus fulfill my duty," replied Burton. Something about this did not feel right. The ability to sense what was about to happen suddenly kicked into full gear. Burton did not like the feeling that stirred inside of him.

"There is much in this that affects us all, Master Myopian. I do not like, nor do I understand it. I must think about this for some time. We will hold council at first light tomorrow." said King Thuron. "Captain," he yelled.

The kings got up from the table and left without as much as a goodbye or thank you.

"If you will follow me, I will show you to some quarters for the night." said the captain.

The three followed silently. Whatever was in that message did not bode well.

The captain led them to a door and pointed.

"Here are your quarters for the night. I will be back to get you just before sunrise, so you may prepare for the council," he said. With that he turned and left three standing dumbfounded in the hall.

"Did I not tell you." said Zander. "You want me to be polite and courteous and look how we are treated. No better than common trash."

"I am as confused as you, brother," said a thoughtful Derfer. "Are you sure you do not know what is in that message?"

"I know nothing of what is contained on the parchment I delivered," said Burton. "My job was to bring the letter here. Nothing more and nothing less. I have done that. What it says or what it means I do not know, nor do I care. I will attend the council tomorrow because the king says I must, but then I am on way home with or without permission of Dwarves or Elves."

Burton pushed open the door and barged into the chamber, leaving Derfer and Zander standing alone in the hall.

"The Myopian has a fiery temper," said Zander.

"Yes, my brother, that he does," replied Derfer. "After you?"

Derfer motioned for Zander to enter the room. Zander playfully bowed to Derfer and walked in, as did Derfer, who gently closed the door behind him.

SeVenTeen

Trust or Consequences

Just before dawn, the Dwarf captain arrived to escort Burton to the council meeting scheduled the day before by King Thuron. Burton, as was his way, was up and ready to meet his visitor before the Dwarf could even knock on the door. The two made their way to the great meeting chamber without uttering a word. The air was thick with anticipation, and Burton wondered what all the fuss was about. He had lain in bed and thought about King Thuron's reaction to the letter that he had delivered from Mindeloria. There was something about it that made him uneasy. Until last night, Burton did not even think about the letter or for that matter, what it might have to say. He was asked to deliver a message from Lord Mindeloria, and that is what he did.

The two entered the great hall, which was filled with Dwarves of all ranks and standing. Burton was directed to sit in a chair to the left of the king, who had not yet arrived, and across from Derfer and Zander. The Dwarf captain took his place at the far end of the table.

"I trust you slept well," said Derfer.

"As well as can be expected, I guess," replied Burton. Burton really hadn't slept much at all as his thoughts of Myopia and this meeting kept him awake and mentally active most of the night.

"What is so important that a person from Myopia brings us words from the Elf Lord?" asked one of the Dwarves at the table.

"It should be enough that word has come," replied Derfer. Burton noticed that Derfer did not appear to be as much at home as Burton thought he would be.

"And why should we welcome word from an Elf?" asked another.

"Lord Mindeloria has been a friend to all beings of Hatu and is considered to be a Dwarf friend and is held in the highest esteem by my people," said a defiant Zander.

Well, no matter what, thought Burton, this should at least be a lively meeting.

A door guard stepped forward carrying a large axe, stamped the handle on the floor, making a loud thumping sound. He did this three times and on the third thump, all of the Dwarves, including Zander, rose to their feet. Burton did the same as King Thuron entered the room from behind his throne.

"Please be seated," said the king. "There is no time for formality. We must conclude our business in the fastest time possible."

Everyone took their seats and the king continued.

"As you have heard, the enemy is on the move and is said to be heading this way with the intention of destroying our people as he did our brothers to the east." King Thuron nodded towards Derfer and Zander, who nodded back in response. "Many of those who have escaped are here with us and have pledged to defend our realm as if it were their own. For that, we are thankful." Again, he nodded at the two Dwarf commanders from the Rolling Hills.

"Their kinsfolk has told us of the might of the army that is marching this way and the devastation that they have wreaked upon all who stand in their way. They tell me this is an army the like of which has never been seen. Now this Myopian," he said while pointing at Burton, "appears and brings word from Lord Mindeloria, Elf of Fallquint. This word was delivered to me yesterday and I can scare believe what it says. Therefore, I will share it with you that we may hold council and have voice in the future of all Dwarf-kind and the free peoples of Hatu."

The king then got out the Elven scroll and read the words out loud.

My dear King Thuron,

As you know, Maloneous, the wizard has risen from the east and brings with him an army of Orcs, Trolls, and Men with the sole purpose of destroying all the peoples of Hatu. He holds in contempt those that fought the Dark King, and in particular those that have blood ties to the destroyer of the Staff of Power. I share your pain in the loss of the Rolling Hills and the destruction of those Dwarves. By now, many have made their way to you and are awaiting your orders. The entire future of the Dwarf nation now lies within your hands. The Elf people of Hatu stand beside you in your hour of need. It is with that fellowship that I make all of my forces available to you in the fight against this evil that threatens us all. Please make haste in coming to Malquint, where we can fight together and stand as one again against a common enemy. All the preparations have been made, and we await word. My friend, I do not think you can defend Doubblegate against such odds as now make their way in your direction. Prudence and trust are our best defense. Please look to Master Brew if you are in need of outside guidance. He is wise beyond his stature. I await you in Malquint.

Lord Mindeloria

So that was the message, thought Burton. Why would Mindeloria want the Dwarves to abandon Doubblegate and defend the Elf port city of Malquint? Surely the Dwarves would not be so willing to leave their home and make a stand with the Elves?

The words of the Elf lord caused quite a commotion in the great hall. For several minutes there was cursing and yelling and axe pounding and such uproar that Burton thought there might be an open rebellion on the spot.

"My lord," yelled one Dwarf at the king. "What madness is this?"

"Leave Doubblegate on the word of an Elf?" yelled another.

"SILENCE!" commanded the king. The commotion died down, so that one could be heard. "There is much to discuss and a difficult decision to be made," he said.

"Surely you cannot consider leaving Doubblegate to the whim of the enemy?" said a Dwarf.

"We must consider all options," replied the king. "I do not take the suggestions of a Lord such as Mindeloria lightly, and I suggest you should pay heed as well." Then he turned to Zander. "Lord Zander, tell us of your defense at the Rolling Hills."

"My people had defenses such as yours" said Zander. "The Orc army broke upon it like small trees in a wind storm. Yet they kept coming. The Trolls hewed their way through rock and steel and kept advancing, row after row. We fought with all of our might, but to no avail. At last, those that did not slip away early in the fight were trapped with no way out. They were slaughtered until there were none left alive. The heads of those that fell adorn the entrance to the city on the ends of Orc pikes."

"Those that ran away lived. Is that what you are saying?" asked a Dwarf.

"Do not imply that my people are cowards," said a stern Derfer. "Many of those that lived through this battle carry the scars of combat. No, my friend, they are not cowards. It is a brave Dwarf who fights, but it is a braver Dwarf who fights and lives to fight again."

"There are none here who call your people cowards, my lords," said the king as he bowed to Derfer. "And I will hear no more I'll talk of a people who fought as our brothers did against such overwhelming odds. But that bring us back to the issue at hand. Surely the odds are as much against us as they were against our brothers."

"This may be true, my lord," said the Dwarf captain from the far end of the room. "But this is our home, and I will not leave it to a horde of marauding Orcs"

"I understand captain, but as Lord Derfer says, it may be in our best interest to live to fight another day," said the king.

"What does the Myopian say?" asked a Dwarf. The cry was immediately taken up by the entire room and only died down when the king made a motion for silence.

"What have you to say, Master Myopian?" asked the King.

All eyes turned on Burton, and the room became deadly silent.

"My Lord," stated Burton. "My Lord, I do not know of the ways of battle, and this is surely a decision that is best left to those who do."

"This is the wise Myopian sent to us by the Elves, and it is expected we listen to this wisdom?" said a Dwarf sarcastically.

"My Lord" continued Burton. "My people are in danger as well. If I had the offer of the aid of the Elves given to me and mine, I would surely accept it. Home and villages can be replaced, crops can be reseeded, gardens and trees regrown, but it is not so with people. Be they Dwarf, Elf, or Myopian when they are gone, they are gone."

The room fell silent. So there it was. Right there on the table for all to see. Should they stay or should they go?

"My Lord" said the Captain. "We will make such a fight that the enemy will be crippled for months."

"Crippled, yes, but defeated, I think not." replied the king. King Thuron looked at Burton as if he was waiting for some form of magic or a sign that would make this decision for him. "I think that it is time to once again trust in the wisdom of those around us. Lord Mindeloria is wise and powerful. If he believes we should make our stand elsewhere, so be it. Raise your companies and sound assembly. We march to Malquint with all haste. Captain, send word to the Elves that we will join them with all possible speed."

Then the King rose, as did the rest of the room. "You have your orders," he said. The king then turned to Burton. "I know that your portion of this journey has ended, but I ask that you accompany me to Malquint, where my people will make what could be our last stand."

Burton wanted to say no. He longed to be home in Myopia to help defend his own home. What a rotten twist of fate, he thought.

"My Lord, I wish only to defend my home and return to my own family and friends. But I think that there may be more for me at Malquint than I realize. Therefore, I will accompany you to the Elf city and take my leave upon our arrival."

"Good," exclaimed the king. "You will travel with my personal body guard and are commissioned lieutenant in the King's Guard. I hereby award you rank and privileges associated with said title. Now, go with your friends from the Rolling Hills and prepare to leave."

Derfer and Zander were standing by waiting for Burton to finish his conversation with the Dwarf king, who immediately turned and exited the room upon completion of his conversation with Burton.

"Dwarf Lieutenant?" laughed Zander. "Never have I heard of such an honor to a Myopian."

"To an outsider for that matter," laughed Derfer.

"It is just a title," Burton replied sheepishly.

"But a proud title just the same," said Zander. "Come my Lieutenant Brew of Myopia, let us take leave and pack for our trek to the Elf city."

The three left the great hall and returned to their sleeping chambers, where they packed and picked up their weapons in preparation for the march to Malquint. They met again in the hall and made their way through the streets to the great gates. The city was alive with activity as the Dwarf army mobilized for the march south. Once they were through the gate's Burton saw one of the most magnificent sights he had ever seen. There, in full battle gear with shields, were some six thousand Dwarves, standing in formation facing the south.

A Dwarf came up to the three and bowed before Zander.

"My Lord" he said. "We await your command."

Burton assumed that these must be the survivors from the massacre at the Rolling Hills. He was in awe of the proud stature of these Dwarves. They looked battle hardened and for the first time in his life, Burton felt proud to be in the presence of such great warriors.

"You will make the way safe for the army that follows," commanded Zander. "It will take many days for the entire population of Doubblegate to assemble and follow our path. We will meet them at the base of the Great Bridge. It is our task that no enemy sword or arrow will touch our brothers on their path, is that understood?"

"I understand my lord," replied the Dwarf. He then took up his position at the head of the column and they started out of the valley through the opening opposite where Burton had arrived. Then a loud cheer arose from the battlements. Burton turned and saw that thousands of Dwarves were looking down on the site and were cheering as the mighty Dwarf army left the field.

"I will go with my people," said Zander. "My brother will stay with you and accompany you on the trail to Malquint. It will be a safe journey, my young Myopian friend, and you must fear not. I will see you when you arrive at your journey's end."

With that, Zander shook hands with his brother Derfer and ran to catch the force that was making it way through the valley. The cheers died down and Dwarves began to pour from the lesser opening in the wall of the city that Burton noticed when they first arrived. There they began to form into companies much like the army that had just left.

"Come, Master Brew. We must find the King's Guard," said Derfer.

So Burton and Derfer returned to the palace and joined the King's Guard as it prepared to leave Doubblegate.

"I shall hate to see what will happen when the wizard gets here and finds no one is at home," said Derfer. Burton noticed a slight smile cross Derfers lips as he said this.

"What do you think will become of the city?" asked Burton.

"I think they will leave it stand and pursue us as quickly as they can," replied Derfer. "It is as you said in council. It is the people they wish to destroy Master Brew, not just the cities. But I think the Wizard Maloneous will not be pleased that no one is here when he comes to call. It may plant a seed of doubt in his head that the Dwarves would so easily leave their greatest city."

Once again Burton's thoughts returned to Myopia and his own people. Would they be safe or were they already defeated by this evil? He longed to see his home and land again, to work in his garden again. These thoughts filled his head as he and the Kin's Guard began their march to join the Elves in Malquint, the largest of the elf sea ports.

EIGHTEEN

MARCH TO MALQUINT

I t took several days to mobilize, equip, and prepare the Dwarf colony for the move from the safety of Doubblegate and begin their march to the Elf city. Over the years the Dwarves had developed many sophisticated weapons, that is, sophisticated to Myopians. Burton was fascinated with one in particular. In the middle of the massive army were Dwarf steam cannons. The Dwarves, known for their work with metal and ore, had made a cannon that could shoot a round iron ball several hundred yards, and then the ball and would then explode on impact. The cannon was built on a large wood and brass platform that had wheels on it so that it could be moved by ten Dwarves, who were attached to the front by a harness made of leather. The barrel of the cannon was in the front, with a large iron and brass boiler behind it. The

Dwarves would build pressure in the cannon by maintaining a fire in the pan located directly beneath the boiler, which was filled water. When the temperature was hot enough to produce steam, a large ball was dropped into the barrel. The ball, which was filled with something the Dwarves called "black fire," also contained something called a fuse, which was lit just before the ball was launched toward the enemy by releasing the pressure that had built up in the boiler. While it was not a very accurate weapon, Burton was sure it would produce a very deadly effect just the same.

Another weapon they had was called an arrow launcher. It was much like a large bow that was laid on its side. The arrow launcher could hold up to one hundred arrows. When released it would send the arrows farther than any Dwarf bowman could shoot. It was a devastating weapon, and when many arrow launchers fired at once, the air would be filled with flying arrows that would block out the light from the sun. For all the posturing that Burton saw, he knew one thing, the Dwarves had been anything but idle and were as prepared for battle as any race could be. Burton was happy they were on the same side and almost felt pity for any foe that would face the onslaught of this Dwarf army.

Once the Dwarves got underway, Burton was amazed with how fast the army moved. He had spent many weeks with Derfer, but it did not prepare him for the pace he was now undertaking. Only the days crossing the great ice field came close to comparison. The Dwarves moved with purpose and traveled night and day, resting only for a few minutes of sleep and food three times a day. At this pace they would reach the Elf city in just a matter of days.

Burton had completely lost track of all time on his journey. He couldn't tell if he had been gone for weeks, months, or years. It seemed like an eternity since he had left Fallquint and Myopia. The hours ran together like streams that empty into a great body of water. He did not know night from day or day from night. Only the rising and setting of the sun told him that a day had come and gone. In particular, he had come to loathe the moment right before the sun went down at night and rose in the morning. In that time, he felt the most homesick, and a feeling of helplessness would overcome him. He didn't mention it to anyone, but somehow he knew that Derfer had noticed how these times had come to affect him. Derfer never said anything, but Burton knew that he was aware.

Tomorrow they would come to the Bridge of Malquint and join back up with the force that had left Doubblegate several days earlier. The bridge was the only way to cross the mighty West River and get to Malquint. The river was located at the eastern end of the West Gulf. The Gulf was the last body of water before the Great Sea that lay between Hatu and the lands beyond the horizon. All of the rivers in Hatu connect to the Great Sea, the West River, the East River, and even the Great River flow to this one place. It was this sea that was crossed in the beginning and brought those who would make Hatu their home. The Bridge of Malquint had been built by the magic of those who were most powerful. It was thousands of years old. It was more than two miles long and built of diamonds and steel. Even the Dwarfs talked of this bridge as a great work and it was said that some even envied the craftsmanship that created it. Burton could not wait to see this wonder of the old world.

"Will we reach the bridge soon?" he asked Derfer.

"Yes, Master Brew. I think we should reach the bridge by tomorrow and be in the great Elf city within the day," replied Derfer.

"It is good that we will reach the city soon," said Burton. "I fear that I cannot keep up this pace for much longer. The army moves as if the enemy were on our very heels."

"That is because time is short, Master Brew" said Derfer. "Our scouts tell us that the army does in fact draw near. Time is no longer on our side. When we get to the great city, we must move quickly and make for our defense. We have put our trust in the Elf Lord, and we must have faith that he has made arrangements for our arrival."

"I am sure that Lord Mindeloria has done that which must be done," said Burton. Burton had all the faith in the world in Mindeloria. If anyone in Hatu knew what to do, it was him.

"I hope you are right, young Myopian" said Derfer. "As I said, there is no time left for discussion and counsel. It is time that we prepare ourselves to fight."

The word then spread through the column to make camp for the night. It seemed that Dwarves had the same lack of love for water that Myopians did. The last thing King Thuron wanted to do was cross the great bridge in the dark. He would camp for the night, and they would make the final leg of their journey under the shining sun. Tomorrow they would join the Elves in Malquint and prepare for the defense of Hatu against the Evil wizard Maloneous. For Burton this meant that he would finally be on his way back to his home. It was his intent to go to the Elf city, say his farewells, and leave for Myopia by nightfall. He would be home within a week and help prepare his people for the onslaught that was to come.

The army made camp and had a late supper. This was fine with Burton, who never could get used to eating just three times a day. He often found himself snacking on fruit or bread or whatever he could find that would fill his stomach and ease the pain that accompanied an empty belly.

After supper, everyone went about their business in preparation for their arrival in Malquint. King Thuron held council with his commanders and discussed how they would deploy their companies and siege engines. He also informed them that the army of Zander and the Dwarves from the Rolling Hills had passed them earlier in the day, through a path to the north and that they now protected their rear flank. Once again, the abilities of the Dwarves filled Burton with respect and admiration. After the meeting, Burton went back to his tent, enjoyed a quiet smoke and laid down for the night.

His dreams were peaceful, and he slept as sound as could be expected. There were no dreamland visitors from faraway lands or mountains or eagles or Myopian gardens or festivals, just a night of peaceful sleep with visions of the night sky and a cool breeze to keep him safe.

Morning came and Burton was awakened by the commotion of the Dwarves as they prepared to get back on the trail and cross the Great Bridge. King Thuron had arranged for Derfer and Burton to join him for breakfast. It was his intent that the three of them would cross the bridge first and lead the mighty Dwarf army across the bridge into the elf city. As was stated before, it appears that Dwarves have a bit of showmanship and drama about them. Burton would have much rather stayed where he was and crossed with the protection of the King's Guard. He would never admit it, but the thought of crossing a two-mile long bridge that was built thousands of years ago and is suspended hundreds of feet above a cold, deep ocean was not exactly his cup of tea. The very thought of it made Burton a bit uncomfortable.

"Would it not be better if I stayed in the ranks and kept my position in the Guard?" said a slightly shaken Burton. "I think it would be much better if My Lord led the way with Master Derfer. It is your army that comes to the aid of the Elves, not I."

"If it were not for your part, Master Brew, we would still be in Doubblegate and more than likely trapped. I think that we would have met the same fate as our brothers if not for the courage you displayed in getting word to me from Lord Mindeloria. No, my Myopian friend, you have earned the right to be by our side as we make our way across the Elf bridge."

"As you wish my Lord," replied Burton. He knew that he had lost this argument, and it would be in his best interest not to pursue the matter any further. He would just have to lead the mighty army, with the King and his companion Derfer, all the while trusting that he would make it across without incident.

"Fear not, Master Burton," said Derfer. "The bridge will hold the weight such as us. The main army will not cross until we reach the other side. I do not think you need worry about falling off the bridge, Master Brew." Derfer must have known that Burton was uneasy about the crossing and made light of the situation. Everyone had a good laugh and finished their breakfast without further discussion of the bridge or the water below.

After breakfast the three made their way to the front of the column, where they would stay until they reached the far side of the bridge. Only a handful of Dwarf scouts were ahead of them. The scouts were trained in such a way that their job was not to engage an enemy, but to report back to the main force and let their commanders make the decision on the proper course of action. During this journey there had been very little that the Dwarf scouts had to report, that is, until now. One of the advance scouts approached the king from trail that led through a patch of trees directly ahead.

"My Lord, the bridge is at hand," said the scout. "But it is not clear to cross."

Not clear thought Burton. Had the enemy made their way ahead of the army? If so, how did they avoid Zander and his people? The thought of being caught in the open sent a shiver down Burton's spine that reached into his very soul. He immediately pulled Warlight to see if there were enemy about, but it did not glow.

"What blocks our way?" asked the Dwarf King.

"The way to the bridge is blocked by two large wolves. They are the biggest wolves I have ever seen. One is black, and the other is grey. They are just sitting at the foot of the bridge as if they were statues." said the scout. "We did not approach, but there is no doubt they know we are here."

"What trickery is this?" asked the king. "Surely, two mere wolves will not slow our advance. We will simple slay the beasts and be on our way."

"No wait," said Burton. "Grey and black wolves you say?"

"Yes, one is grey and one is black," replied the scout.

"Milo and Silo, I'll bet." exclaimed Burton, as he raced ahead, leaving his befuddled Dwarf companions behind. It had to be Milo and Silo, he thought. No other great wolves would be alone in the middle of nowhere guarding a bridge that led to a great Elf realm.

Burton ran down the path and entered into a clearing that stretched about a quarter mile to the base of the great bridge. There sat Milo and Silo, wolves from the wizard Erideous who had traveled with him to Fallquint and were his constant companions at the outset of this wondrous adventure. When the great wolves saw Burton, they both let out the loudest howl that he had ever heard. He had to stop and cover his ears, the noise was so loud. Then the great wolves came down from the bridge and took their usual positions on each side of him. They bowed down, so that Burton could pat the heads of the mighty beasts as if they were pets. Both Milo and Silo looked at Burton, as if they too had just been reunited with a long lost friend. Burton was sure that they missed him almost as much as he had missed them. He was glad to know they had made it safely to Malquint.

The rest of the Dwarf scouts appeared from the woods, along with Derfer and King Thuron. Milo and Silo just looked over their shoulders at the Dwarves and did not move.

"What magic is this?" asked the king.

"These are my friends, Milo and Silo," replied Burton. "They are on loan to me from the wizard Erideous. I think that they will be accompanying us across the bridge, my Lord."

"I think you are right, Master Brew," replied the King. "And if your friends are ready, I suggest we get on our way"

It was then that Burton finally looked at the Bridge of Malquint that stood majestically before him.

It was a great archway that left the shore and climbed up until it reached a crest that Burton could not see over. Above the roadway were mountainous columns that stood high over the bridge. The tops of the columns were so high that Burton could not see them as they disappeared into the clouds that hung overhead. The ground that led to the entrance of the bridge ended abruptly and went straight down to the jagged rocks below. The water pounded against the rocky shoreline and broke high into the air as it crashed onto the rocks. A steady mist rose from the bay below and sprayed into the air, creating a rainbow of colors that radiated against the blue sky. From the columns were large cables of some type of metal that actually held that bridge in the air. Burton was both in awe and afraid at the same time. Of all of the buildings and floating Ice Mountains he had seen, this was by far the most beautiful, yet most ominous structure he had ever seen. And he was about to step foot where no Myopian had ever been before.

"Come Master Brew, let's go visit the Elves that live on the other side of this cavernous divide," said King Thuron, as he started to cross. "I think your companions will keep you safe."

Burton started toward the bridge and immediately Milo and Silo got up and walked beside him. The great beasts forced Burton into the very middle of the bridge and because of the height of both wolves, he was unable to see anywhere but directly ahead of him. While a small part of him wanted to look over the side and see the water below, most of him was very happy that he was unable to do so. Just the rise of the road ahead filled him with dread. Occasionally he would have visions of the road just ending and the party falling into the sea below. But he summoned up all his strength and courage and forged ahead until he reached the halfway point at the very crest of the bridge. He felt much better when he could see down and knew that there was in fact another side and they would not fall into the waters below. Burton let out a slight laugh as he realized just how foolish he had been in his fear of the bridge.

When he looked below he could see the great Elf city of Malquint in the distance. It sparkled in the sunlight as if it were a jewel that had been crafted by the finest hand. Its mighty towers stood tall and proud against the skyline, as if they had been painted into the very fabric of the earth. The sight was simply breathtaking. Burton soon lost all fear of the bridge, and was filled with wonder as he gazed at the city that stretched below.

At the foot of the bridge stood two Elf guards wearing full battle armor. They each held a long spear that was at least twelve feet in length, or twice their body height. On their heads they wore helmets that were topped with large white feathers on each side directly above the ear holes. On their chest plates and shields were large white ships on a blue field with three golden stars above the ship. They were tall and slender, but Burton knew them to be High Elves. Much like the Elves who lived in Fallquint, these were Elves of the Beginning Days and still possessed the bloodline of the old days.

They first greeted King Thuron, who arrived well ahead of Burton at the foot of the bridge. It seemed that the king was in more of a hurry to get across the bridge than Burton or Derfer. Burton always suspected that the king was as much afraid of the bridge as he was, although he would never admit it. The two guards and the king headed toward the city.

Another Elf, dressed like the others, approached Burton as he reached the end of the bridge. Milo and Silo took off at a full sprint towards the city and were gone before Burton could get out a single word. He guessed their entire duty was simply to accompany him across the bridge. The very thought of this brought a smile to Burton's face, and he could not help but laugh at the unthinkable situation he had put himself in.

"Master Brew," said the Guard. "I am to escort you and Master Derfer to the Great Hall of Malquint, where My Lord Mindeloria and Lady Lindeloria await you. They wish me to bid you well, and they hope your journey has not caused you any discomfort or hardship. They bid you make haste and come with me."

The guard turned and Burton and Derfer followed both, with almost running to keep up with the Elf guard, who moved as if he walked on air. It was not an easy task for a Myopian and Dwarf to keep up with a long-legged Elf who was in a hurry.

As they approached the city Burton noticed that they were indeed prepared for war. Stockade and palisade fortifications were everywhere. The city itself was surrounded by the same type of stone work that surrounded Fallquint. Atop the walls were Elf archers and other types of defensive fortifications that Burton had never seen. They entered the city without any fanfare or salute at all. As a matter of fact, with the exception of the guards at the gate, the Elves were so busy with their work that they did not even seem to notice Burton or Derfer as they made their way to the Hall of Malquint.

At last they came to a large building that was built directly against the sea. They entered and went through a large set of doors into a room that was filled with all kind of people. There were Myopians, Elves, Dwarves, and even Gnomes assembled within the hall. At the far end was a table where Mindeloria, Lindeloria, Warrant, Tordin, King Thuron, and Tisiron all sat. The guard led Burton to the table and then bowed to Mindeloria and left the room.

"I see you are none the worse for wear, Master Brew," said the Elf lord.

"It was not any easy task, but I have completed it and the Dwarves are here as you requested." replied Burton. "Now I wish to be on my way and return home in defense of my own realm."

"I do not think that will be necessary, Master Burton" said Mindeloria. "You see, we have brought your people here and they are safe within these walls."

"All of Myopia? You have brought them here?" exclaimed Burton. "Where are they? I would love to see my friends."

"In time Master Brew, in time," said Mindeloria in a very relaxed tone. "There will be time for reunions soon enough, my young friend, but first we must prepare for the battle to come. The enemy will arrive with days, and there is much to do. I'm afraid we do not have the luxury to waste time right now, Master Burton. I must speak with you, and we must prepare ourselves for the great battle that is about to unravel before us."

With that Mindeloria motioned for chairs to be brought in for Burton and Derfer and requested that the room be cleared of all but those who would have an active part in the planning of the defense of Malquint.

And so was forged the plan for the last stand against tyranny in preparation for the battle that would decide the future of the free peoples of Hatu.

NineTeen

The Calm Before the Storm

While the defense for Malquint was laid out, the Dwarf forces deployed in preparation of the battle to come. It was decided that the main gate would be defended by the Dwarves from the Rolling Hills. This made Zander very happy, as he wanted the opportunity to engage the forces that had destroyed his homeland. His six thousand Dwarves would anchor the line and be supported by the Dwarf steam cannons that were being placed upon the ramparts of the city walls. Elf archers, the finest in all of Hatu, would take a position upon the walls and rain down arrow fire before the enemy got within striking distance of the Dwarves. The Dwarves from the Mystic Mountains, some twenty to twenty-five thousand in all, would take up a position on the left flank and extend their line all the way to the Bay of Malquint.

The Bridge of Malquint would be the very end of the line and should the enemy gain this position all would be lost. The right flank would be the Rangers, numbering approximately fifteen hundred, along with Elves from both Fallquint and Malquint. Mindeloria had brought ten thousand with him from Fallquint. Malquint would be able to put another fifteen thousand on the field of battle. Burton did the math and to his best account that meant that the defense of Hatu would stand with some sixty thousand, compared with the two hundred and fifty thousand who would be knocking on their door in less than a couple of days. Just fewer than five to one: not the kind of odds that makes a person feel secure at all.

"And what if they should cross the bridge?" asked Zander. "It would only make sense that they follow our path when they find that we have left the defenses of Doubblegate. Who will stop them then?"

"I think that will not be a problem, my dear Dwarf" said Lindeloria, once again with that famous smile crossing here lips. "My father has placed a spell on the bridge, and the Orcs will not even know it exists. To them it will just be a two-mile-wide strait of water with nowhere to cross"

"But will this magic stand up to a wizard?" insisted Zander.

"I agree Commander," said Thuron. "Elf magic is no match for a wizard."

"You are quite correct, Lord Thuron, Elf magic is no match for a wizard." said Tordin. "But I must remind you that Lord Mindeloria is not just any Elf. He is high born, and his magic is unsurpassed by any other in Hatu. He may be as powerful as any who as ever lived, and I would not hesitate to say that he may be as powerful as my grandfather and those of his time. I am not concerned that his magic will fail us, Lord Zander. My fear is that we will fail it."

"How do you mean that? I do not like what you have implied, Master Ranger," said a defiant Zander.

"What I think he means, Master Dwarf, is that my magic draws on the strength of those around me and will depend on the strength of our army," Mindeloria calmly replied. "My magic is of the old ways, and there are few who can understand it and how it works. I will be in battle with you my friend. I choose to stand at the gate with my Dwarf allies, and I will lend all that I have to their defense. Should we falter or lose faith, then my magic will fade and the bridge will appear to our enemies. But I do not fear such an event my friends, as the enemy will undoubtedly throw all of his strength against us and should the bridge appear, there will be no one there to cross it."

"But will not the wizard sense such magic and cast a spell to block it and make the bridge appear?" continued Zander. "Surely, he will know of its existence."

"Yes, he will know it is there, and, yes, I think he will try to block my spell. But he will fail," replied Mindeloria.

"And if he does not?" stubbornly asked Zander.

"If my father says he will fail, then he will fail," said Lindeloria, putting a stop to this line of conversation.

"My lord, what of the Elf cavalry?" asked Tisiron.

"They are deployed south of here and upon my signal will descend upon the enemy with all possible haste," said Mindeloria.

"And how many ride with them?" asked Burton.

"They number five thousand and are mounted on the fastest war steeds this side of Forlosha," replied Tordin.

"Then all is ready," said Thuron.

"That is, all but the Myopians" replied Mindeloria.

"Myopians? Unless you have more such as Lord Brew here, I think they had best hide with the women and children," laughed Zander.

"We have a right to fight for our homes, too," replied Burton. At times he was not sure if he really liked Zander or not. And this was one of those times.

"He is quite right. They will join the Elves on the walls that support the Dwarves. I have directed that special platforms be built, which will allow them to see over the rampart and look down upon the field as the battle unfolds," replied Mindeloria. "Do not take the Myopians so lightly, Lord Zander. They have been far more engaged with the enemy these past few months than any, save your people. They have proven to be valiant warriors and very skilled with bow and sling. While we have been preparing for battle, it is they who have fought it."

"I meant no disrespect to any, my Lord," said Zander. "I did not think that any with such stature could be of much use against the enemy that now approaches."

"I think you will be pleasantly surprised with the skills of my people," said Burton, as he stuck his chest out and sat taller in the chair. "While you may be stouter than us, you are not all that much larger over all."

Everyone got a laugh at this statement there was a large difference between a Myopian and a Dwarf. Even Zander allowed a smile to cross his lips as he stroked his long brown beard.

"All right Master Brew," he said. "We will see your worth in battle soon enough."

"Before we all go to join our brethren in the too few hours of peace we have left, there is some unfinished business which we must conclude," said Mindeloria. My Lord Derfer, I understand that you happened upon a Dwarf Battle axe in your travels. May I see it?"

Derfer took the axe from its sheath and placed it on the table before Mindeloria. Everyone in the room was mesmerized by the beauty of this grand weapon. Even the Elves who were in attendance took a deep breath at the remarkable blade.

"In the first age there were two such weapons made. One was the axe of Tyrindos, the finest Dwarf weapon ever made. The other is this" said Mindeloria. "It is the brother to the Axe of Tyrindus and until now had been thought lost in the great war against he who will go unnamed. It has many magical powers and is said to sense the type of enemy it is about to engage. Did you notice any such signs in your travels?"

"It made music when we met our friends in the wilderness," said Derfer.

"And a different sound when we fought the Trolls," chimed in Burton.

"This is the magic of this weapon," continued Mindeloria. He then reached down and picked up the blade, examining it before he swung it in the air. Once again the great axe sung out in a melodic voice that could only be compared to a magnificent choir of a thousand voices. Everyone in the room was filled with calmness, and a gentle peace flowed through the air. Mindeloria stopped swinging the axe, and the music faded as it caressed the very soul of all who sat at the table.

"Never have I seen such a weapon," exclaimed Thuron. "Truly, this is an heirloom of the line of Tyrindus and belongs in the hands of its king." As he said this he reached out to take the axe from the table. Zander and Derfer both reached for it at the same time, and as they touched the handle of the axe a great sound filled the room. There was not music in the air. It was more of a single note that was so loud everyone had to cover their ears. Derfer, who had carried the great weapon for several weeks, let go. Zander did not. The great axe stopped making any noise and began to glow. Burton had seen this same kind of magic before when Lindeloria and Tordin went into battle frenzy.

"I think the axe has chosen its new master," said Mindeloria, as he and everyone else uncovered their ears. "This axe was made explicitly for the line of Tyrindus, and I think it has made its way home to the rightful line"

"But why did it not act like that when it was wielded by Derfer?" inquired Burton.

"Because they are brothers and the same blood flows through their veins," replied Mindeloria. "The axe knew that Derfer was of the line of Tyrindus, but not the true heir to the throne."

"What evil is this?" said an incensed Thuron. "I will not have some usurper appear and steal the very realm I have sworn to defend. This cannot be."

"Remember, King Thuron, there were many Dwarf kings, and all Dwarves are related to one another. The blood line flows throughout your entire race. It is now that it has emerged, in your greatest hour of need, that it has reestablished itself through the chance finding of this weapon," said Mindeloria. "It does not mean that you are not king of your people. It simply means that Zander has the true blood of Tyrindus, and the weapon has chosen him."

"I do not want your kingdom or your throne, King Thuron," said Zander. "If it is my destiny to take this magnificent weapon into the greatest battle that has ever been known, then that is what I will do. I wish no followers or worshippers, nor do I want land or title. My task is to fight the enemy of all our peoples, and with this blade in my hand I will wade into my foes and they will pay for what they have done to my people."

As Zander talked he looked directly at the great blade, and it glowed even more as he talked. To everyone in the room, even King Thuron, it was obvious that the two were meant to be.

"And what of Derfer, what will he carry to battle?" asked Burton.

Once again the host at the table laughed at the simple question of a Myopian.

"I think you need not worry about that my friend," laughed Derfer.

"No, I think not," followed Zander. "We Dwarves have brought plenty of weapons with us. My brother does not need this magic axe to kill his enemies."

"No, that I do not," said Derfer. "But I will miss the music from the great blade."

"I think that will not be a problem my brother. Stand beside me and wield this." Zander then reached under the table and threw a white rolled linen on the table. He gripped the linen and with one mighty pull unraveled it. An axe fell from the cloth and hit the table, making a loud clang.

The room fell silent as all eyes looked upon the magnificent axe as it lay gleaming in the light from the torches that lit the room.

"You did not think that we would let the vermin that fouled our lands make off with one of our greatest treasures, did you?" laughed Zander. "Smelter, the Great War axe, will once again vanquish our enemies. I will have you, my brother, carry it by my side. With weapons such as these, the three Dwarfs kings will stand in battle, and all will tremble to look upon us"

Smelter was an axe of great renown and was carried by Dwarf kings in the days of old, many, many years ago. When the last known king of the Rolling Hills died, the axe was laid to rest upon his tomb. Apparently it was rescued from Maloneous and his marauding army before the fall of the Rolling Hills and the desecration of the Dwarf king's resting place. It was presented to Zander when he found his people after he left Fallquint to return to his homeland. And he was giving it to Derfer, who gladly accepted it.

"You said three Dwarf kings?" asked Burton.

"That is if King Thuron will unfurl his banner with mine and stand with my brother and me in the face of our enemy?" said Zander, as he looked at the proud Dwarf king from the Mystic Mountains.

"I humbly accept this great honor, my Lord," replied Thuron.

"Then all is ready, and I suggest we look to our people in the time we have left." said Mindeloria as he rose from the table.

Everyone else got up. and the members of council went their separate ways. For Burton it was a time to catch up with his friends and find out what had happened in his absence these many months.

Myopians had been under constant harassment by bands of Orcs as Mindeloria had already related. Between the Rangers and the local sheriffs and militias, the Orcs suffered many a humiliating defeat, and with the exception of the outset of the war, the people of Myopia had not suffered too terribly. As the plan was developed to evacuate Doubblegate and the Mystic Mountains, there was much debate on what to do with the Myopians and the folks from their outlying cities and towns. By vacating Doubblegate it would force the invading army to take a path back toward the south and cross the West River. Unfortunately, this would place Myopia directly in the path of the main army. Mindeloria arranged for a council with the local mayors. It was decided that the Myopians would join in the defense of Malquint. So the Rangers gathered up all the cities and towns of people and brought them to the Elf city. They were camped several miles from the main gate, and Burton would have a chance in the morning to visit with all his family and friends. This brought great joy to him. He could not wait to finish with his business here, so that he could go and see them.

Most of the folk from the larger cities in the east decided not to join in the defense of Malquint. For whatever reason, they choose to travel south and make their way towards Forlosha and the Horse People. Many of the Rangers, including Warrant and Borgon, shadowed them much of the way and kept them as protected as they could. To the best of their knowledge, they made it to Forlosha and were given safe haven.

Lindeloria and Tordin spent much of their last few days in preparation for the defense of Malquint. After the Myopians were safely protected, they began reinforcement of the battlements and oversaw placement of the Dwarf steam cannons. Mindeloria must have known that the Dwarves were going to accept his offer because when the Dwarves finally arrived everything was already in place for their equipment. Hoists were already built, and it took very little time for everything to be put in its proper place.

Milo and Silo spent much of their time running between Fallquint and Malquint. The two great wolves could come and go as they desired and did not attract very much attention.

Before Burton could visit his fellow Myopians, he had one more stop to make. For some unknown reason he felt he had to go to the docks and overlook the bay that led into the great waters beyond. He asked Lindeloria, to join him and she accepted. So the two of them made their way through the bustling city until the came to the bay and found the last dock on the row. They walked out to the end and just stood there looking at the water.

"To think, this is the very spot where those that fought the last Great War all left for faraway lands to live forever." said Burton. "But I have seen this place before."

He told Lindeloria of his dream of sitting on the dock with the man dressed in wizard garb. He had finally figured out that this man was an image of none other than Quickfoot. The two others who had visited him in his dreams before were Milton Brew and

Nuldoria, the Great Elf Lord. It was their visits in his sleeping hours that had given him hope and provided him the strength he needed to survive his great ordeal. Lindeloria said nothing; she just looked at Burton and gave him one of her smiles. Burton looked back into the city and then once again out over the water.

"It will not be long now, I suppose," he said. "I guess the enemy will arrive and we will fight. We may die, I think, or we may not. Either way, I assume, everything will change. I suppose our life will be different when this is over. I think that if we win, the price will be high, and I guess that if we lose, there will be no life, unless it is that of a slave. But I suppose that is the way of things."

"Maybe not, Burton," Lindeloria softly spoke. "We do not know what tomorrow will bring, or the day after, or the day after that. Yes, there will be a terrible battle, and yes, the price may be high, but who is to say what may come after that. All we know is that we must fight or surely we will die. If not in death, then through slavery and torture, will not our souls die a little at a time? For only time will tell if our struggle against this evil is in vain. I believe that no matter what the outcome of this battle, there is no evil that can destroy good forever. Just as I believe that there can be no good without evil. It is simply the nature of things. Should we lose this fight, there will be another, and another, and even more after that; and in time we will win. What we do here now Burton Brew will affect all life in Hatu for generations to come. And to be a part of that is truly a great gift, do you not agree?"

Burton looked down into the water as if he had not heard a word that was said. After a few seconds all that came out of his mouth was, "I suppose."

Twenty

A Promotion Is Given

B urton spent most of the night visiting with the Myopians from his home area who had been given refuge in the Elf city, and he was very happy to know that for the most part, Myopia was safe. He talked with all of his neighbors and the friends of neighbors and the neighbors of neighbors, many of whom he did not even know. He found out his home was intact and none of his immediate neighbors or family was ever in any danger. This was due to the vigilant effort of both the local militias and the Rangers. Burton discovered that many a Ranger paid the ultimate price to keep his people from being in harm's way. To listen to the Myopians talk, one would have thought they had never seen a Ranger before. They all explained how until recently they took the Rangers for granted, and for the first time, they realized just how important these strange men were to their quiet way of life. Of course, when the time came to leave Myopia, they were none too happy about that turn of events. They spent almost three days and nights in council, and it wasn't until Mindeloria himself came to the meeting that the Myopians gave in and marched to the safety of Malquint.

Many of the younger Myopians wanted to know all about Burton's adventures and hounded him for hours to tell them of his travels. At first, Burton was reluctant to talk about his adventures, but eventually, he gave in and told anyone who would listen about the path that brought him to this place. Myopian's love a good story and listening to any tale that is out of the ordinary. But even more, they loved to tell stories. Most of the early morning was monopolized by Burton and his rendition of what he had experienced. Of course, he left out the parts about his magic. He thought there would be chance enough for them to learn of his powers soon enough.

Finally, at about three or four in the morning he reluctantly returned to his quarters to get some sleep. That is, after a couple of Elf guards made it perfectly clear that they had been sent to retrieve him and make sure he got at least a few hours of rest. So he tossed off his gear and climbed in to the soft, down-filled bed that had been set for him hours ago. As soon as his head hit the pillow, he was fast asleep. No dreams or visitors came to him, he simply slept as a weary Myopian sleeps.

A mere few hours later, a Dwarf knocked on the chamber door and woke Burton from his deep sleep.

"Master Brew," said the voice. "Master Tordin has sent for you. He wishes me to fetch you and bring you to him immediately"

"I will be right there," replied Burton, still wiping the sleep from his eyes and trying to figure out what time it was. He quickly threw some water on his face, dressed, buckled on his sword, and opened the door.

"What time is it?" he asked sleepily.

"It is almost ten," replied the Dwarf.

"At night?" asked Burton.

"In the morning, Master Myopian," laughed the Dwarf. "You act as if you have been drinking ale all night. The Ranger said you were out late, but he didn't tell me you'd been out all night"

By now Burton was coming around and was beginning to realize that it was indeed daytime. He found he was slightly embarrassed by the incident, but just shrugged his shoulders and went with the Dwarf without any further comments.

The two made their way through the city back towards the main gate. Along the way Burton did not see many people. He noticed that the city had become very calm and quiet. He assumed that this was because of the impending attack and that everyone was either safety in hiding or preparing for the events to come. Finally, they reached the main gate and ascended the ramp that led to the parapet directly over the gates. Here he found a hub of activity. Dwarves were aiming their steam cannon and arrow machines. The Elves were firing their arrows towards markers that had placed at various distances in the field before the gate. The accuracy that they displayed was incredible.

Tordin was waiting rather impatiently when Burton arrived.

"Good morning, my young friend," said Tordin. "I hope I did not disturb you too much, but there is much to do and very little time to do it."

"I am sorry Tordin, I stayed far longer with my kinsfolk last evening than I had intended too," replied Burton.

"I understand, but there is no time for such luxuries anymore. The enemy will be within sight of this wall by night fall," said Tordin. Burton noticed a hint of disgust in Tordin's voice.

"I had not seen my friends for so very long, and there was so much to catch up on. I am much relived to find them safe, but I understand that my attention must now focus elsewhere," said Burton. "What is it you need me to do?"

"You have not asked where you will be during this battle," said Tordin. "This will be your position. You and the Lady Lindeloria will have total control of all of the forces within these walls. Be they Elf, Dwarf, or Man. Is that understood?"

"Yes, I understand," replied a stunned Burton. "But I am no general. What if I don't make the right decision? What if I give the wrong order at the wrong time?"

"Have you not learned anything about yourself in these past few months Master Brew?" replied Tordin. "You have the abilities you need within you; all you have to do is use them. This is the order of Lord Mindeloria, and I do not think that he would give such a command if there was even the slightest chance it would diminish our chances of victory"

"Victory?" said Burton. "Do you really think that we can succeed in the face of such odds? These are the same forces that routed the Dwarves in the Rolling Hills; they have marched half the distance of Hatu and now are outnumbering us by more than four to one. Surely, you do you expect to win in the face of all that is against us?"

"You surprise me, Master Burton," replied Tordin. "I did not think that you had fallen into such despair. Have you lost all hope? You have been instrumental in bringing the Elves and the Dwarves together. Do you think that they would have done so if an Elf had delivered the message from Lord Mindeloria to the King? Do you think that King Thuron and King Zander would have come to such a peaceful agreement if it were anyone else but you who sat at the table? Burton, if not for your leadership and faith, all would already be lost. I believe the Dwarves would have already been defeated, and Malquint would be engulfed by the enemy if you had not played your part. Your people would never have left their lands if Lord Mindeloria had not told them of your exploits and urged them to come here under your protection. No, Master Brew, you do not give yourself enough credit."

It had been a long time since Tordin had been this strict with Burton. So long in fact that Burton had completely forgotten how it felt.

"I have not lost hope Lord Tordin," said the shattered Myopian. "It is just that all of this is so overwhelming. I did not ever think that I would be in this position, doing the things that I am doing. I did not, for a second, ever think that such evil as this would come along and that I would be not only involved, but possibly the very focal point of such hatred. And now, as the enemy approaches, I am told that it falls on me to act as a general in the defense of thousands of Elves and Dwarves and Men. Even the fate of the very protectors of my people, the Rangers, may rest in the decisions that I make in the next few hours. Surely, you can understand how much of a burden this has become?"

"I understand much Master Burton," said Tordin. "Much of what you have said is true. There is a tremendous burden on your shoulders, and it may grow even heavier before this war is over. But you are not alone with such baggage. Do you not think that Lord Mindeloria and the Lady Lindeloria feel such pressure as well? Do you think that our Dwarf allies are impervious to the responsibility that now lies upon their respective shoulders? What of Warrant and Tisiron, who have spent much of their life defending your land against intruders such as these, only to have such a force march to their door so that they had no choice but to bring their charges here? Even I have felt the strain that this conflict has created. Make no mistake about it, Burton Brew, you are not alone. And if hope and trust in one another is all we have in the face of such adversity, then I say we are the better off for it."

At that moment, Burton Brew came to realize just how selfish he had become in the past few weeks. He tried to think back to the last time that he thought about others and not just himself. He had been so caught up in his own responsibilities that he forgot that others were involved in this great struggle as well. Not just himself. While he was concerned with thoughts about Myopia, it was really his own land and property that he had been concerned with losing, as well as his family and friends. Not those he barely knew or those he didn't know at all. He gave no real thought to the Dwarves, an entire race of beings who had lost their homes in defense of all races, not just themselves. Or the Elves who risked everything to bring these people together. He'd given little thought to the realms of Ancintron and Forlosha and the future they faced should this city fall. He struggled with the words, but no matter what he tried to say he knew it would not come out right.

Finally, he said, "I am sorry, Tordin, for having doubted such wisdom as that which controls our destiny. I have forgotten how many others have been affected by the war and how their lives have been destroyed as the events unfolded. I still do not want such responsibility placed on my shoulders, but if it must be there, and it appears it must, then I will promise to make the very best of it. As I said my friend, I am no general, but I will do the best I can. If we are to fall, so be it. But it will not be because of my selfishness that victory will slip from our grasp. If I have a part yet to play in this adventure, then I will play it to the best of my ability and with all of my heart."

"That sounds more like the Myopian that I have spent these many years with," said Tordin. "Now enough talk of burdens and choices, we have a battle to plan for."

Tordin and Burton spent the next few hours talking of strategy and plans. Burton actually caught on very quickly in how the battle was expected to play out. It was expected that the Orc army would hit the line directly in the middle, making for the entrance to the city. It was a single-minded battle plan, and if successful, would spell instant defeat for the forces defending the fortified walls, both in and out of the city. So all they had to do was keep the Orc army from the gates to the city. It sounded simple enough to Burton, but deep down inside he knew it could not possibly be that easy.

Late in the afternoon, Burton and Tordin had discussed all that there was to discuss. So they decided to leave the upper parapet and return to the dining area for some dinner and relaxation. There they met Derfer and Zander, and the four sat down for a meal and general discussion. They laughed and talked as if they had not a care in the world. An observer would not have known there was an enemy army bearing down on them and that within days the peoples of Hatu could all be captured or worse. They talked of olden days, days when the world was in fellowship and lived in peace. They talked of Tyrindus and Cyrus, Quickfoot and Nuldoria, even of the Tree People and the Mountain People. The conversation ranged among many different topics. Every topic, that is, but war.

It was just about dark when the alarm sounded and the command given that all personnel were to report to their battle stations. The enemy had been sighted and a small party was approaching the city.

Everyone went their separate ways, and the calm of the evening was shattered as if a fine china plate had been tossed to the ground and splintered into a hundred pieces. Burton ran to his place on the wall as quickly as his legs would carry him. His heart raced, and he thought it would pound right out of his chest. This was it! The battle he had been dreading for so many months was about to begin.

Burton got to the parapet and looked out over the field.

The field was dark, except for a small band that was approaching the city. It looked like there were three companions making their way towards the city gate. He could see that one of the men, or at least he thought it was a man, was sitting on some sort of large beast, probably a horse, he thought to himself. Beyond the horizon, the night sky was aflame with the dancing lights from the fires of the enemy encampment. It was so bright, and there were so many fires, that Burton thought the ground of Hatu itself was on fire. Soon Lindeloria joined him, and the two stood side by side as they looked over the field and watched the approaching party. Neither said a word, but Lindeloria shone and glimmered in the night darkness, making Burton feel safe and confidant as the gates opened and a single rider rode from the city to meet the advancing party. It was Lord Mindeloria on his white horse, and it became apparent to Burton that whoever was approaching the city was both of importance and very, very powerful.

The two parties met, and the stranger mounted on the great beast spoke in a loud and powerful voice. His voice bounced off the very walls and mountains.

"I am Maloneous, the Wizard of the Hatu, King of the East, and I have come to accept your surrender. But I will not barter with Elf, or Dwarf, or Man. It is the Myopian Burton Brew that I will speak with and none other. I demand that you send me the Last of the Line of those that destroyed my Master so that he may choose if you shall live or die."

All eyes turned towards Burton, who looked immediately at Lindeloria. She looked down at the Myopian with the soft look she knew so well, and smiled. She was about to speak when another loud voice was heard. It, too, echoed off the very walls and mountains. But it was far clearer and had a much calmer, less hateful sound to it. It was Mindeloria, the mighty Elf lord.

"Do not come to this place and make demands, Master Wizard. If it is Burton Brew you wish to speak to, then you need but ask. But it is his choice to converse with you, and it will not be because you have demanded him to do so"

The air was filled with the power of the Wizard and Elf Lord as they sat in silence after this exchange of words. If it were an encounter designed to intimidate the inhabitants of the city, it did not. Trumpets sounded and voices yelled in defiance; both Dwarf and Elf in unison cheered at this turn of events. But the wizard did not move nor was there a reply from the Orc army, and soon the din died down. When all was quiet again, a single solitary voice could be heard coming from the rampart, above the city gates. It was a small voice, but it was clear and amazingly powerful.

"If it is I, Burton Brew, that you wish to speak to, then so be it."

Burton walked down the ramp to the ground then he turned towards the great gates. The gates were opened, and all eyes were glued to him as he walked bravely towards the Wizard and his companions. Only the gentle white light of Mindeloria, and the cheers of those on the wall, gave him the courage to continue on his way.

"So this is what it has come to. Curse you, Milton Brew, for having brought this upon me," he thought as he approached the four figures in the field.

"I am Burton Brew. Say what you will and be off!" commanded the Myopian.

Maloneous reared his horse, which let out a snort, and then he laughed.

"What a brave Myopian who comes to a meeting of peace and talks as if he were the king of the world," said Maloneous. "But I will have my say, you stupid little man, and it is you who will listen or you, and this Elf, will die on the spot!"

And so began the conversation that would decide if there would be a battle that would determine the fate of all of the races that dwelt in Hatu.

TWENTY-ONE

MALONEOUS

As Burton approached the evil wizard and his henchmen, he took a few seconds to evaluate the situation and find out who the other two beings were. One was an Orc, a big ugly Orc, who was in battle armor, carrying a full body shield, with a scimitar-type sword hung at his side. The other being was a Man. He was a tall man with a dark beard that reminded Burton of the beard of a Dwarf, only not as full or long. It was not even long enough to even reach down to the top of the breast plate that he wore. On the breast plate was a picture of a black dragon flying over a green forest. The rest of his clothing was very foreign, to Burton and he did not recognize anything about it. The man wore a red cloak that was pinned at the shoulders with large black orbs. Burton thought that these were images of the Crystal Stone that was represented on all of the shields that he had seen the Orcs carrying.

Maloneous, on the other hand, was a very, very old looking man who was dressed as a wizard from head to toe. He had a long dark beard, and from what Burton could surmise, had dark hair under his large brimmed pointy hat. He sat on top of a large black horse that had red eyes; it had huge hooves that were covered in black hair. Just the look of this horse gave Burton a feeling of dread. And worst of all, the beast smelled terrible.

"I will make this simple Myopian," said Maloneous. "Give yourself up, and the others may live. What is your answer?"

Burton looked at Mindeloria as if he was hoping the Elf would answer for him. The chance that his kinsmen would go free and live if he would give himself freely to the wizard, sounded like an offer that was too good to be true.

"And what guarantee do I have that you will keep your word?" asked Burton. He knew that the Evil Wizard was not to be trusted.

"It is you that I want Myopian," replied Maloneous. "Because of you, and your kind, my master was defeated and all that we had worked for nearly destroyed. I will have my revenge on you. Then I will be satisfied, and I will bother your friends no more." A sneer crossed the evil wizard's face as he spoke these words. Burton knew that the words that he heard could not be believed.

"If it were me you were after, then why did you attack the Dwarves in the Rolling Hills?" asked Burton, already knowing that the wizard had intended to destroy the Dwarves from the very beginning.

"That was very unfortunate for those that dwelt in the Rolling Hills," replied Maloneous. "My emissaries told me that you were visiting the Dwarves and when they said you were not there…. Well, how sad for the Dwarves. But worry not my, silly Myopian, I have dealt with those who were mistaken about your presence, and I apologize for the misunderstanding."

"So you attacked and wiped them out anyway? And now you expect me to take your word that you will turn and leave should I choose to give myself to you?" said Burton. A kind of anger was growing in Burton that he had only felt a couple of times before in his life. The last time was in his battle with the Trolls right before they met up with the Rangers.

"I do not come here to talk to you about the Dwarves," said Maloneous. "Nor do I feel I need to justify my actions to one such as you." Turning to Mindeloria he said, "Or you for that matter." He turned again to Burton. "I am here to offer you a way to save your friends. Take it or not?"

"If I must choose now," started Burton.

"And you must," interrupted Maloneous. "I did not come all this way to leave empty-handed. I will have you, Myopian, you alone, or with your friends. It makes no difference to me. I have spent many, many hours in the planning of your demise. And now I have the strength at hand to simply wish it so. You are mine. This city, this Elf city, will not stand against the army that I have brought to this place. I will fall upon you like rain to the ground. My army will destroy this city until there are none left in Hatu to stand against me. I will rule these lands, as is my destiny. And when I am done here, I will rebuild Mertain, and it will be my castle. From there I will be the lord of all. There will be none left to oppose me. You think you have been wise in coming to this place. But I say you are fools. You are trapped, and there is no way out. Your back is to the sea, and no ship is there to carry you away. There is no escape." Once again he turned to Mindeloria. "Give me the Myopian, and you may live in service to your king. I will be fair and just to those that follow me. And those that do not follow me will fall and be ground into the dust of the earth. That is the offer I bring to this meeting. It is your destiny that you shall kneel before me. I am your king and you will obey me."

As Maloneous talked, Burton could feel the power rise within the wizard. The Orc and the Man with Maloneous became restless, as if waiting for word to strike. The situation was quickly escalating from one of conversation to one of confrontation. Mindeloria must have sensed it as well, as the light around him began to increase as the hatred from Maloneous wound its way from his heart to the lips that spoke. As the light from Mindeloria grew, the Orc and the Man began to back away from the Elf and despite being in the presence of their master, Burton thought that they would turn and run if the situation continued to deteriorate. Deep down, Burton knew that something had to be done or the situation would get out of hand, and there was no telling what would happen.

"May I have time to talk to my friends?" he asked the wizard. "I must assure them that if I choose to go with you that it is of my free will, and they must not attempt to stop me."

"No, Myopian. I will have an answer now." yelled the wizard. A fire burned from his eyes and the lines in his weathered face disappeared as his skin grew taut. Burton knew that there was no way out of this situation. He knew that now was the time to decide.

"Then my answer is no! I choose to fight!" yelled Burton. At that moment he began to unsheathe his sword, but before he could pull the weapon Mindeloria reached down and jerked him onto his horse. Then the horse turned, and they headed back towards the city so fast that Burton could not even catch his breath. The black horse once again reared up and let loose a terrible sound as the wizard turned and broke back toward his lines beyond the horizon. The Man and Orc were caught flat-footed and stood looking at each other for a few seconds before they realized what had happened. They scurried back in the direction of their lines as well. Loud cheers went up from the city as they saw the wizard turn and leave the field. It was a small victory, but a victory just the same.

After they returned to the city and closed the gates behind them, Mindeloria released Burton from his horse. Lindeloria had come down from the wall and was standing, waiting for their return, as were Tordin and Zander.

"I take it the Wizard did not like the conversation," laughed Zander.

"No, I think not," said Mindeloria as he lightly leaped from the back of his horse. "I think he found there is much more here than he anticipated,"

"What did you say to anger him so?" inquired Zander.

"It was not I, Lord Dwarf. It was the Myopian." replied Mindeloria.

"And what did you have to say then?" Zander asked Burton.

"He said that if I gave myself up, without a fight, he would let you all go free" replied Burton, finally catching his breath following the confrontation with Maloneous.

"I take the fact that you are here, means you said no?" laughed Zander. Ever since the incident with the axe in the council meeting, Zander's demeanor had changed. Burton didn't know why, but Zander was no longer the hateful, spite-filled Dwarf that he first met in Fallquint. Maybe it was that he was the undisputed leader of the Dwarves, maybe it was that they were about to go into battle against those that murdered his kinsmen in the Rolling Hills. Whatever it was, Burton liked it, and he liked the new Zander much more than the old one.

"I think if I had not snatched up our young Myopian, he may have tried to end this battle on the spot," said Mindeloria.

"I think you are right," said Burton.

"Lucky for you my father was there then," chimed in Lindeloria. "As powerful as you are, Master Brew, you are no match for a wizard."

"That is true, my young friend" said Tordin. "But I know he would have felt your wrath."

"I believe you are right, my friend" said Mindeloria. "But I fear that this conversation has sealed our fate, that is, if it were not already so. I expect that we will hear from Maloneous in short order. He will not take lightly the insult that Master Brew has laid at his feet this evening. I suggest we make preparations for the advance of his army. There is not much time left. Send word to deploy." He turned to an Elf guard who was standing by. "Please ask Lord Derfer to join Master Brew and myself in my quarters. Master Brew, if you will come with me"

And so the Elf lord turned and headed towards his quarters with Burton hot on his heels. Walking with Elves had never been an easy task for a Myopian. Elves were so graceful and took such long, lanky strides. Whereas the small legs of a Myopian have to work almost three times as hard just to keep pace. They arrived at Mindeloria's quarters and sat in the waiting area of his main room. Soon Derfer arrived, and the three moved to a small corner of the room, away from any windows or doors.

"I must tell you I have just received a message that the enemy will attack as the sun reaches it zenith in the midday" the Elf Lord quietly spoke. "Erideous has his animal agents in the field and they have sent word that at noon he will begin his assault. The reason I have asked you here is that I need the two of you to be my eyes and ears in the battle that will become chaotic and unnerving as they day goes on. It will take all of my concentration and ability to attempt to combat the spells that the Wizard will cast our way."

"Would this not be a better job for my brother Zander? He is the leader of our people," inquired Derfer.

"I think not my friend," replied Mindeloria. "Your brother will be in Dwarf battle lust and he will be difficult, at best, to control. I do not believe that we will be able to depend on him to make sound, decisions when the time comes. While I can think of no other I would want to fight beside on the field, I do not think that he will prove to be the most dependable should wisdom be needed over brawn"

"On that I can agree, my lord," replied Derfer. "What exactly would you have us do?"

"On the field, Lord Derfer, we will need a general who will know if it is time to press the enemy or time to give way," said Mindeloria. "For that, I will look to you."

Then he turned to Burton.

"And of you, my young friend, I ask that you keep a level head about you as you will have total sight of the battlefield and may be able to anticipate our enemy's movements before they actually occur. It is a great gift you have, Master Brew, and I believe now is the time to use that intuition of yours to its fullest extent."

"But, my Lord, I have never been able to control it or make it come and go as I choose." said Burton.

"That is why it is intuition, Master Brew. Just let it come to you, and when it feels right or wrong, as the case may be, go with it," said Mindeloria. "You have been given a gift that is very rare indeed."

"I will do what I can, my Lord," said Burton.

"Master Burton" said Mindeloria, "the outcome of this battle may very well depend on you and the unexpected. It is you that Maloneous wants, and it is you that he shall not have. I will have you as my general in the city and Derfer as my general on the battlefield. You are my generals, and it is by your choices that we may win or lose this war. I have faith in both of you. I believe that if you believe in yourselves and trust your instincts, all may yet work out and we will prevail."

The words from Mindeloria filled Burton and Derfer with a great swelling of pride and confidence. They left the meeting with him and walked back to their positions as laid out in the overall defense of the city. The forces that were placed outside of the walls quietly took their positions and by midnight were ready for anything that might be thrown their way. The Rangers had previously dug hundreds of small holes at various places in the fields that led to the city. They then filled the holes with oil and now were secretly making their way through the fields to light the oil. This provided a wonderful light source that illuminated the countryside, thus eliminating any chance of the enemy's sneaking up on the fortifications in the middle of the night.

The Dwarves, while not nearly as quiet as the Rangers or Elves, took up their positions in the middle and the left of the line. They had built several wooden fortifications from behind which they could fight. While they did not provide the protection they were used to, that of iron and stone, they did provide enough protection that the enemy could not easily reach the Dwarves. They would be delayed long enough that the Elves from the walls would be able to rain down several additional volleys of arrows before the Orcs would be too close to the Dwarves. Once the enemy got that close, only the very best archers would be able to continue to fire. The remaining Elves on the walls would become the last line of defense against ladders, or a breach in the wall, or the main gate.

The rest of the night was quiet, except for the occasional patrol or scout that would wander too close to the city. They were dispatched quickly, and none got within a distance where they would be able to see anything that might help before the attack. The enemy would attack at noon tomorrow, and it would not be until first light that they would be able to see the defenses that would lie before them. Everything had been checked, double-checked, and checked again. If a battle were to come, and come it would, those friends that stood together in defense of each other's freedom would be ready.

TWENTY-TWO

AN ANCIENT DEBT REPAID

B urton and Derfer spent much of the night and well into the next morning working on a way to signal each other during the battle. Derfer determined that most horn calls would be useless and could be easily duplicated by the enemy. Besides, each race had their own set of horn calls that meant one thing to them and nothing to anyone else. The plan they devised would be various colored flags that could be seen from a distance. One color, meant one thing and another meant something else. More signals could be sent by using different color combinations. They then trained multiple "signalmen" from the different races who could pass commands from one organization to another. While slightly complicated, this method might prove more easily understood than horn calls, which were the standard in most armies. Even the Orcs and Trolls used standards horn sounds to direct an army on the battlefield. By using the flag signals Burton could signal those on the ground from the parapet above the gate. Burton was surprised at how fast the signalmen caught on, and the various commanders were able to use their new innovation when they brought it to Mindeloria. The Dwarves, in particular, were impressed. Zander said it was because it would cut down on those blasted Elf horns and their high pitched-squeals. The Rangers liked them because the flags were on the end of long poles and could be seen from a distance. Thus they would not have to reveal themselves as much when concealed in the underbrush.

Around ten o'clock in the morning the Orcs started to harass the defending army with small raids and false attacks at various points of the line. Since the word had already been passed on that the main attack would not happen until noon, the Orcs got very little response or information from these probing missions. Mindeloria made it a point to make sure everyone was aware of their battle plans and knew that any information the enemy received could be devastating to their defenses when the main attack came. This proved to be very difficult for the Dwarves. Each time even so much as one Orc approached the line, Burton thought the entire Dwarf army would run off in pursuit and attempt to press the attack to Maloneous. Burton had heard of Dwarf Battle Lust but had never seen it until now. He could only imagine what would happen if the dwarves were turned loose to rain destruction upon an enemy. He realized that before this battle was over the Dwarves would break from the line and pursue the enemy. He had a long discussion with Zander and Derfer concerning this issue and was assured that only when given the command to do so would the Dwarves pursue the enemy to their death. Despite the outward appearance, he was told that the Dwarves were an extremely disciplined army. They would press on an enemy until told to do otherwise, and they would, in fact, do no more then ordered. This made Burton feel a little better, but he still was not totally convinced. He finally gave in and decided that what was to be would be, and he must have faith that Zander and the Dwarves would follow the battle plan and not risk defeat of a war for victory in one battle or one skirmish within a battle.

About eleven o'clock Burton told Lindeloria that he was going to go down to the docks for a few minutes to try to clear his head. Lindeloria, in her usual way, simply smiled and said that he should not to be too long. So Burton took leave of his post and went down to the docks, where he walked to the end and sat down. There he lost himself in thought. He thought about Myopia and his home, about his friends and his journey here, about Mindeloria and Derfer and Tordin, about the beautiful Dwarf city of Doubblegate. So many thoughts ran through his head. He thought about when he was a young Myopian and would play in the farmers' fields and how the farmers would chase him off with their dogs. He thought of how he would skip school and go down to the brook and fish for hours at a time. Burton loved to fish. For an instant he thought that he could drop a line in the water right now if he only had his pole with him. But he doubted he would ever see his fishing pole again, let alone use it. He wondered how so much responsibility could be laid upon him and how he would perform in the great battle that was to come. But he was ready and promised himself he would do as Lord Mindeloria had asked. He would trust his instincts and intuition and do whatever it took to help his friends in this new Great War that had marched to his very doorstep. He must have sat there for thirty or forty minutes before he rose and started to return to his post. There, right in front of him was an Elf from Mindeloria's guard who had been sent to get him.

"I am ready," he told the guard, who had not said a word. The two moved through the city towards the parapet that stood above the city gates. The city was deathly quiet. All of the civilians, the women, children, the elderly folk, had been sent to the farthest regions of the Elf city, where they would be as safe as possible. Burton scampered up the ramp to his position and took a few seconds to look to his left and right. He was most impressed with what he saw, and his heart was filled with hope that all was not lost. To his immediate right he saw both Men and Elves in full battle dress with weapons at the ready. The Elves had strong bows that were at least six feet long, and they wore helms that glimmered in the midday light. Above each ear hole there was a white wing that stretched two more feet into the air. These were the Sea Elves of Malquint. Sea Elves were of the first born and a very rare sight to see. They lived primarily in Malquint and the other Elf seaports. They very rarely were seen anywhere but on the sea or near its shore. Although Burton had spent the last few days with them, it was the first time he had seen them in battle dress, that is battle dress like this.

The Myopians also were in battle dress. They wore the traditional plate mail and small helms with no consistent marking that could be seen. Some had feathers, some did not. However, they all wore the traditional cape and bright colors that had been Myopian battle fashion from the beginning of time itself. Many different colors were displayed for the many different towns or cities represented. Some carried bows, and some had slings. Myopians were extremely deadly with slings, and many a wild pig or stray duck had fallen to the deadly eye of an expert Myopian marksman. But it was not pig they faced today. Burton felt tremendous pride to be with those of his race this morning.

Scatted along the parapet were the mighty Dwarf steam cannons. Mountains of black smoke billowed from the furnaces that built the steam to fire these engineering marvels. Each cannon was manned by four Dwarf gunners, each having his own specific duty to perform. The Dwarves on the walls were not in full armor, but wore leather in place of chain mail. Burton assumed this was so they could move more easily and perform their function at a faster pace. They did, however, wear their steel helms and carried their axes strapped across their back. The cannons were ready, and as soon as the enemy got within range, they would release their shot.

Standing near him was the Lady Lindeloria with her bodyguard of forty-five High Elves. They, too, were dressed for battle. Each guard carried a large sword with serrated edges. They also carried large Elf body shields. These shields were very unique in that they were slightly curved at the top. If the lower tip was placed directly on the ground in the standing position, the Elf that carried it could see through a U-shaped opening at the very top of the shield. Each shield was made specifically for one Elf and was marked with a large blue star on a golden field. This must be the sign of the Lady Lindeloria, thought Burton. Then he looked out on to the field before him.

There he could see the defenses of the city that had been so well carefully thought out. He could see the banners of Zander and Derfer and Mindeloria directly in the middle. To his left was the banner of King Thuron of the Mystic Mountains. Even though the king himself stood with Zander and Derfer, his banner flew above his people, and rightfully so thought Burton. To the right were the banners of Fallquint and Malquint, along with the banner of the Rangers. Once again a white star on a green field stood high in the golden sunlight. Burton knew that this was where Tordin, his lifelong friend and companion stood. Burton thought hard about him and hoped, no prayed, that he would survive this battle.

Finally, he looked back at the Lady Lindeloria as she stood about five feet from him. She was not in battle dress nor was there any sign of a weapon. The mighty Elven blade that she carried during their trip together was not to be seen. She wore a flowing white dress that shone and shimmered. Burton was unsure if this was Lindeloria or the dress shining in the sunlight, but somehow it didn't really matter. Either way, he was convinced that this was the most beautiful sight he had ever seen. She stood tall and regal and was surrounded by a light that shone as if it protected her like a suit of armor. Her golden hair flowed in the breeze, and she looked like a queen of days gone by. Burton could not take his eyes off her. He could sense her power and thought that she would explode upon the enemy with a violence that the Dwarves would envy. Burton was mesmerized. Then, a single horn sounded from the distance. Followed by another, and then another, until so many horns were sounding in the valley before the entrenched defenders that there was nothing but a wall of Orc horn that vibrated the very walls of the city. Burton looked up and saw that the sun was at its zenith and noon had come. And with it, the battle he had so dreaded was about to be unleashed.

The sight before Burton filled him with terror as he looked out toward the enemy. The horizon was nothing but a long line of Orcs and Trolls. It filled his vision as far as he could see. Tens of thousands of Orcs in battle formation now stood but a few thousand yards from him. He could not make out specifics, but his Myopian eyesight did tell him that there were thousands of Trolls in the direct center of the army and to his extreme left. As the horns changed their song, the army began to march forward. Rank after rank, column after column, the pure numbers of the enemy were staggering. Drums began to beat and the Orc army pressed forward. "How could anything stand against such a force?" wondered Burton. Yet, stand they must, and he reached down inside to summon all the courage he could find.

"My lady," he said to Lindeloria. "I do not think they intend to attack in the middle as they are indicating. I believe they will press us hard on the left. I think their first target is the banner of King Thuron and the Dwarves from the Mystic Mountain. I do not know why, but I sense we must concentrate our fire on the Trolls that approach there."

"Then we must send the signal, Master Brew." replied Lindeloria, looking at the Myopian with that familiar smile on her face. She turned to the signalman who stood beside her. "Send word to Dwarves of the Mystic Mountain and tell King Thuron to join them as soon as he can," she said.

The signalman flashed his colored banners and received a response from the Dwarf king.

"They are ready," said the signalman.

A group of about ten Dwarves could be seen leaving the middle of the line and making their way to the left. Burton knew that this was King Thuron and the handful of his King's Guard that were making their way to the Mystic Mountain Dwarves.

Just then the Dwarf cannons opened fire. The sound of them releasing the pent up steam was deafening. A loud cheer went up from the Dwarves as these monsters unleashed a barrage upon the approaching hoard. But the enemy was far from unready and unleashed a volley from their entrenched siege weapons. Maloneous had several hundred catapults with him and they hurled large boulders towards the city walls. Because the city was Elf built, the projectiles had very limited impact when they struck the mighty fortress. Burton now understood why Mindeloria wanted to make the last stand here. While Dwarves were expert craftsman, they did not have the ability to place magic in their building, such as the Elves had placed in Malquint. The bigger concern was for the troops that were deployed on the battlefield and facing the oncoming army. Many a projectile founds its mark and was making short work of the dirt and wood palisades that the entrenched army was using for protection. Of course, the explosions from the fused weapons of the Dwarves were having a similar impact as well. Large holes were created in the lines of the advancing Orcs with impacts killing several at one time. Unfortunately, the Orcs were so numerous that they simply filled in the holes and kept advancing.

"I think we need to direct more fire on the left flank," said Burton to the signalmen, who immediately signaled the cannon to redirect their fire. Two out of three cannons now concentrated on the portion of the line that was advancing towards King Thuron and his troops. The effect was as planned. Hundreds of Orcs and Trolls were cut to pieces by such a large concentration of firepower in one area. Maloneous must have seen this, and it soon became apparent that he, too, was redirecting his catapult fire. He was now aiming at the Dwarf steam cannons. One not very far from Burton was hit, and the impact knocked him to the ground. As he stood, he saw that the cannon was destroyed and three of the four Dwarf crewmen killed. The remaining crewman simply went to another cannon and began working as if nothing had happened. Burton was very impressed with the discipline the Dwarves had displayed and regretted his earlier concerns that they would be hard to control.

The first lines of the enemy army now were within archery range. The signal was given and the Elf archers on the wall let loose their first flight of arrows. The sky darkened and the sun was all but blocked out as thousands of arrows were sent into the ranks of the Orcs. Hundreds found their mark and many an Orc would advance no more. A second, then a third volley, was unleashed. Hundreds, maybe thousands of Orcs fell yet, the army continued to advance.

"I think they will show their plans soon," said Burton, as he looked out over the field.

"I think you are right, Master Brew" said Lindeloria. "I suggest you find a safer place to observe, and keep your head down."

No sooner did the words come out of her mouth then the Orcs let fly with a return volley of arrows. The sky once again was dark and tens of thousands of arrows flew towards the defenders of Malquint. Thousands of staunch defenders perished in this first wave of fire. At the same time, the center of the advancing line changed direction and joined in the attack on the left flank. Burton's intuition was correct and the first test of their defenses would be King Thuron and the Dwarves of The Mystic Mountains.

The Orc army broke into a full charge and struck what was left of the Dwarf palisades with a fury that left Burton awestruck. The sound of steel upon steel echoed throughout the valley. The attack was so well planned that the rest of the approaching army stopped and did not engage the defenses. The Orcs concentrated firepower on the center and right in the form of arrow and catapult. Thus, there was no way to send any assistance to the left, leaving King Thuron and his folk truly on their own.

Burton directed that as much support as could be given be sent from the parapets and that arrow fire be directed toward the now-engaged army. So every third Elf from the center of the line left his post and raced to support the Dwarves.

So much dirt and dust was created from this encounter that Burton could not see what was happening and who was winning the battle. He could only watch as more and more Orcs and Trolls waded into the fray. Lines were no longer discernible, and the advancing army was backed up onto itself. It could neither go forward, to join the fight, nor retreat, as more and more Orcs were coming up from the rear. This was the opportunity that they needed to turn the tide.

Burton directed that all cannon, catapults, and arrow launchers fire upon the stalled Orcs and continue firing until none were alive. All weapons were brought to bear on the stalled army, and the largest barrage in Hatu history rained down upon the now hopelessly trapped Orc army.

Tens of thousands were slaughtered in the open field. The Orcs at the very rear finally started to retreat, and before long the entire left side of Maloneous' army began to turn and run. It was a major victory for the goodly forces, and trumpets sounded from every battlement and defensive position both inside and outside the walls. Soon it was a complete rout and all of Maloneous' army withdrew to well out of arrow range. But the enemy catapults continued to fire and the large columns of smoke from the steam cannons made them easy targets. For the next several hours Maloneous concentrated all of his firepower on the cannons, and before long the desired effect was achieved. Soon the fire from the cannons became almost nonexistent. All but a few were knocked out of commission, and there would be no devastating barrage when the next attack came.

As for King Thuron and the mighty Dwarves from the Mystic Mountains, they survived the encounter with the Troll-led army, but as a battle force, they were no more. King Thuron was wounded in both arm and leg and was carried from the battlefield after the last Orc was no longer in range and there was nothing left to defend. Of the twenty thousand who had stood proudly under the banner of the King, only five thousand remained. King Zander dispatched one thousand Dwarves from his command to reinforce them and another fifteen hundred Elves were dispatched from the city. They hurriedly repaired defenses and did what they could to prepare for another attack. But they would have no chance if another wave such as the first wave were to strike them again.

Lord Mindeloria returned to the city and council was held just outside of the range of the Orc projectiles.

"It is good you followed your instincts Master Brew," said Mindeloria to Burton. "I fear we would have been defeated had you not done so."

"What do you think will be the next move our enemy will make, Master Burton?" inquired Zander.

Burton thought hard for a minute. Thousands of possible plans ran through his head. Finally, he spoke.

"I do not think that Maloneous will take this defeat well at all," said the Myopian. "I fear he will return with even more of a vengeance and drive his troops even harder. I am not sure, but I think he will drive straight for the city gates and the next attack will be his last. His forces will no longer retreat, and I do not think we have seen the worst yet."

"I think you are right, Master Burton," said a thoughtful Mindeloria. "We have won a minor victory today but the cost was extremely high. While our Dwarf brothers fought valiantly and with honor, they cannot survive another onslaught such as they faced today. Today, Maloneous struck us hard and weakened us considerably. His next attack will be more furious and his forces more committed to our defeat. Because of our anticipation and resolve, we fought the good fight this day. But it is the next attack that will seal our fate. We must prevail or all is lost."

Mindeloria then looked towards the sea and said; "But we still have hope and with that hope, faith. We must keep faith in one another and hold to that faith that we all serve a higher purpose. What that purpose may be, I do not know. But together we still stand, and we will persevere. No matter what the enemy may throw at us next, we will be ready, and we will be victorious. I suggest we return to our posts and prepare for the next assault."

And so Burton returned to his position on the wall above the main gate. There he stood and watched as the remaining forces prepared for the advance of Maloneous and his evil army.

Twenty-Three

One Final Stand

Burton sat quietly at his post and thought about how his first major battle had gone. He reflected upon the losses the Dwarves had suffered and wondered if there was anything different he could have done. By his account, his side of the battle had lost nearly a third of their total forces. The enemy had lost only about a fifth of their estimated numbers. So now it was forty thousand against only two hundred thousand. Not very favorable odds, Burton thought. He tried to stay positive and look for anything that he could consider being a bright spot. The only favorable thing he could come up with was that the enemy had committed most of its Trolls in the first attack. They had done the job they were sent to do and took a heavy toll on the defenders in the first wave. But that meant they would not have to contend with many Trolls during the next attack. He convinced himself that this would greatly increase their odds at winning this battle, and in effect, the war.

Hours passed and the sun was just about to set when the horn calls once again started from the enemy camp. Burton jumped to his feet and looked across the field toward the enemy lines. Once again the enemy lines filled the horizon and the skyline was full of red banners with the black orb right in the middle. He had surmised correctly and there were but a handful of Trolls to be seen. However, he was far from prepared for what he did see. Directly in the center of the Orc army sat Maloneous. He was seated upon his great black horse and surrounded by his cavalry. Burton estimated there must have been at least ten thousand. He and Mindeloria were correct in their assessment that this would be an all-out attack. If they failed, the war would be lost and with it Hatu and their way of life.

In the dying light, Burton could see the advance of the army begin. They walked slowly and with purpose toward his position and the gate that guarded the entrance to the city. Once again, as soon as they got in range, the Dwarf cannon began to fire. There was no loud cheer or sounding of trumpets this time, just a barrage of what cannon, catapults, and arrow launchers as were left. Yet, Burton was still surprised by the damage they inflicted upon the enemy as the Orc army continued its advance.

Once again the Rangers lit the fires in the field as they had done the night before. This provided just enough light that they could make out the army as it got closer. Burton began to notice that dark clouds began to roll towards them as the enemy advanced closer and closer. The work of a Wizard, he thought. Occasionally, great bolts of light would shoot into the clouds from Maloneous, tremendously brilliant flashes of yellow light that would momentarily blind anyone who was looking directly at

Maloneous when he sent a bolt skyward. Once again, as soon as the Orcs got within archery range, a hail of arrows was unleashed from both sides. Maloneous had a dark circle around him that none of the projectiles could pierce. Again, thought Burton, wizard magic.

Burton could easily see the Elves and some of the Rangers. They, too, had a light around them. But instead of making them easy targets it acted as a shield and arrows simple whizzed by or were deflected to the ground. Lindeloria had this same light around her as she stood at the very front of the parapet and looked out upon the battlefield. Burton had noticed this before, but tonight it was as bright as a shining star.

"Fear not Master Brew," she said. "Arise and stand by me. No arrow or Orc stone, or wizard magic will touch you as long as I stand."

Burton stood by Lindeloria and looked out over the field. Directly below he could see Mindeloria sitting on his horse in the very middle of the Dwarf battle line. Mindeloria, too, was bathed in a light. But this was the purest, whitest light Burton had ever seen. Once, years ago, Burton saw a light like this. But it was the white light that burns hot in a fire. The kind of fire needed to form ore into metal. Around Mindeloria was his bodyguard. They, too, were in a light. But Mindeloria shone so brightly that his light nearly drowned out the others. Yet they were there. Burton knew that it would take more than a handful of Orcs to extinguish this light.

Suddenly he had an idea.

"My Lady," he said to Lindeloria. "We need a breeze from the sea and we must make smoke! Lots of smoke!"

As she turned her back on the enemy, she said "I will make the wind blow."

Immediately, Burton could feel the sea air on his face as the breeze picked up from the waterfront.

Lindeloria turned to one of her bodyguards.

"Tell the Dwarves to make smoke from their cannons." she commanded.

The guard immediately gave the command. The cannons ceased to fire and white smoke began to billow from the few cannons that were left. Burton hoped it would be enough for what he had in mind.

At this moment, the Orc horns sounded and a great charge was sent forth in the direction of the line of defenders. Loud horns and screams came from the evil horde as it began to charge along the entire line. First, struck were the Rangers and Elves on the right. The arrow fire from the Rangers and Elves had been particularly devastating to the Orcs, and by engaging them first, the Orcs would force the defenders to do combat in close quarters. But Burton knew that the Orcs had greatly misgauged this advantage. While the preferred weapon of Rangers and Elves was the bow, they were still very effective with sword and spear.

Next to be engaged was the left flank. Burton was particularly worried about this side of the line because of the heavy fighting they had been involved in not more than seven hours ago. But they did not yield. They stood heroically against the overwhelming odds they now faced.

That left the middle of the line. Maloneous and Mindeloria would meet somewhere in this engagement, Burton knew it. If the middle fell, the city was lost.

As the Orcs got to Mindeloria's position, they drove to the right and to the left. Burton almost smiled as he realized the Orcs, however driven on, wanted no part of the Elf Lord. Instead, they focused on the Dwarves. The Dwarf front line of shield and spear bearers took the brunt of the initial strike. But these

Dwarves were ready for a direct assault, and the Orcs took severe losses. Both horse and rider were driven back and made little impact upon the defensive line. The second line of Dwarves was the traditional axe men. The handful of Orcs that managed to make it through the front line were immediately eliminated. And, finally, the third line was the Dwarf archers. Dwarf archers are not very accurate at long distance. But the power of a Dwarf is unsurpassed, and at close range, there is very little a Dwarf archer cannot penetrate.

But by sheer numbers they were still at a tremendous disadvantage. With Maloneous in the battle, there was little hope of a rout and retreat as had happened earlier in the day. The situation would soon become desperate if this engagement lasted too long. The defenders were inflicting heavy losses on the enemy, but they, too, were starting to take more losses then they could afford. And they could afford none when the battle began. So Burton decided it was time to implement his plan and hope it worked.

Thinking back to when he was trapped in the burning house, when Derfer found him, he reached into his cloak and grasped both the Elven pin and the brooch given him by Lady Elladoria. He then put out his right hand and concentrated with all of his might. Soon the white light he was able to produce began to dance into the night sky. This was amplified by the smoke created by the Dwarf engines, and with the breeze blowing from the sea it produced a kaleidoscope of colors and images. The effect was exactly as Burton had hoped. The Orcs were completely caught off guard by this new magic and became confused and disoriented. At the same moment two other things occurred that caused even more confusion and panic in the stunned army.

When Burton opened his eyes the first thing he saw was both Mindeloria and Lindeloria let loose with the deadly white bolts that they were able to produce. He was awestruck as the mighty Elves held out their hands and literally blew holes in the enemy lines. Thirty to forty Orcs at a time fell under these mighty blasts. And unlike before, the blasts came one after the other. Burton knew that it was now or never and that both Mindeloria and Lindeloria had committed themselves to either winning or dying in this fight.

Then Burton heard a similar sound. It was a song. He knew that Zander had begun to swing the magic axe that had chosen him in this hour of need. The song grew louder and louder until it almost drowned out every sound of the battle. Then Burton could see a green light coming from Zander's direction. The light grew brighter and brighter. Occasionally, it would spark as it struck down a foe. The enemy forces faltered, and their advance was halted. Now was the time for the only desperate act Burton could think of. Once again his intuition told him it was time to do the one thing that no one would expect.

"My Lady," he called to Lindeloria. "I do not totally understand, but now is the time to charge. We must open the gates and attack the enemy."

Lindeloria looked at Burton, and the broadest smile he had ever seen crossed her face.

"Then let us take the fight to him." she said. turning to her guards. "Bring me my sword and open the gates. But do not run to the fight yet. Master Myopian, your intuition serves you well, but so must your trust and faith."

"I do not understand my Lady." replied Burton.

Just then he heard the sound of approaching cavalry. Not from outside the city but from within. He turned and was astonished by what he saw. Coming directly at him from the direction of the harbor was row after row of heavily armored cavalry. At the head of the column flew the flag of Ancintron. These were some of the famous heavy cavalry of South Isle.

"The breeze has brought much more than a vehicle to spread smoke, Master Brew," said Lindeloria.

"But how?" asked Burton.

"Do you not remember that the founders of the Great City of South Isle were of both Elf and Man descent? Children of the sea?" she replied. "My father has long arms and the world still has memory, Master Brew."

The cavalry rode directly into the battle. Burton could only imagine the effect this must have had on the enemy. Directly behind the cavalry came columns of foot soldiers. They were in the black and silver of South Isle and carried long spear-like weapons. Burton had never seen such a weapon. They were twice the size of the man who carried it and thicker then anything he had ever seen. Behind them came a small company dressed in black and gold. Each wore a diamond helmet adorned with large white wings. On the front of their armor, directly upon their chest, was a Griffon with two stars above its head. They only numbered about one hundred, but they were Guardsmen of Ancintron, the very bodyguard of the king and the best that land had to offer. At the head of this group was Battlehelm. They were still heavily outnumbered, but the very sight of such a force would have to raise the morale of the entire army. Burton even noticed the Myopians on the wall began to fire their bows and sling their rocks at a faster pace.

"Now we may join the fight, Master Brew," said Lindeloria as she directed the horns to sound and the entire city garrison to join the fight. Only the Myopians would stay behind to man the parapets. This was because of their skill with the sling and actually was quite an honor. They were entrusted to be the final line of defense of the oldest city in Hatu.

Burton raced down the ramp and ran into the fray. Much of the smoke had been blown away, and he could see rather clearly how the battle was progressing.

Both the right flank and the center of the line were advancing, however slowly, and driving the enemy back. Only the heavily outnumbered left flank remained in question. Burton directed that all of the Elves from the city join that flank. He rushed headlong into the battle and found Derfer and Zander right in the middle of the thickest fighting. Derfer was wielding Smelter and cutting through the Orcs as if they were made of butter. The Great Axe of old was singing and burning bright green in the hand of the mighty Dwarf King Zander. The two fought as if they were possessed. Burton finally had a chance to see Dwarf Battle Lust firsthand. It was both rewarding and scary at the same time.

"We have saved some for you, Master Myopian," said Zander.

Warlight burned brightly in the night, brighter than Burton had ever seen. He waded into the fight and attacked with the same ferocity that had served him well in battles past. His speed and agility caught the Orcs off guard. Unlike the other times he had been in battle, Burton could see everything and knew exactly what he was doing. He was not only aware this time, but he was actually thinking ahead and planning his next attack before he finished the one he was engaged in. Orc after Orc fell to the three warriors as they cut a path through the enemy lines. Burton, Zander, and Derfer struck down so many Orcs that they could not begin to count or keep track. The sight of the three inspired the rest of the Dwarves, and they joined in the slaughter. Ahead of the quickly advancing party, Burton could see the light from the Elves. Lindeloria and her bodyguard had gone directly to be with her father and the two Elf groups joined to form one very large, powerful Elf contingent.

The reinforcements that joined the left flank had turned the tide there. Now all three sections were advancing on the Orc army and driving their foes away from the city. Burton thought that they were just about to turn and run when a large clap of thunder came from directly overhead. Bolts of lightning came down from the dark clouds and struck several places in the ally lines. This halted the advance and turned the tide once again in the direction of Orcs. Maloneous had called down his trump card and saved his greatest piece of magic for just the right time. The Orcs were spurred on by this magic and attacked on all fronts as if the whip of their master were right behind them. Only the center stood and fought. Burton knew that they would not move from this spot and their last stand would take place here.

A messenger from the Rangers found him in the midst of the fighting.

"Lord Tordin sends word," said the messenger. "He is in need of assistance. They are almost surrounded and will soon be cut off if help does not arrive soon."

Tordin, Burton's friend, was in trouble and he was unable to help him. He was torn about what to do. Large parts of him wanted to run and join his friend and provide whatever relief he could. But his role was to the entire army and not just to Tordin and the Rangers.

"I will send help as soon as I am able," replied Burton, as he pulled Warlight from yet another Orc. "Tell him to buy as much time as he can and help will come."

"I will tell him, My Lord, but I do not know how much time we have left." said the messenger as he raced to join his companions.

Word came from the Dwarves of the Mystic Mountains that they too, were in a serious predicament and that if help did not arrive, they would not be able to hold out much longer. Only the middle remained intact, but the bolts from the wizard and the overwhelming numbers of Orcs were taking their toll there as well. The situation was desperate, and Burton could only think of one answer. It was time to send for the cavalry.

Some five thousand Elves were still safely hidden away and waiting for the order to attack. Burton knew that now was the time to give that order. This was one of those times that the old way was the best way. He found an Elf trumpeter and ordered him to sound the cavalry charge. The Elf sounded the call three times and after the third time received two answers. But there should only have been one. One came from the direction of the Elf cavalry, and the other came from behind the enemy lines. And the second horn was not Elf, nor was it an Elf call. Whatever it was once again caused the Orcs to lose focus on the battle and look over their shoulders.

From the right rode five thousand of the best Elf cavalry Hatu had ever known. They traveled in light armor and their horses were quick and nimble. On horseback, they were the finest archers and spearmen this side of Forlosha. They rode directly to the aid of Tordin and the right flank. This introduction of fresh forces turned the tables on the Orcs once again and a rout was soon underway. The arrival of the Elf cavalry caused immediate displacement of several other Orc companies, and before long the middle of the line was advancing again, with the Orcs in full retreat.

From behind the Orc army came another sight that Burton had not been prepared to see. The only other cavalry in Hatu that could strike fear into the very being of an Orc was that of Forlosha. And how they got there, or where they came from, Burton did not know. But there they were, light cavalry from Forlosha. And at the head of the charging line was Handil, Lieutenant of Forlosha. They bore into the retreating Orcs with a vengeance. It was now a complete rout on all fronts. Many Orcs tried to stand and fight, but most simply tossed away their weapons, their shields and their armor, and tried to run. But there was nowhere to run. They were slaughtered by the thousands. Elf, Man, and Dwarf bore into the enemy forces and made them pay for every evil they had ever committed. The Dwarves from the Rolling Hills began chanting "Remember the Rolling Hills". Burton stopped and watched the rest of the army chase the decimated Orc army into the night. He was exhausted. He had never felt so tired. He stood and looked at the carnage that lay at his very feet. Dwarf, Elf, Horse, Orc, Ancintron Guardsmen, Knights from South Isle, Ranger, and even his own Myopian brothers lay dead. The sight sickened him so that he just turned and walked back into the city. He walked back up the ramp to his post on the parapet. There he sat down, and with his back against the wall, put his head in his hands and wept. They had won the battle, and quite possibly the war but Burton Brew found no joy in the events that had unfolded on this day. Many a cheerful soul would no longer grace Fallquint or Doubblegate or even Myopia. They had won their freedom, but it came at an extremely high price.

TWENTY-FOUR

PONDERING THE NEXT STEP

"War is not the glorious thing we make it to be, is it Master Brew?" asked a familiar voice.

Burton looked up to see Erideous standing before him. On one side of him stood Milo, and on the other side Silo, his constant wolf companions.

"I have never seen such carnage," replied a still slightly shaken Burton.

"It is not a pretty thing at all, war," continued Erideous. "Too many times in my life have I seen such as this. Too many times have I bid farewell to a good friend. But it is almost over now, Master Brew. Look and you will see they bring the evil one to us."

Burton rose and looked out towards the battlefield. There he could that see a large contingent of Elves, including Lindeloria and Mindeloria, was coming into the city. In the middle of the party he could see Maloneous. He was without staff and hat, and his hands were bound together with diamond chain.

"And what will become of him?" inquired Burton.

"That, I do not know. But I think we will have an answer soon enough." replied Erideous. "Come, Master Brew, let us go meet to my wizard brother."

The two walked down the ramp and awaited the party at the base of the entrance to the parapets. There they stood until the party entered the city. Maloneous glared at one and all, but none could feel the cold hatred that consumed the malignant wizard more than Burton. Their eyes locked only for a moment, but Burton instantly felt the wrath that had festered for so long. As they passed, Erideous and Burton fell in behind the procession as it marched through the city to the great hall.

Tordin fell back in line and joined Burton.

"I am glad to see you have made it through this battle in one piece," he said to the Myopian.

"I am glad you are well, too. What of Tisiron and Borgon?" asked Burton.

I am afraid they were not so lucky." replied a saddened Tordin. "Many of the Rangers that served Myopia so well will not see the sunrise. If not for the timely arrival of the Elf cavalry, I would not be here to talk with you this early morning. Warrant is alive, but barely. He will be in healing for many weeks. He does not yet know that his brother has been killed, and it is my hope to be there when this news is passed on to him."

"We have lost many true allies this day." added Erideous. "But now we must look to the living. Our next task is at hand, and it is one that must not be taken lightly."

Burton knew he was referring to Maloneous and what was to become of him. What fate he would suffer lay at the very hands of those he had sought to exterminate? And what does one do with a wizard? Burton tried to imagine what the fate of Maloneous would be. But he would not have to wait for long. The party arrived at the great Elf hall, where only the representatives from each race were allowed in. That is with the exception of the four Elf guards who had surrounded Maloneous since his capture.

Into the hall went Mindeloria and Lindeloria. Lindeloria was not really a representative of the Elves, but it was thought wise to allow her into the great hall because it was the combination of her power and that of her father that subdued the evil wizard and allowed him to be captured.

Next went Zander and Derfer. Zander was there as the representative of the Dwarves of the Rolling Hills. Derfer went on behalf of Thuron, who was unable to attend because of his battle wounds.

Then went the contingent of Men. Tordin would represent the Rangers. He would be the voice of those who had fought so long and hard to keep the peace in western Hatu. Battlehelm would represent the men of Ancintron. He had proved himself to be worthy of his name. The arrival of his forces was one of the reasons the tide turned in their favor. Burton noticed how tall and unassuming he now appeared. Not like he looked when last Burton saw him, barging out of the room in Fallquint. The war must have had a calming effect on him, and somehow Burton could sense that he had changed.

Then in came Handil of Forlosha. He walked in next to last and appeared to be the same, quiet person Burton took an instant liking to in Fallquint. He sat at the far end of the table, and it became apparent that while he was here physically, his thoughts were elsewhere.

Lastly, in walked Burton and Erideous. They took their seats alongside of Handil in the very back of the room. Burton knew he was there because someone had to be the voice of the Myopians. Once again though, he wished it were someone else.

Mindeloria took his traditional seat at the head of the table, and as soon as all had settled in he began the meeting.

"It is time that we end the war and decide what to do with Maloneous," he said.

Instantly, Zander slammed his axe on the table and yelled "Kill Him. He does not deserve the right to live for what he has done to us."

"I agree with the Dwarf," yelled Battlehelm. "My city is still under siege and thousands have perished because of his evil. I, too, say kill him and let's be done with it."

"You fools," said Maloneous in a voice that filled the room. It was so commanding that everyone immediately became quiet. "You think you have won? You have won nothing. You cannot kill me. You do not have the power to do so. I have lost this battle, but how will you stand against the army that follows this, or the one after that? You cannot kill me. And to lock me away will simply prolong your agony. Why not simply give up and set me free?" he held his fettered arms out as he spoke. "I will allow you to live if you just set me free. We can live in harmony, you and I." As he spoke his voice became softer, almost hypnotic in its effect.

"I did not wish this war with you," he continued. "But you would not listen to reason. All I ever wanted was the Myopian. Do I not have the right to avenge the wrongs done to me? Have I not suffered these many long, lonely years because of the evil his kind brought to me and my people? It was the Myopians who started this war many generations ago when they destroyed my friend and ally. Is it so hard to understand that I simply wanted to right what was wrong? Have you not all suffered because of these Myopians? I am not your enemy. I am your friend. I have come to help you, not hurt you."

"Enough," cried Zander. "Enough of his dark tongue, I say. I will not listen to such rubbish from the mouth of a fool."

"Fool you say?" replied Maloneous. "You dare to call me a fool? It is not I who has been taken in by this treachery and deceit, but you. You who now sit here and dare to pass judgment on me. I demand you set me free and I will be gone from this place where it is you who are the fools."

"Silence! Both of you." commanded Mindeloria. "It is your fate that will be decided here Maloneous, not ours. We are free to choose our own path. It is you who is not. Tordin, what say you?"

Tordin stared long at the table and was deep in thought. Finally, he raised his head and looked directly at Maloneous. "I say we imprison him in the dark places of Hatu. There he can rot in the filth and mire of the old ways."

Burton could see the two locked in a mental battle as Tordin spoke.

"And what of Forlosha?" said Mindeloria, looking at Handil.

"Forlosha wants what is best for all in this matter. We will cast our voice to whatever the majority decides. But I say we decide quickly, as there is still a battle to be fought if Ancintron and Forlosha are to survive. We have won this battle, but I fear there are many more to fight before the war is over. King Bulclius still has a mighty army at the throat of Ancintron."

"And they will not fight alone, my friend," said Zander. "Once this council is over, what is left of the Dwarves will march in defense of those who have defended us. But Lord Mindeloria is right. This is our appointed task, and it is here and now that it must be dealt with. You know what I say, Master Elf. Kill him and let's be done with it."

"And I agree." chimed in Battlehelm. "We waste precious time with talk. Now is the time to act, and I say we deal with him here and now and be done with it"

"Killing a wizard is not so easy, Lord Zander." said Lindeloria. "It can be done, but it will take much effort and energy to break his life spell. And the power of those who can accomplish this deed are needed elsewhere." She looked at Handil as she finished speaking. "Captain Handil is correct. The war is not yet over. What is left of our armies is needed in defense of Forlosha and Ancintron. The easterners' king is a very formidable foe in deed."

"Well, if he cannot be killed, then imprisonment is the only other option." said Derfer. "Then I say lock him away and let's be done with it."

"But could he not escape someday and once again spread his evil?" asked Burton.

"The Myopian is right," said Zander. "To simply lock him away is not the answer either. If we cannot kill him and we cannot lock him away, what other choice is there?"

"Only one I am afraid," said Mindeloria as he looked directly as Erideous.

A silence filled the room as each member contemplated what the third option could be. Finally, Erideous spoke.

"You are right, Lord Mindeloria, there is only one other choice. And it is I who will pick up this burden and see it through until its end. I will return him to the land beyond the sea."

Beyond the sea! Erideous would take Maloneous back over the seas to the faraway lands.

"Long have I been away from home and until now, did not know why." continued Erideous. "He is of my race, and it is I who will end this struggle once and for all. My part in these events has been tiring. I have not the strength I once had. I no longer wish for war and death but miss the quiet of my home and my friends. It is long since I have spoken with Quickfoot. I look forward to sitting with him again."

"Is there any further discussion required?" asked Mindeloria.

The room sat in silence at the revelation that had just occurred. Surely, the powers of old and the wizard race will know how to deal with Maloneous, they all thought.

"Then it is decided," said Erideous, as he rose to his feet. "I will leave within the hour for home." Then he spoke directly to Maloneous. Burton could sense the power struggle between them. "I am sure, my brother, that you will be dealt with appropriately upon your return to the First Lands. I think they will be very happy to have you return, very happy, indeed"

Burton could almost hear the sound of laughter in Erideous's voice as he finished his statement to Maloneous. It was obvious to all that this was, by far, the worst fate that they could impose upon the wizard. He would return to his lands a prisoner at the hands of a fellow wizard.

"I will have a ship readied immediately." said Mindeloria. "It will be light soon, and it is time we tend to our wounds and make ready for a new day. Go and join your people. Let them know the evil of this Wizard will be no more!"

And so Mindeloria directed that Maloneous be led away and preparations be made for a ship to sail over the seas within the hour. Burton and the others did not leave the meeting straight away. Instead they spent some time reviewing the events that had led to the victory over the dark forces.

Handil had taken a special message back to Forlosha, and, with the aid of Mindeloria, assisted in negotiations that led to the forces of Forlosha being able to appear just in the nick of time. The Dwarves would not only be allowed to resume mining, but it was decided that the lands around Moewirth Lake would be given to them in payment for their years of service to the people of Forlosha. Thus the Dwarves of the Rolling Hills, who had their homes destroyed in the battle with Maloneous, would have a new realm to inhabit and mine. Needless to say, this made

Zander, Derfer, and the rest of the Rolling Hills Dwarves very happy indeed. Handil was then sent back to Fallquint to provide whatever assistance he could to Mindeloria and the High Elves. When he and his forces arrived at Fallquint, he was informed that the Elf Lord had made his way to Malquint and that a great battle was about to begin. They had arrived only a few hours before the call for cavalry was given. Because Handil was educated in various forms of combat, he knew the Elf attack call and decided to answer when that call was given.

Battlehelm had returned to Ancintron to find the armies of Maloneous on the march and at the very doorsteps of the mighty capital. He secretly went to the northern most Ancintron city of Sinford, where he raised an army of northern peoples. They also enlisted the aid of several hundred Dwarves who made their way south from the Rolling Hills. Having had the opportunity to fight side by side with them these past few months, Battlehelm had a new respect for the Dwarves. When word was received that the Orc army was moving west, he returned to capital and later was sent to South Isle in order to raise an army that would sail to Malquint. Approximately half of the forces available loaded onto ships and left for their destination. However, it was the sudden increase of the breeze over the water that gave them the speed to make their journey in time. If Burton had not asked Lindeloria to assist with the wind, Battlehelm doubted the force would have made it to Malquint and been able to be a part of the engagement that turned the tide of the fight.

Zander gave much of credit for their victory to Burton. He was convinced that the magic of his light show and his ability to read the thoughts of the enemy played the biggest part of their victory.

One thing became clear in the conversations Burton had with his friends. The battle was over, but not the war. He was convinced that the side of good would prevail, but not before many more lives were lost. Once again, he left his friends thinking about those who had fallen in battle and just how important their sacrifice had been. The sixty thousand or so that had launched the defense of Hatu now numbered about twenty thousand. Over forty thousand warriors had fallen in this battle alone. Burton wondered how many more must die before the evil of Maloneous would be extinguished and things were once again made right.

But for now he was content to return to his fellow Myopians and prepare for whatever lay ahead.

Twenty-Five

The Journey Home

First light found Burton Brew and his friends on a dock in Malquint. There they watched quietly as Maloneous was unceremoniously loaded into the hold of a beautiful Elven ship anchored at the end of the longest dock. Several Elves also boarded the ship, as it was their time to leave Hatu to sail back home to the place where their race was born. Lindeloria and Mindeloria would not be leaving as their adventures in defense of the realm were not yet completed. Lindeloria mentioned to Burton that one day soon they, too, would board a ship and sail home, but today was not that day.

"Well Master Brew, it is time for me to take your leave," said Erideous as he prepared to board the ship. "I have met many great Myopians, Master Brew, and you stand tall in their presence. It has been both a pleasure and an honor. I leave to you my two greatest companions and the only thing I value in Hatu. To you, I leave Milo and Silo. May they serve you well as they have served me. They will meet you later as you journey to Myopia and return home."

"Return home?" exclaimed Burton. All this time, Burton had assumed that he would be traveling with the rest of the army to Forlosha, and eventually to Ancintron, to help fight the remaining Maloneous army that lay siege to the capital.

"Yes, my brave Myopian," said Lindeloria. "Your role in the adventure is over. Now you must return home and help your kinsmen rebuild your country. Your days and nights of battle are over."

"But there is still so much to do," said Burton.

"Yes, Master Burton, there is," replied Mindeloria. "And your place is back in Myopia, where you belong. You have served Hatu well. It is time you resume the life that was meant for you. War is no longer your concern, and the time has come for you to go back to your peaceful existence in Myopia."

"Your job here is done," said Erideous. "You have played your role in the downfall of Maloneous and helped to defeat my brother, as was your destiny. I thank you, as we all do, but now it is truly the age of men. With my leaving, there will be no more wizards in Hatu, and that is as it should be. No, Master Brew, when Maloneous and I leave, the age of magic and conjurers will be ended. The Dwarves and Elves will once again return to their quiet ways and live in the twilight of our imaginations. The Rangers will once again become the shadows of things that might be. They will go unseen unless they wish to be seen."

"But what of the Orcs and Trolls that escaped into the night? Surely they are not totally destroyed," said Burton.

"Orcs and Trolls will never be totally destroyed, Master Burton" replied Mindeloria. "They are a part of the night and a part of this world. They belong here as much as you or I. They are evil, and evil they will always stay. But I think you will never see another army rise or such a concentrated gathering as you have seen here. I believe that this was the beginning of their end. Unlike in the past, there is no longer a force that can control or twist them to its way of thinking and use them as pawns in the subjugation of others. I think from here on out they will become much like the stories that are told around campfires in the dark. They will no longer have substance. In time, they will be forgotten and simply fade away in to dust."

"We have more fighting yet to do Master Burton," said Zander. "But I think they are right. It is no longer a place for Myopians. You should do as they say and go home and live the life that is meant for you. As we will lead the life that is destined for us when this war is over. Once again, we Dwarves will return to the ground from which we sprang. And that, my mighty Myopian, is a moment I cannot wait to get back to"

"I agree brother," said Derfer. "I, too, cannot wait until I return to the caves and live a life that is full of diamonds and gold."

"Dwarves," said Battlehelm with a laugh. "If I had not the chance to fight with you, I would never have understood."

"All this will come in time, my friends," said Mindeloria. "But there is much to do and not much time to do it. Even as we speak, the noose around the neck of Ancintron grows tighter. It is time we bade Erideous goodbye and got back to the business at hand."

With that there were the traditional goodbyes as Erideous boarded the ship that would take him and Maloneous back home. As soon as the ship cleared its moorings, most of those on the docks left and went about their business in town. That is, most save Burton and Tordin. The two stood quietly and watched the Elf ship sail gracefully into the morning sky, which glowed red from the light of a brilliant sun.

"Is that the last I shall see of Erideous?" Burton quietly asked.

"No, I think not" replied Tordin. "His time has ended here in Hatu, and he now returns home. And do not be sad my young friend, he goes to the lands far away where he will be reunited with those of our past."

"Do you mean Quickfoot and Milton?" said Burton.

"They could not visit you in your dreams if they did not still exist." replied Tordin. "I think that one day that is where you will once again see Erideous."

The thought that Erideous would one day appear in his dreams gave great comfort to Burton.

"And he will be with his other brothers, the Wizards." said Burton.

"I think you may have missed something here, Master Brew" said Tordin, with a slight smile on his face. "Erideous has one brother, and he is taking him home."

"You mean he and Maloneous are really brothers?" said a startled Burton. "I thought he meant that they were brothers in spirit, or wizardry? I did not know they were brothers of the same flesh"

"That they are," said Tordin. "And Quickfoot is their cousin. So, yes, Erideous is truly going home to his family and friends, as we all must."

The ship had at last sailed out of sight when Burton and Tordin left the dock.

The dock was full of activity as the Knights from South Isle and the Ancintron King's Guard loaded their equipment onto the ships that carried them here, not but a few hours ago. The contingent from Forlosha had returned to the site of the battle and begun to ceremoniously pick up the bodies of those who had fallen in the great battle. They then made arrangements with the Elves that the bodies of their fallen warriors would be transported back to their homeland after the main force left on the return journey to Forlosha.

The Elves and Dwarves also began to clean up from the previous day's battle. They carefully collected their dead and laid them out so that their women could prepare the bodies for burial. For the first time Burton got a look at Dwarf women, and the rumors were correct. There were a few physical differences, but otherwise there were not a lot of other noticeable ways to tell the genders apart.

The Rangers were gone when Burton returned from the dock. Tordin informed him that they had gone ahead to make sure the path would be safe for the Myopians to return to their homes. As for their dead, they left this task to the Elves, who were more than happy to assist in the grim task of caring for the dead. As Tordin had once told Burton, the work of a Ranger is never done.

As for the Orcs and Trolls and Men of the defeated army, they were piled up, according to tradition, and burned. The thick black smoke rose straight into the air and was quickly dissipated by the strong wind that blew in from the sea.

The Myopians went back to their tents and began packing to go home. Myopians, who don't like to travel in the first place, could not wait to begin their journey home and to see what damage had been done to their crops and gardens in the past few days.

"Well, I guess I had best prepare to leave as well." said Burton.

"As do I," replied Tordin. "I will go with you on the journey home as well as few others. That is, if you do not mind the company?"

Burton was beside himself as he answered.

"Of course not, my friend" he said to Tordin. "I welcome all that will join us on the road back to Myopia."

Then I will meet you here in a few hours," said Tordin. "I do not know about you, Master Brew, but I have had a very long night and would not mind a little rest before I journey."

Burton failed to realize that he had been a wake for over twenty-six hours and with the exception of some bread had eaten very little.

"I think you are right. I will see you back here in four hours." replied Burton.

Burton then went back to the Myopian tent area and informed them that they would leave for home soon. He also recommended that they all get some rest and have a big meal before they departed. Of course, all of the Myopians agreed that a large afternoon snack was just what they needed.

And so Burton went back to his sleeping area and fell fast asleep. He once again had his dreams, but there were no visitors from distant lands. No Myopians or Elves long since departed, no Orc armies or evil wizards. Just dreams, normal everyday dreams.

Burton awoke and despite only sleeping for a few hours was well rested and ready to go. He thought they would march for a few hours and just before sundown they would make camp. Of course, they would have to put out guards and do all of the things that a group moving in time of war would do. But he was not overly concerned. His friend Tordin was with him, and the Rangers were already miles ahead. He expected the journey home would be quite uneventful.

He picked up his backpack, placed his cloak around his neck, and walked toward the gate. He passed many Dwarves and Elves on the way who all bowed and gave him wonderful greetings. Burton felt a little embarrassed by the attention, but after all, he had played a major role in the defeat of a powerful, evil Wizard.

When Burton got to the gates, they were closed, with only Tordin, who face was covered by his cloak hood, standing in front of them as he approached. Burton could only see a few of the guards on the parapet that served as his observation point but a day ago.

"Are you ready my friend?" asked Tordin.

"I am," replied Burton. "But where is everyone else?"

"I told you we would have a few companions on the way home," replied Tordin. And he tossed the hood from his cloak off of his head.

Trumpets sounded, and as the gates opened, a great cheer rose from outside of the city. To Burton's amazement, the road leading out of Malquint was lined with Dwarves and Elves and Men and even Myopians. And they were all cheering for him.

As Burton made his way down the road, he was congratulated by everyone he passed. They called him a hero, the last of a brave line, all sorts of titles. Burton was both embarrassed and proud as he walked through the gauntlet of well-wishers. As he passed the Myopians, they all filed in behind him, and before long all of the men and women of Myopia of Hatu were marching behind their leader, Burton Brew.

And at the very end of each line stood a great wolf. On one line was Milo, on the other was Silo. They immediately took up positions on Burton's left and right and walked with him as he approached the final two figures that stood before him and the road home.

There on white horses, trimmed in ceremonial silver and gold, sat Lindeloria and Mindeloria.

"Master Brew," said Mindeloria. "I believe it is time that you took us home."

Mindeloria and Lindeloria then led their horses behind Burton, opening the road toward Myopia and the path home.

Burton looked behind him at the cheering throng and could feel the emotion of the moment swell inside of him. So he did what all brave Myopians do. He turned back to the east, tossed his cloak over his shoulder and with a great wolf on each side, began the journey home.

CPSIA information can be obtained
at www.ICGtesting.com
Printed in the USA
BVHW031747210722
642703BV00017B/564